Finding a Girl
in America

Other Books by Andre Dubus

The Lieutenant
Separate Flights
Adultery & Other Choices
The Times Are Never So Bad
Voices from the Moon
The Last Worthless Evening
Selected Stories
Broken Vessels *(non-fiction)*

Finding a Girl in America

A NOVELLA AND TEN SHORT STORIES

ANDRE DUBUS

David R. Godine, Publisher
BOSTON

First edition published in 1980 by
David R. Godine, Publisher, Inc.
Horticultural Hall
300 Massachusetts Avenue
Boston, Massachusetts 02115

Library of Congress Cataloging-in-Publication Data
Dubus, Andre, 1936–
Finding a girl in America.
Contents: Killings – The dark men. – His lover – [etc.]
I. Title.
PZ4.D824Fi[PS3554.U265]   813'.5'4   79-90371
ISBN: 0-87923-393-1

ACKNOWLEDGMENTS

'Killings' and 'The Winter Father' first appeared in *The Sewanee
Review*; 'The Dark Men' in *Northwest Review*; 'His Lover' in *The
William and Mary Review*; 'Townies' in *The Real Paper*; 'At St.
Croix' in *Ploughshares*; 'The Pitcher' in *The North American
Review* and *Fielder's Choice, an Anthology of Baseball Fiction*; 'Wait-
ing' in *The Paris Review*; and 'Delivering' in *Harper's*.

Fourth printing, 1993
PRINTED IN THE UNITED STATES OF AMERICA

To Peggy

I am grateful to the John Simon Guggenheim Memorial Foundation, The National Endowment for the Arts, and the Artists Foundation of Massachusetts.

Contents

PART ONE

Killings · 3

The Dark Men · 21

His Lover · 31

Townies · 37

PART TWO

The Misogamist · 51

At St. Croix · 65

The Pitcher · 75

Waiting · 91

PART THREE

Delivering · 99

The Winter Father · 109

Finding a Girl in America · 129

One is never talking to oneself, always one is addressed to someone. Suddenly, without knowing the reason, at different stages in one's life, one is addressing this person or that all the time, even dreams are performed before an audience. I see that. It's well known that people who commit suicide, the most solitary of all acts, are addressing someone.

Nadine Gordimer, *Burger's Daughter*

PART ONE

Killings

O N THE AUGUST morning when Matt Fowler
buried his youngest son, Frank, who had
lived for twenty-one years, eight months,
and four days, Matt's older son, Steve, turned to him as the family
left the grave and walked between their friends, and said: 'I should
kill him.' He was twenty-eight, his brown hair starting to thin in
front where he used to have a cowlick. He bit his lower lip, wiped
his eyes, then said it again. Ruth's arm, linked with Matt's, tightened; he looked at her. Beneath her eyes there was swelling from
the three days she had suffered. At the limousine Matt stopped and
looked back at the grave, the casket, and the Congregationalist
minister who he thought had probably had a difficult job with the
eulogy though he hadn't seemed to, and the old funeral director
who was saying something to the six young pallbearers. The grave
was on a hill and overlooked the Merrimack, which he could not see
from where he stood; he looked at the opposite bank, at the apple
orchard with its symmetrically planted trees going up a hill.

Next day Steve drove with his wife back to Baltimore where he
managed the branch office of a bank, and Cathleen, the middle
child, drove with her husband back to Syracuse. They had left the
grandchildren with friends. A month after the funeral Matt played
poker at Willis Trottier's because Ruth, who knew this was the second time he had been invited, told him to go, he couldn't sit home
with her for the rest of her life, she was all right. After the game
Willis went outside to tell everyone goodnight and, when the others
had driven away, he walked with Matt to his car. Willis was a
short, silver-haired man who had opened a diner after World War

3

II, his trade then mostly very early breakfast, which he cooked, and then lunch for the men who worked at the leather and shoe factories. He now owned a large restaurant.

'He walks the Goddamn streets,' Matt said.

'I know. He was in my place last night, at the bar. With a girl.'

'I don't see him. I'm in the store all the time. Ruth sees him. She sees him too much. She was at Sunnyhurst today getting cigarettes and aspirin, and there he was. She can't even go out for cigarettes and aspirin. It's killing her.'

'Come back in for a drink.'

Matt looked at his watch. Ruth would be asleep. He walked with Willis back into the house, pausing at the steps to look at the starlit sky. It was a cool summer night; he thought vaguely of the Red Sox, did not even know if they were at home tonight; since it happened he had not been able to think about any of the small pleasures he believed he had earned, as he had earned also what was shattered now forever: the quietly harried and quietly pleasurable days of fatherhood. They went inside. Willis's wife, Martha, had gone to bed hours ago, in the rear of the large house which was rigged with burglar and fire alarms. They went downstairs to the game room: the television set suspended from the ceiling, the pool table, the poker table with beer cans, cards, chips, filled ashtrays, and the six chairs where Matt and his friends had sat, the friends picking up the old banter as though he had only been away on vacation; but he could see the affection and courtesy in their eyes. Willis went behind the bar and mixed them each a Scotch and soda; he stayed behind the bar and looked at Matt sitting on the stool.

'How often have you thought about it?' Willis said.

'Every day since he got out. I didn't think about bail. I thought I wouldn't have to worry about him for years. She sees him all the time. It makes her cry.'

'He was in my place a long time last night. He'll be back.'

'Maybe he won't.'

'The band. He likes the band.'

'What's he doing now?'

'He's tending bar up to Hampton Beach. For a friend. Ever notice even the worst bastard always has friends? He couldn't get work in town. It's just tourists and kids up to Hampton. Nobody knows him. If they do, they don't care. They drink what he mixes.'

'Nobody tells me about him.'

'I hate him, Matt. My boys went to school with him. He was the same then. Know what he'll do? Five at the most. Remember that woman about seven years ago? Shot her husband and dropped him off the bridge in the Merrimack with a hundred pound sack of cement and said all the way through it that nobody helped her. Know where she is now? She's in Lawrence now, a secretary. And whoever helped her, where the hell is he?'

'I've got a .38 I've had for years. I take it to the store now. I tell Ruth it's for the night deposits. I tell her things have changed: we got junkies here now too. Lots of people without jobs. She knows though.'

'What does she know?'

'She knows I started carrying it after the first time she saw him in town. She knows it's in case I see him, and there's some kind of a situation –'

He stopped, looked at Willis, and finished his drink. Willis mixed him another.

'What kind of a situation?'

'Where he did something to me. Where I could get away with it.'

'How does Ruth feel about that?'

'She doesn't know.'

'You said she does, she's got it figured out.'

He thought of her that afternoon: when she went into Sunnyhurst, Strout was waiting at the counter while the clerk bagged the things he had bought; she turned down an aisle and looked at soup cans until he left.

'Ruth would shoot him herself, if she thought she could hit him.'

'You got a permit?'

'No.'

'I do. You could get a year for that.'

'Maybe I'll get one. Or maybe I won't. Maybe I'll just stop bringing it to the store.'

Richard Strout was twenty-six years old, a high school athlete, football scholarship to the University of Massachusetts where he lasted for almost two semesters before quitting in advance of the final grades that would have forced him not to return. People then said: Dickie can do the work; he just doesn't want to. He came home and did construction work for his father but refused his father's offer to learn the business; his two older brothers had learned it, so that Strout and Sons trucks going about town, and signs on construction sites, now slashed wounds into Matt Fowler's life. Then Richard married a young girl and became a bartender, his salary and tips augmented and perhaps sometimes matched by his father, who also posted his bond. So his friends, his enemies (he had those: fist fights or, more often, boys and then young men who had not fought him when they thought they should have), and those who simply knew him by face and name, had a series of images of him which they recalled when they heard of the killing: the high school running back, the young drunk in bars, the oblivious hard-hatted young man eating lunch at a counter, the bartender who could perhaps be called courteous but not more than that: as he tended bar, his dark eyes and dark, wide-jawed face appeared less sullen, near blank.

One night he beat Frank. Frank was living at home and waiting for September, for graduate school in economics, and working as a lifeguard at Salisbury Beach, where he met Mary Ann Strout, in her first month of separation. She spent most days at the beach with her two sons. Before ten o'clock one night Frank came home; he had driven to the hospital first, and he walked into the living room with stitches over his right eye and both lips bright and swollen.

'I'm all right,' he said, when Matt and Ruth stood up, and Matt turned off the television, letting Ruth get to him first: the tall, muscled but slender suntanned boy. Frank tried to smile at them but couldn't because of his lips.

'It was her husband, wasn't it?' Ruth said.

'Ex,' Frank said. 'He dropped in.'

Matt gently held Frank's jaw and turned his face to the light, looked at the stitches, the blood under the white of the eye, the bruised flesh.

'Press charges,' Matt said.

'No.'

'What's to stop him from doing it again? Did you hit him at all? Enough so he won't want to next time?'

'I don't think I touched him.'

'So what are you going to do?'

'Take karate,' Frank said, and tried again to smile.

'That's not the problem,' Ruth said.

'You know you like her,' Frank said.

'I like a lot of people. What about the boys? Did they see it?'

'They were asleep.'

'Did you leave her alone with him?'

'He left first. She was yelling at him. I believe she had a skillet in her hand.'

'Oh for God's sake,' Ruth said.

Matt had been dealing with that too: at the dinner table on evenings when Frank wasn't home, was eating with Mary Ann; or, on the other nights—and Frank was with her every night—he talked with Ruth while they watched television, or lay in bed with the windows open and he smelled the night air and imagined, with both pride and muted sorrow, Frank in Mary Ann's arms. Ruth didn't like it because Mary Ann was in the process of divorce, because she had two children, because she was four years older than Frank, and finally—she told this in bed, where she had during all of their marriage told him of her deepest feelings: of love, of passion, of fears about one of the children, of pain Matt had caused her or she had caused him—she was against it because of what she had heard: that the marriage had gone bad early, and for most of it Richard and Mary Ann had both played around.

'That can't be true,' Matt said. 'Strout wouldn't have stood for it.'

'Maybe he loves her.'

'He's too hot-tempered. He couldn't have taken that.'

But Matt knew Strout had taken it, for he had heard the stories too. He wondered who had told them to Ruth; and he felt vaguely annoyed and isolated: living with her for thirty-one years and still not knowing what she talked about with her friends. On these summer nights he did not so much argue with her as try to comfort her, but finally there was no difference between the two: she had concrete objections, which he tried to overcome. And in his attempt to do this, he neglected his own objections, which were the same as hers, so that as he spoke to her he felt as disembodied as he sometimes did in the store when he helped a man choose a blouse or dress or piece of costume jewelry for his wife.

'The divorce doesn't mean anything,' he said. 'She was young and maybe she liked his looks and then after a while she realized she was living with a bastard. I see it as a positive thing.'

'She's not divorced yet.'

'It's the same thing. Massachusetts has crazy laws, that's all. Her age is no problem. What's it matter when she was born? And that other business: even if it's true, which it probably isn't, it's got nothing to do with Frank, it's in the past. And the kids are no problem. She's been married six years; she ought to have kids. Frank likes them. He plays with them. And he's not going to marry her anyway, so it's not a problem of money.'

'Then what's he doing with her?'

'She probably loves him, Ruth. Girls always have. Why can't we just leave it at that?'

'He got home at six o'clock Tuesday morning.'

'I didn't know you knew. I've already talked to him about it.'

Which he had: since he believed almost nothing he told Ruth, he went to Frank with what he believed. The night before, he had followed Frank to the car after dinner.

'You wouldn't make much of a burglar,' he said.

'How's that?'

Matt was looking up at him; Frank was six feet tall, an inch and a half taller than Matt, who had been proud when Frank at seventeen outgrew him; he had only felt uncomfortable when he had to reprimand or caution him. He touched Frank's bicep, thought of the young taut passionate body, believed he could sense the desire, and again he felt the pride and sorrow and envy too, not knowing whether he was envious of Frank or Mary Ann.

'When you came in yesterday morning, I woke up. One of these mornings your mother will. And I'm the one who'll have to talk to her. She won't interfere with you. Okay? I know it means—' But he stopped, thinking: I know it means getting up and leaving that suntanned girl and going sleepy to the car, I know—

'Okay,' Frank said, and touched Matt's shoulder and got into the car.

There had been other talks, but the only long one was their first one: a night driving to Fenway Park, Matt having ordered the tickets so they could talk, and knowing when Frank said yes, he would go, that he knew the talk was coming too. It took them forty minutes to get to Boston, and they talked about Mary Ann until they joined the city traffic along the Charles River, blue in the late sun. Frank told him all the things that Matt would later pretend to believe when he told them to Ruth.

'It seems like a lot for a young guy to take on,' Matt finally said.

'Sometimes it is. But she's worth it.'

'Are you thinking about getting married?'

'We haven't talked about it. She can't for over a year. I've got school.'

'I *do* like her,' Matt said.

He did. Some evenings, when the long summer sun was still low in the sky, Frank brought her home; they came into the house smelling of suntan lotion and the sea, and Matt gave them gin and tonics and started the charcoal in the backyard, and looked at Mary Ann in the lawn chair: long and very light brown hair (Matt thinking that twenty years ago she would have dyed it blonde), and the long brown legs he loved to look at; her face was pretty; she had probably never in her adult life gone unnoticed into a public place. It was in her wide brown eyes that she looked older than Frank; after a few drinks Matt thought what he saw in her eyes was something erotic, testament to the rumors about her; but he knew it wasn't that, or all that: she had, very young, been through a sort of pain that his children, and he and Ruth, had been spared. In the moments of his recognizing that pain, he wanted to tenderly touch her hair, wanted with some gesture to give her solace and hope. And he would glance at Frank, and hope they would love each other, hope Frank would soothe that pain in her heart, take it from her eyes; and her divorce, her age, and her children did not matter at all. On the first two evenings she did not bring her boys, and then Ruth asked her to bring them next time. In bed that night Ruth said, 'She hasn't brought them because she's embarrassed. She shouldn't feel embarrassed.'

Richard Strout shot Frank in front of the boys. They were sitting on the living room floor watching television, Frank sitting on the couch, and Mary Ann just returning from the kitchen with a tray of sandwiches. Strout came in the front door and shot Frank twice in the chest and once in the face with a 9 mm. automatic. Then he looked at the boys and Mary Ann, and went home to wait for the police.

It seemed to Matt that from the time Mary Ann called weeping to tell him until now, a Saturday night in September, sitting in the car with Willis, parked beside Strout's car, waiting for the bar to close, that he had not so much moved through his life as wandered through it, his spirit like a dazed body bumping into furniture and corners. He had always been a fearful father: when his children were young, at the start of each summer he thought of them drowning in a pond or the sea, and he was relieved when he came home in the evenings and they were there; usually that relief was his only acknowledgment of his fear, which he never spoke of, and which he controlled within his heart. As he had when they were very young and all of them in turn, Cathleen too, were drawn to the high oak in the backyard, and had to climb it. Smiling, he watched them, imagining the fall: and he was poised to catch the small body before it hit the earth. Or his legs were poised; his hands were in his pockets or his arms were folded and, for the child looking down, he appeared relaxed and confident while his heart beat with the two words he wanted to call out but did not: *Don't fall*. In winter he was less afraid: he made sure the ice would hold him before they skated, and he brought or sent them to places where they could sled without ending in the street. So he and his children had survived their childhood, and he only worried about them when he knew they were driving a long distance, and then he lost Frank in a way no father expected to lose his son, and he felt that all the fears he had borne while they were growing up, and all the grief he had been afraid of, had backed up like a huge wave and struck him on the beach and swept him out to sea. Each day he felt the same and when he was able to forget how he felt, when he was able to force himself not to feel that way, the eyes of his clerks and customers defeated him. He wished those eyes were oblivious, even cold; he felt he was withering in their tenderness. And beneath his listless wandering, every day in his soul he shot Richard Strout in the face; while Ruth, going about town on errands, kept seeing him. And at nights in bed she would hold Matt and cry, or sometimes she was silent and Matt would touch her tightening arm, her clenched fist.

As his own right fist was now, squeezing the butt of the revolver, the last of the drinkers having left the bar, talking to each other, going to their separate cars which were in the lot in front of the bar, out of Matt's vision. He heard their voices, their cars, and then the ocean again, across the street. The tide was in and sometimes it smacked the sea wall. Through the windshield he looked at the dark red side wall of the bar, and then to his left, past Willis, at Strout's car, and through its windows he could see the now-emptied parking lot, the road, the sea wall. He could smell the sea.

The front door of the bar opened and closed again and Willis looked at Matt then at the corner of the building; when Strout came

around it alone Matt got out of the car, giving up the hope he had
kept all night (and for the past week) that Strout would come out
with friends, and Willis would simply drive away; thinking: *All
right then*. *All right*; and he went around the front of Willis's car,
and at Strout's he stopped and aimed over the hood at Strout's blue
shirt ten feet away. Willis was aiming too, crouched on Matt's left,
his elbow resting on the hood.

'Mr. Fowler,' Strout said. He looked at each of them, and at the
guns. 'Mr. Trottier.'

Then Matt, watching the parking lot and the road, walked
quickly between the car and the building and stood behind Strout.
He took one leather glove from his pocket and put it on his left
hand.

'Don't talk. Unlock the front and back and get in.'

Strout unlocked the front door, reached in and unlocked the
back, then got in, and Matt slid into the back seat, closed the door
with his gloved hand, and touched Strout's head once with the
muzzle.

'It's cocked. Drive to your house.'

When Strout looked over his shoulder to back the car, Matt
aimed at his temple and did not look at his eyes.

'Drive slowly," he said. "Don't try to get stopped.'

They drove across the empty front lot and onto the road, Willis's
headlights shining into the car; then back through town, the sea
wall on the left hiding the beach, though far out Matt could see the
ocean; he uncocked the revolver; on the right were the places, most
with their neon signs off, that did so much business in summer: the
lounges and cafés and pizza houses, the street itself empty of traffic,
the way he and Willis had known it would be when they decided to
take Strout at the bar rather than knock on his door at two o'clock
one morning and risk that one insomniac neighbor. Matt had not
told Willis he was afraid he could not be alone with Strout for very
long, smell his smells, feel the presence of his flesh, hear his voice,
and then shoot him. They left the beach town and then were on the
high bridge over the channel: to the left the smacking curling white
at the breakwater and beyond that the dark sea and the full moon,
and down to his right the small fishing boats bobbing at anchor in
the cove. When they left the bridge, the sea was blocked by abandoned beach cottages, and Matt's left hand was sweating in the
glove. Out here in the dark in the car he believed Ruth knew. Willis

had come to his house at eleven and asked if he wanted a nightcap; Matt went to the bedroom for his wallet, put the gloves in one trouser pocket and the .38 in the other and went back to the living room, his hand in his pocket covering the bulge of the cool cylinder pressed against his fingers, the butt against his palm. When Ruth said goodnight she looked at his face, and he felt she could see in his eyes the gun, and the night he was going to. But he knew he couldn't trust what he saw. Willis's wife had taken her sleeping pill, which gave her eight hours—the reason, Willis had told Matt, he had the alarms installed, for nights when he was late at the restaurant—and when it was all done and Willis got home he would leave ice and a trace of Scotch and soda in two glasses in the game room and tell Martha in the morning that he had left the restaurant early and brought Matt home for a drink.

'He was making it with my wife.' Strout's voice was careful, not pleading.

Matt pressed the muzzle against Strout's head, pressed it harder than he wanted to, feeling through the gun Strout's head flinching and moving forward; then he lowered the gun to his lap.

'Don't talk,' he said.

Strout did not speak again. They turned west, drove past the Dairy Queen closed until spring, and the two lobster restaurants that faced each other and were crowded all summer and were now also closed, onto the short bridge crossing the tidal stream, and over the engine Matt could hear through his open window the water rushing inland under the bridge; looking to his left he saw its swift moonlit current going back into the marsh which, leaving the bridge, they entered: the salt marsh stretching out on both sides, the grass tall in patches but mostly low and leaning earthward as though windblown, a large dark rock sitting as though it rested on nothing but itself, and shallow pools reflecting the bright moon.

Beyond the marsh they drove through woods, Matt thinking now of the hole he and Willis had dug last Sunday afternoon after telling their wives they were going to Fenway Park. They listened to the game on a transistor radio, but heard none of it as they dug into the soft earth on the knoll they had chosen because elms and maples sheltered it. Already some leaves had fallen. When the hole was deep enough they covered it and the piled earth with dead branches, then cleaned their shoes and pants and went to a restaurant farther up in New Hampshire where they ate sandwiches and drank beer and watched the rest of the game on television. Looking at the back of Strout's head he thought of Frank's grave; he had not been back to it; but he would go before winter, and its second burial of snow.

He thought of Frank sitting on the couch and perhaps talking to the children as they watched television, imagined him feeling young and strong, still warmed from the sun at the beach, and feeling loved, hearing Mary Ann moving about in the kitchen, hearing her walking into the living room; maybe he looked up at her and maybe she said something, looking at him over the tray of sandwiches, smiling at him, saying something the way women do when they offer food as a gift, then the front door opening and this son of a bitch coming in and Frank seeing that he meant the gun in his hand, this son of a bitch and his gun the last person and thing Frank saw on earth.

When they drove into town the streets were nearly empty: a few slow cars, a policeman walking his beat past the darkened fronts of stores. Strout and Matt both glanced at him as they drove by. They were on the main street, and all the stoplights were blinking yellow. Willis and Matt had talked about that too: the lights changed at midnight, so there would be no place Strout had to stop and where he might try to run. Strout turned down the block where he lived and Willis's headlights were no longer with Matt in the back seat. They had planned that too, had decided it was best for just the one car to go to the house, and again Matt had said nothing about his fear of being alone with Strout, especially in his house: a duplex, dark as all the houses on the street were, the street itself lit at the corner of each block. As Strout turned into the driveway Matt thought of the one insomniac neighbor, thought of some man or woman sitting alone in the dark living room, watching the all-night channel from Boston. When Strout stopped the car near the front of the house, Matt said: 'Drive it to the back.'

He touched Strout's head with the muzzle.

'You wouldn't have it cocked, would you? For when I put on the brakes.'

Matt cocked it, and said: 'It is now.'

Strout waited a moment; then he eased the car forward, the engine doing little more than idling, and as they approached the garage he gently braked. Matt opened the door, then took off the glove and put it in his pocket. He stepped out and shut the door with his hip and said: 'All right.'

Strout looked at the gun, then got out, and Matt followed him across the grass, and as Strout unlocked the door Matt looked quickly at the row of small backyards on either side, and scattered tall trees, some evergreens, others not, and he thought of the red and yellow leaves on the trees over the hole, saw them falling soon, probably in two weeks, dropping slowly, covering. Strout stepped into the kitchen.

'Turn on the light.'

Strout reached to the wall switch, and in the light Matt looked at his wide back, the dark blue shirt, the white belt, the red plaid pants.

'Where's your suitcase?'

'My suitcase?'

'Where is it.'

'In the bedroom closet.'

'That's where we're going then. When we get to a door you stop and turn on the light.'

They crossed the kitchen, Matt glancing at the sink and stove and refrigerator: no dishes in the sink or even the dish rack beside it, no grease splashings on the stove, the refrigrator door clean and white. He did not want to look at any more but he looked quickly at all he could see: in the living room magazines and newspapers in a wicker basket, clean ashtrays, a record player, the records shelved next to it, then down the hall where, near the bedroom door, hung a color photograph of Mary Ann and the two boys sitting on a lawn—there was no house in the picture—Mary Ann smiling at the camera or Strout or whoever held the camera, smiling as she had on Matt's lawn this summer while he waited for the charcoal and they all talked and he looked at her brown legs and at Frank touching her arm, her shoulder, her hair; he moved down the hall with her smile in his mind, wondering: was that when they were both playing around and she was smiling like that at him and they were happy, even sometimes, making it worth it? He recalled her eyes, the pain in them, and he was conscious of the circles of love he was touching with the hand that held the revolver so tightly now as Strout stopped at the door at the end of the hall.

'There's no wall switch.'

'Where's the light?'

'By the bed.'

'Let's go.'

Matt stayed a pace behind, then Strout leaned over and the room was lighted: the bed, a double one, was neatly made; the ashtray on the bedside table clean, the bureau top dustless, and no photographs; probably so the girl—who *was* she?—would not have to see Mary Ann in the bedroom she believed was theirs. But because Matt was a father and a husband, though never an ex-husband, he knew (and did not want to know) that this bedroom had never been theirs alone. Strout turned around; Matt looked at his lips, his wide jaw, and thought of Frank's doomed and fearful eyes looking up from the couch.

'Where's Mr. Trottier?"

'He's waiting. Pack clothes for warm weather.'

'What's going on?'

'You're jumping bail.'

'Mr. Fowler—'

He pointed the cocked revolver at Strout's face. The barrel trembled but not much, not as much as he had expected. Strout went to the closet and got the suitcase from the floor and opened it on the bed. As he went to the bureau, he said: 'He was making it with my wife. I'd go pick up my kids and he'd be there. Sometimes he spent the night. My boys told me.'

He did not look at Matt as he spoke. He opened the top drawer and Matt stepped closer so he could see Strout's hands: underwear and socks, the socks rolled, the underwear folded and stacked. He took them back to the bed, arranged them neatly in the suitcase, then from the closet he was taking shirts and trousers and a jacket; he laid them on the bed and Matt followed him to the bathroom and watched from the door while he packed his shaving kit; watched in the bedroom as he folded and packed those things a person accumulated and that became part of him so that at times in the store Matt felt he was selling more than clothes.

'I wanted to try to get together with her again.' He was bent over the suitcase. 'I couldn't even talk to her. He was always with her. I'm going to jail for it; if I ever get out I'll be an old man. Isn't that enough?'

'You're not going to jail.'

Strout closed the suitcase and faced Matt, looking at the gun.

Matt went to his rear, so Strout was between him and the lighted hall; then using his handkerchief he turned off the lamp and said: 'Let's go.'

They went down the hall, Matt looking again at the photograph, and through the living room and kitchen, Matt turning off the lights and talking, frightened that he was talking, that he was telling this lie he had not planned: 'It's the trial. We can't go through that, my wife and me. So you're leaving. We've got you a ticket, and a job. A friend of Mr. Trottier's. Out west. My wife keeps seeing you. We can't have that anymore.'

Matt turned out the kitchen light and put the handkerchief in his pocket, and they went down the two brick steps and across the lawn. Strout put the suitcase on the floor of the back seat, then got into the front seat and Matt got in the back and put on his glove and shut the door.

'They'll catch me. They'll check passenger lists.'

'We didn't use your name.'

'They'll figure that out too. You think I wouldn't have done it myself if it was that easy?'

He backed into the street, Matt looking down the gun barrel but not at the profiled face beyond it.

'You were alone,' Matt said. 'We've got it worked out.'

'There's no planes this time of night, Mr. Fowler.'

'Go back through town. Then north on 125.'

They came to the corner and turned, and now Willis's headlights were in the car with Matt.

'Why north, Mr. Fowler?'

'Somebody's going to keep you for a while. They'll take you to the airport.' He uncocked the hammer and lowered the revolver to his lap and said wearily: 'No more talking.'

As they drove back through town, Matt's body sagged, going limp with his spirit and its new and false bond with Strout, the hope his lie had given Strout. He had grown up in this town whose streets had become places of apprehension and pain for Ruth as she drove and walked, doing what she had to do; and for him too, if only in his mind as he worked and chatted six days a week in his store; he wondered now if his lie would have worked, if sending Strout away would have been enough; but then he knew that just thinking of Strout in Montana or whatever place lay at the end of the lie he had told, thinking of him walking the streets there, loving a girl there (who *was* she?) would be enough to slowly rot the rest of his days. And Ruth's. Again he was certain that she knew, that she was waiting for him.

They were in New Hampshire now, on the narrow highway, passing the shopping center at the state line, and then houses and small stores and sandwich shops. There were few cars on the road. After ten minutes he raised his trembling hand, touched Strout's neck with the gun, and said: 'Turn in up here. At the dirt road.'

Strout flicked on the indicator and slowed.

'Mr. Fowler?'

'They're waiting here.'

Strout turned very slowly, easing his neck away from the gun. In the moonlight the road was light brown, lighter and yellowed where the headlights shone; weeds and a few trees grew on either side of it, and ahead of them were the woods.

'There's nothing back here, Mr. Fowler.'

'It's for your car. You don't think we'd leave it at the airport, do you?'

He watched Strout's large, big-knuckled hands tighten on the wheel, saw Frank's face that night: not the stitches and bruised eye and swollen lips, but his own hand gently touching Frank's jaw, turning his wounds to the light. They rounded a bend in the road and were out of sight of the highway: tall trees all around them now, hiding the moon. When they reached the abandoned gravel pit on the left, the bare flat earth and steep pale embankment behind it, and the black crowns of trees at its top, Matt said: 'Stop here.'

Strout stopped but did not turn off the engine. Matt pressed the gun hard against his neck, and he straightened in the seat and looked in the rearview mirror, Matt's eyes meeting his in the glass for an instant before looking at the hair at the end of the gun barrel.

'Turn it off.'

Strout did, then held the wheel with two hands, and looked in the mirror.

'I'll do twenty years, Mr. Fowler; at least. I'll be forty-six years old.'

'That's nine years younger than I am,' Matt said, and got out and took off the glove and kicked the door shut. He aimed at Strout's ear and pulled back the hammer. Willis's headlights were off and Matt heard him walking on the soft thin layer of dust, the hard earth beneath it. Strout opened the door, sat for a moment in the interior light, then stepped out onto the road. Now his face was pleading. Matt did not look at his eyes, but he could see it in the lips.

'Just get the suitcase. They're right up the road.'

Willis was beside him now, to his left. Strout looked at both guns. Then he opened the back door, leaned in, and with a jerk brought the suitcase out. He was turning to face them when Matt said: 'Just walk up the road. Just ahead.'

Strout turned to walk, the suitcase in his right hand, and Matt and Willis followed; as Strout cleared the front of his car he dropped the suitcase and, ducking, took one step that was the beginning of a sprint to his right. The gun kicked in Matt's hand, and the explosion of the shot surrounded him, isolated him in a nimbus of sound that cut him off from all his time, all his history, isolated him standing absolutely still on the dirt road with the gun in his hand, looking down at Richard Strout squirming on his belly, kicking one leg behind him, pushing himself forward, toward the woods. Then Matt went to him and shot him once in the back of the head.

Driving south to Boston, wearing both gloves now, staying in the middle lane and looking often in the rearview mirror at Willis's headlights, he relived the suitcase dropping, the quick dip and turn of Strout's back, and the kick of the gun, the sound of the shot. When he walked to Strout, he still existed within the first shot, still trembled and breathed with it. The second shot and the burial seemed to be happening to someone else, someone he was watching. He and Willis each held an arm and pulled Strout face-down off the road and into the woods, his bouncing sliding belt white under the trees where it was so dark that when they stopped at the top of the knoll, panting and sweating, Matt could not see where Strout's blue shirt ended and the earth began. They pulled off the branches then dragged Strout to the edge of the hole and went behind him and lifted his legs and pushed him in. They stood still for a moment. The woods were quiet save for their breathing, and Matt remembered hearing the movements of birds and small animals after the first shot. Or maybe he had not heard them. Willis went down to the road. Matt could see him clearly out on the tan dirt, could see the glint of Strout's car and, beyond the road, the gravel pit. Willis came back up the knoll with the suitcase. He dropped it in the hole and took off his gloves and they went down to his car for the spades. They worked quietly. Sometimes they paused to listen to the woods. When they were finished Willis turned on his flashlight and they covered the earth with leaves and branches and then went down to the spot in front of the car, and while Matt held the light Willis crouched and sprinkled dust on the blood, backing up till he reached the grass and leaves, then he used leaves until they had worked up to the grave again. They did not stop. They walked around the grave and through the woods, using the light on the ground, looking up through the trees to where they ended at the lake. Neither of them spoke above the sounds of their heavy and clumsy strides through low brush and over fallen branches. Then they reached it: wide and dark, lapping softly at the bank, pine needles smooth under Matt's feet, moonlight on the lake, a small island near its middle, with black, tall evergreens. He took out the gun and threw for the island: taking two steps back on the pine needles, striding with the throw and going to one knee as he followed through, looking up to see the dark shapeless object arcing downward, splashing.

They left Strout's car in Boston, in front of an apartment building on Commonwealth Avenue. When they got back to town Willis drove slowly over the bridge and Matt threw the keys into the Merrimack. The sky was turning light. Willis let him out a block from his house, and walking home he listened for sounds from the houses he passed. They were quiet. A light was on in his living room. He turned it off and undressed in there, and went softly toward the bedroom; in the hall he smelled the smoke, and he stood in the bedroom doorway and looked at the orange of her cigarette in the dark. The curtains were closed. He went to the closet and put his shoes on the floor and felt for a hanger.

'Did you do it?' she said.

He went down the hall to the bathroom and in the dark he washed his hands and face. Then he went to her, lay on his back, and pulled the sheet up to his throat.

'Are you all right?' she said.

'I think so.'

Now she touched him, lying on her side, her hand on his belly, his thigh.

'Tell me,' she said.

He started from the beginning, in the parking lot at the bar; but soon with his eyes closed and Ruth petting him, he spoke of Strout's house: the order, the woman presence, the picture on the wall.

'The way she was smiling,' he said.

'What about it?'

'I don't know. Did you ever see Strout's girl? When you saw him in town?'

'No.'

'I wonder who she was.'

Then he thought: *not was: is. Sleeping now she is his girl.* He opened his eyes, then closed them again. There was more light beyond the curtains. With Ruth now he left Strout's house and told again his lie to Strout, gave him again that hope that Strout must have for a while believed, else he would have to believe only the gun pointed at him for the last two hours of his life. And with Ruth he saw again the dropping suitcase, the darting move to the right: and he told of the first shot, feeling her hand on him but his heart isolated still, beating on the road still in that explosion like thunder. He told her the rest, but the words had no images for him, he did not see himself doing what the words said he had done; he only saw himself on that road.

'We can't tell the other kids,' she said. 'It'll hurt them, thinking he got away. But we mustn't.'

'No.'

She was holding him, wanting him, and he wished he could make love with her but he could not. He saw Frank and Mary Ann making love in her bed, their eyes closed, their bodies brown and smelling of the sea; the other girl was faceless, bodiless, but he felt her sleeping now; and he saw Frank and Strout, their faces alive; he saw red and yellow leaves falling to the earth, then snow: falling and freezing and falling; and holding Ruth, his cheek touching her breast, he shuddered with a sob that he kept silent in his heart.

The Dark Men

THEIR DARK CIVILIAN clothes defied him. They were from the Office of Naval Intelligence, they sat in his leather chairs in his cabin, they poured coffee from his silver pot, and although they called him Captain and Sir, they denied or outmaneuvered his shoulder boards by refusing to wear their own. He did not know whether they were officers or not, they could even be civilians, and they came aboard his ship and into his cabin, they told him names which he had already forgotten and, in quiet inflectionless voices, as if they were bringing no news at all, they told him that three months ago, during a confession in San Francisco, someone gave them Joe Saldi's name; and they told him what they had been doing for those three months, and what they had discovered. Then for a few moments they were talking but he wasn't listening and there were no images in his mind, not yet; he didn't see their faces either, though he was looking at them. If he was seeing anything at all, he was seeing the cold, sinking quickening of his heart. Then he entered their voices again, met their eyes, these men who looked for the dark sides of other men, and then he looked at his watch and said: 'I've forgotten your names.'

They told him. He offered them more coffee and they took it, and as they poured he watched their hands and faces: they appeared to be in their late thirties. Their faces were drained of color, they were men who worked away from the sun. Todd pinched his earlobe; Foster breathed through his mouth. At times it was audible. Foster now had a dispatch case on his lap; the raised top of it concealed his hands, then he lifted a large manila envelope and handed it to Captain Devereaux. The Captain laid it in front of him; then slowly, with a forefinger, pushed it aside, toward the photograph of his wife.

'I wonder how much you've missed,' he said.

'We have enough,' Foster said.

'That's not what I meant. I suppose he doesn't have much of a chance.'

'I wouldn't think so,' Foster said. 'But we don't make recommendations. We only investigate.'

'They always resign,' Todd said.

Captain Devereaux looked at him. Then he picked up the envelope and dropped it across his desk, near Foster.

'I don't want to read it.'

Foster and Todd looked at each other; Todd pinched his ear.

'Very well,' Foster said. 'Then I suppose we could see him now.'

'I suppose you could.' He dialed Joe's stateroom, waited seven rings, then hung up and told them Commander Saldi's plane was ashore and he might have gone flying. He went to the door and opened it and the Marine orderly saluted. The Captain told him to get Commander Saldi on the phone; he told him to try the pilots' wardroom and the commanders' wardroom and the officers' barber shop.

'I'll try the OOD too, sir.'

'Do that last.'

Then he sat at his desk and looked at them. Out of habit he was thinking of a way to make conversation but then he decided he would not. He looked away and tried not to hear Foster breathing.

'He should be flown home tomorrow,' Foster said. 'It's better for everyone that way.'

'Before the word gets out,' Todd said. 'It always gets out.'

'You shouldn't complain.'

'What's that, Captain?'

'It's how you make your living, isn't it? On word that gets out?' Now he looked at them. 'And where do you think he'll be flown to? I mean where do you think he will choose?'

'I don't know where he'll go, Captain,' Foster said. 'Our job is only to make sure he does.'

'You contradict yourself. You said your job was only to investigate.'

'Captain—'

'Yes, Mr. Foster?'

'Never mind, Captain.'

'Have some coffee, Mr. Foster. Don't be disappointed because I'm not making your work easy. Why should it be?'

'We understand you're a friend of his,' Todd said. He was trying to sound gentle. 'We understand that.'

'Do you, Mr. Todd?' The orderly knocked. 'It's strange to talk to you gentlemen; you don't wear ribbons. I have no way of knowing where you've been.'

'It doesn't matter where we've been,' Foster said.

'Maybe that's my point.'

He rose and went to the door. The orderly saluted.

'Sir, the OOD says Commander Saldi went ashore. He'll be back at eighteen hundred.'

'When did the boat leave?" Foster said.

Captain Devereaux looked at him. He was twisted around in his chair.

'What boat is that, Mr. Foster?'

'The one Commander Saldi took.'

Captain Devereaux looked at the orderly.

'Fifteen minutes ago, sir.'

Foster took the envelope from the Captain's desk, put it in his dispatch case, and he and Todd stood up. Captain Devereaux held the door. When they were abreast of him they stopped.

'I don't know what you think you've gained,' Foster said.

'Have a good day in Iwakuni,' the Captain said.

'We'll be back tonight.'

From his door he watched them cross the passageway and start down the ladder. Then he turned to the orderly.

'Have my boat alongside in thirty minutes. Wait: do you know Commander Saldi? What he looks like?'

'Yes sir.'

'Then make it an hour for the boat. Then go eat your lunch. I want you to come with me.'

The carrier was huge, it was anchored far out, and the ride in the launch took twenty minutes. It was a warm blue summer day and, to go ashore, he had changed from khakis to whites. He sat in the rear of the launch, his back against the gunwale, holding his cap so it wouldn't blow off; Corporal Swanson sat opposite him, wearing a white pistol belt and a .45 in a spit-shined holster, his cap chin-strapped to his head, dozing in the warm sun, his chin sinking slowly till it touched his necktie, then he snapped his head up and glanced at the Captain who pretended he hadn't seen, and in a few moments the sun did its work again and Swanson—who looked hung over—fought it for a while and then lost until his chin again touched the knot of his tie, and it stayed there; soon his mouth was open. The Captain looked back at the carrier, diminished now but still huge against the sky and the sea beyond; then he turned away and looked up at the blue sky and at the green and rocky shore, his vision broken once by the hull of a British freighter, then shore line again, while in his mind he saw Joe in the orange flight suit, helmet under his arm, crossing the flight deck and turning his face into the wind; sometimes Joe looked up at the bridge and smiled and waved: thinning black hair, a suntanned face that never seemed weary, and the Captain, looking down through glass and lifting his arm in a wave, felt his own weariness, and he yearned for the wind out there, away from the bridge that could make him an admiral, and away from the cabin where he slept little and badly and smoked too much and drank too much coffee and took Maalox after his meals; and Joe would move on to his plane near the catapult and beyond him the Pacific glittered under the sun, and the endless blue sky waited to lift him up; but now images collided in the Captain's mind, images of night and shame, and he actually shook his head to cast them out and to cast out memory too, thinking he must move from one moment to the next and that no matter what he did the day held no hope, and that memory and imagination would only make it worse; he gazed ahead at the white buildings of the Marine air base and he looked at the boat's wake, and kept himself from thinking about what had happened in his heart this morning when, as soon as Foster spoke Joe's name, he had known what was coming next and though he had been Joe's friend for thirteen years this was the first time he knew that he knew it.

As the boat neared the wharf Corporal Swanson was rubbing his neck and blinking his eyes. When the engine slowed, the Captain leaned forward and told him what to do.

'After that,' he said, 'you can sack out till I get back.'

It was early Thursday afternoon, so there weren't many people in the Officers' Club. A commander and his handsome wife were finishing lunch. The commander was a flight surgeon. Three Marine pilots were drinking at the bar. They were loud and happy and the Captain liked being near them. He chose a small polished table with two leather chairs, and he sat facing the door. A Japanese girl took his order. She was pretty and she wore a purple kimono of silk brocade, and as she walked back to the bar he felt an instant's yearning and then it was gone and he was both amused and wistful because either age or responsibility or both had this year kept him clean. He was finishing his second drink when Joe stepped in, wearing whites with short sleeves, four rows of ribbons under the gold wings on his breast, his white cap under his arm like a football; he stood looking about the room while his eyes adjusted and Captain Devereaux raised his hand and Joe saw him and waved and came forward. The Captain stood and took his hand and nodded toward the laughing pilots at the bar.

'It is peacetime and the pilots are happy pretending to make war. I'm about to start my third gimlet. Are you behind?'

'I am.'

They sat, and the Captain signalled to the Japanese girl at the end of the bar, pointed at his glass and at Joe and then himself. Under the table Joe clicked his heels, and briskly raised his hand and held it salute-like at his brow: 'Commander Saldi, sir. Captain Devereaux wishes the Commander to join him at the O Club sir. In the bar sir. He says if the Commander wishes to go back to the ship instead, sir, he is to send me to get the Captain and the Captain will take the Commander back to the ship in the Captain's boat. Sir.' He snapped off the salute. 'Jesus Christ, Ray, I'll drink with you. You don't have to send them out with .45's.'

The girl lowered the drinks and Joe reached for his wallet but the Captain was quicker and paid.

'What about lunch,' Joe said. 'Have you had lunch?'

The girl was waiting.

'I'll buy you a lunch,' the Captain said.

He watched the girl going back to the bar, then he looked at Joe, and Joe raised his glass and the Captain raised his and they touched them over the table.

'Old Captain Devereaux.'

'Old is right. I don't sleep much, out there. My gut's going too.'

'Gimlets'll back up on you.'

'It's the lime, not the gin.'

'Right.'

'How do you know? Is yours on the blink too?'

'Not now. It has been.'

'Not an ulcer.'

'Oh hell no. *You* don't have one, do you?'

'Just acid. I ought to retain the booze and get rid of cigarettes and coffee.'

The girl gave them the menus and then went away.

'You ought to have the lasagna, Joe.'

'Where is it?'

'It's spelled sukiyaki.'

'I don't like lasagna anyway.'

'Really?'

'Too heavy.'

'I'll have the sukiyaki.'

'So will I.'

'Should we have sake too?'

'How's your gut?'

'Fine. I'm going to lay off this lime juice.'

'Then let's have hot sake.'

When they laid down the menus the girl came and took their order and the Captain told her to bring his friend another drink but to leave him out.

'It's my stomach,' he told her. 'It needs gentleness.'

'Oh? I could bring you some nice milk.'

'No, not milk, thanks.'

'What about Asahi?'

'Yes: fine. Bring me a big Asahi.'

She brought Joe's gimlet and his beer, and after a glass of it he quietly belched and felt better but not good enough, so he told Joe he'd be right back and he went to the men's room and took from his pocket the aspirin tin containing six Maalox tablets and chewed two of them. He went back into the bar, approaching the table from Joe's rear and, looking at his shoulders and the back of his head, he felt a power he didn't want but had anyway, and he felt like a traitor for having it.

'You ought to get up more,' Joe said.

'I know.'

'Let's do it then.'

'When?'

'After lunch. We can walk over to the field and go up for an hour.'

'With gin and beer and sake.'

'Oxygen'll fix you up.'

'I can't though. I have things at the ship.'

'Let them wait.'

'They won't.'

'Tomorrow then.'

'Tomorrow?' He frowned, pretending he was trying to remember what tomorrow held for him, then he said: 'All right. Tomorrow,' and saying the word gave him a sense of plaintive hope that somehow and impossibly this moment with drinks and waiting for lunch would flow into a bright afternoon of tomorrow with Joe off his wing as they climbed from Iwakuni and out over the blue sea. And with that hope came longing: he wanted Foster and Todd to vanish, he wanted to go to sea next week and launch Joe into the wind, he wanted to not know what he knew and, with this longing, fear came shivering into his breast, and he did what he could not recall doing since he was a boy trying to talk to his father, a young boy, before he finally gave up and became silent: he promised himself that when a certain thing happened he would tell Joe: when his cigarette burned down; when he finished his beer; when the girl brought the sukiyaki; when Joe finished telling his story; and as each of these occurred, a third and powerful hand of his clutched his throat and squeezed.

The girl stood smiling and serving them until all the sukiyaki was on their plates and then she left, and he was chilled by her leaving because he had been flirting with her, praising the meal and her kimono and her face and small delicate hands, he had been cocking his head to her and glancing up at her, not up very high because he was a tall man and sat tall and she was barely over five feet and maybe not even that; now she was gone. He started to look at Joe, then poured sake into the china tumbler and carefully pinched rice with his chopsticks and dipped it into raw egg and, leaning forward, quickly raised it to his mouth, and heard over Joe's voice the drinking talk of the Marines at the bar, and he chewed his rice and hated his fear and silence and when he took another swallow of sake the acid rose to his throat and he held his breath for a moment till it went down, and then took another swallow and that one was all right. Joe was laughing: '—and he said I couldn't bail out, Commander. I'm afraid of sharks. You see, he really meant it but the bombardier and the crewman didn't believe him. They thought he believed he had a chance to make it, and he was just being cheerful to help them along. Truth was, he thought he'd go down, but he wasn't going into the water without that plane around him. So he kept telling them: look, you guys better jump, and they'd say what about you, and he'd say not me, I ain't getting down there with no sharks. So they stuck with him and he hit the ship first try, he said if he'd got waved off that time he'd have gone in and too low for anybody to bail out and he was cussing the other two for making him responsible for them going down too. But then he made it and I gave him a shot of rye in my room and he told me, You see, I don't even wade. Not in salt water. I haven't been in salt water for fourteen years. He was shot down, you see, in the Pacific, and he swam to his raft and he was climbing aboard when a shark got his co-pilot. He said the water turned red. He said I heard that scream every night for ten years. He said I ain't been in the water ever since and if any shark's going to get Chuck Thomson he's going to be the most disguised shark you ever saw because he's going to cross two hundred feet of sand walking on his tail and wearing a double-breasted pinstripe suit and some of them reflecting sunglasses—' Then Joe was laughing again, and the Captain was too, his body jerked and made sounds and then he was telling a story too, listening to it as it took shape, just as he had watched and listened to his own laughter: another story of men who had nearly gone into the sea and then had laughed, and after that Joe told one and then he told another, and they kept going. They did not tell stories of valor without humor, as though valor were expected but humor was not, and the man who had both was better. And they did not talk about the dead. Sometimes they spoke a name but that was all. Three o'clock came and the girl brought more tea and Captain Devereaux went to the men's room and chewed two more tablets, standing alone at the mirror, but Joe's ghost was with him, and he went back to the table and looked at Joe and he could not feel the wine now, his heart was quick, his fingers tight on the tumbler of tea, and he said : 'There are two men, Joe. On my ship. Or they were. They're coming back tonight.' And already Joe's eyes brightened, even before the Captain said: 'They're from ONI, Joe, and it's about you.'

Joe turned in his chair and gazed off toward the bar and shut his eyes and rubbed his forehead and murmured something he couldn't hear and didn't want to, and then it was over, the long bantering friendship between them, he felt it go out of him like dry tears through his ribs and for an instant, watching Joe's profiled face that could never look at him again, he raged at the other face he had never seen, impassioned and vulnerable in the night, then the rage was gone too and he sat watching Joe rubbing his forehead, watched Joe profiled in that place of pain and humiliation where he had fallen and where the Captain could never go. Yet still he kept talking, threw words into the space, bounced them off the silent jaw and shoulder: 'Listen, I hate the bastards. I don't want you to see them. They're going to tell you general court or resign, but I'm going to tell them to get the hell off my ship, and I'll handle it. No one will know anything. Not for a while anyway. Not till you've written your letter and gone. And still they won't know why. I don't care about what they told me, I want you to know that. They brought paperwork and it was sealed and it still is and it'll stay that way. I don't give a good Goddamn and I never *did*. You hear me, Joe?'

He waited. Joe nodded, looking at the bar.

'I hear you, Captain.'

For perhaps a minute they sat that way. Then Captain Devereaux got up and touched Joe's shoulder and walked out.

Corporal Swanson was sleeping in the sun, his cap over his eyes, and he did not wake when the Captain and the coxswain and crew descended into the gently rocking boat, did not wake until Captain Deveraux softly spoke his name. Then he stood quickly and saluted and the Captain smiled and asked if he'd had a good nap. All the way back to the ship he talked to Swanson; or, rather, asked him questions and watched him closely and tried to listen. Swanson was not staying in the Marines; in another year he'd get out and go to college in South Dakota. He wasn't sure yet what he wanted to be. He had a girl in South Dakota and he meant to marry her. The Captain sat smiling and nodding and asking, and sometimes he leaned forward to listen over the sound of the engine, and it wasn't until the launch drew within a hundred yards of the ship that he knew Joe wasn't coming back, and then at once he knew he had already known that too, had known in the Club that Joe's isolation was determined and forever, and now he twisted around and looked back over his shoulder, into the sky above the air base, then looked forward again at the huge ship, at its high grey hull which now rose straight above him, casting a shadow across the launch.

At six-thirty Foster and Todd found him on the flight deck. He had been there for an hour, walking the thousand feet from fore to aft, looking into the sky and out at the sea. When they emerged from the island and moved toward him, walking abreast and leaning into the wind, he was standing at the end of the flight deck. He saw them coming and looked away. The sun was going down. Out there, toward the open sea, a swath of gold lay on the water. When they stopped behind him he did not turn around. He was thinking that, from a distance, a plane flying in the sunset looks like a moving star. Then shutting his eyes he saw the diving silver plane in the sunset, and then he was in it, his heart pounding with the dive, the engine roaring in his blood, and he saw the low red sun out the cockpit and, waiting, the hard and yielding sea.

'Commander Saldi is not here,' he said.

'Not here?' It was Foster. 'Where is he?'

'He's out there.'

Foster stepped around and stood in front of him, and then Todd did, and they stood side by side, facing him, but he continued to stare at the sun on the water.

'Out there?' Foster said. 'You let him fly? In a million dollar—'

Captain Devereaux looked at him, and he stopped.

'Iwakuni lost contact with him an hour ago,' the Captain said.

'You told him,' Foster said. 'You told him and let him go up—'

This time the Captain did not bother to look at him; he stepped through the space between them and stood on the forward edge of the flight deck. He stood there, motionless and quiet, then he heard Foster and Todd going away, only a moment's footsteps on the deck before all sound of them was gone in the wind, and still he watched as the sun went down and under the pale fading light of the sky the sea darkened until finally it was black.

His Lover

W HEN SCOTTY stopped the police car, Moissant opened the door and put his cane out
first. He had both legs out when Scotty said:
'Leo? It's funny you never asked her anything. Where they went at
night.'

He did not turn his head; he had been blind for over a year, and it
had taken him almost that long to break the habit of looking at
people whenever they spoke.

'It didn't matter,' he said.

He got out and shut the door but kept his hand on it. The breeze
came from the sea, and he knew from the smell of the salt marsh
down the road that the tide was out. He lowered his head to the
window so Scotty wouldn't have to talk to his belt buckle, and said:
'She really liked killing those people?'

'She liked talking about it too. I didn't mean you *should* have
asked her anything.'

'She was pretty, wasn't she?'

'She's pretty. You give a man something to look forward to.'

'That's what her name means. In Spanish.'

He walked away, touching with his cane the grass and earth
ahead of him. He stopped and listened to the car going east, and
when he couldn't hear it anymore he went around his trailer to the
back lawn, to the hammock Linda had hung from two pines, and he
settled into it and took off his sunglasses. He felt shade across his
ankles and feet but that was all, and he unbuttoned his shirt and
opened it to the sun. Sometimes in the afternoon Linda took him to
the hammock; they left his cane inside and she held his hand. She

told him the hammock and the van could not be seen from the road, they were hidden by his trailer and the woods, and it was nice to be quiet and secret back there. She sat on the ground beside him. Usually he fell asleep on the hammock and when he woke she was gone to the van where the other girl and the boy were. He could hear their radio music. She always came back to him, soon after he woke.

He rarely spoke to the other two, and they never came to his trailer. It was Linda who had talked to him that first day, had asked if they could park their van in his backyard for a few days. They were from New Mexico and they wanted to spend some time at the Atlantic. He had put on his sunglasses and stepped out of the morning cool of his trailer to talk to her, and he liked her voice coming out of the sun. He almost said no because he knew it was the same van that had gone past his trailer three times in the last two days, once while he was pushing the lawnmower, walking barefooted so he'd know where he had been; he had stopped mowing and turned his face with the van as if he could see it. But he said yes. He had outlived everyone he cared about and now had outlived his eyes too. There was nothing they could take from him.

Then on the first night Linda knocked on his door and he regretted saying yes that morning because now they would want more, it would start with borrowing salt and end with them swarming all over the life he had learned to live. But she did not want to borrow anything. She wanted to cook his dinner. He told her he could do it himself; and while she cooked and he waited to hear the other two coming to move the chairs around and eat with them, he told her how he cooked by smelling and time-guessing and sticking and touching with a fork. She asked how he got his food and he said the grocer's son delivered it. The other girl and the boy did not come, and when she put the plates on the table he thought he should have been able to tell by listening that she had brought and cooked two steaks, not four. For a while they ate quietly, then she asked if he had put on his sunglasses when she knocked on the door. Yes: he didn't wear them when he was alone. Gently she lifted them from his face: it was the first time she touched him. They must be ugly, he said. No: no, they looked like egg whites: like the white of a soft-fried egg, and the eyeballs were like blue marbles under milk.

She washed the dishes while he sat near the screen door and felt the sun going down, the air cooling, and he imagined the long shadows of the pines on the trailer and the lawn and the road. She brought him a beer and sat at the table and asked if she could smoke. Sure, he'd given them up when he was sixty-two and that was eight years ago and if he hadn't gone through such hell to quit he'd have one with her. A smile was in her voice: she didn't mean a cigarette. Oh: marijuana; no, he didn't care. He liked the smell, and he thought her inhaling was funny. Do you have to draw that deep on it? She said mmmm with her breath held. Then she let it out. Is it like booze? Better; quicker; you want to try it? He smiled. He wanted to. But maybe some other time. It took him a while to get around to something new. He had been a boozer. You could say he had been a bad one. But he had retired from whiskey a long time ago, before it caused him any more trouble with either men or women. Only a little beer now at night.

He felt her watching him and then, incredulous and slow to hope, he felt the way she was watching him and he lowered his face to hide his eyes, and basked in her watching. Then her chair slid back and she came lightfooted around the table and stood behind him. Her hands slipped under his shirt and slowly and softly rubbed his chest. She licked his ear and whispered and his body quivered yet his loins were stalled by the question he didn't ask: Why him? Then rising he received her arm around his waist and went with her to his bed. Slowly she took off his clothes while he touched her.

In the morning he listened to her sleeping. Her naked back was against his side. When the trailer warmed she turned to him with her hands and tongue, and he told her he'd thought he would never have a woman again; it had been six years; six years last May. A widow up in Portsmouth. Named Florence. She wasn't as old as he was but she might as well have been. She grew up in Alabama and she still talked like it. It was warm weather, and you could see the girls' legs again. One day Florence saw him watching and she said the young girls come out in spring, like snakes.

On their third night he felt her getting out of bed and he listened to her dress and creep out of the trailer; after a while the van drove slowly out to the road and toward the sea. He lay awake and told himself it was all right, it would be easy enough to start tomorrow without her. Finally he even felt peaceful, and he slept. Then the van came back, and she sneaked into the trailer and undressed and cautiously got into bed. After that he was amused when her leaving waked him; he thought of the night clubs and the beach in the moonlight; he slept until the van returned, and when she was naked in his bed he slept again. Last night he woke because the van did not return; he lay waiting until he knew it was morning, then he dressed and made coffee and was still at the kitchen table when the car came up the road and into the driveway; he put on his glasses and turned his face to the screen door, and then Scotty standing outside told him they had three young people for the murder of a summer couple in a beach house and the one girl who did all the talking said they'd stayed at his place for the past month and if that was true would he mind coming to the station just to make a statement.

She cooked all his meals, and she ate with him. She bought fish and fresh vegetables and fruit in town; she never placed an order with the Peters boy, was never in the trailer when he delivered groceries. One night Moissant said he'd smoke with her. He let her roll it for him but he lit it himself, slowly moving the flame's heat up to his mouth. He laughed and wanted a shower and they stood under the spray till the water turned cold, then went to bed without drying and he pressed his face into her long wet hair. Then all the nights after dinner he smoked with her.

Last night she had blood on her clothes when she talked to Scotty. She couldn't even count the houses they had broken into up and down the coast. She didn't want to talk about that. She wanted to talk about stabbing the man and woman. She said she liked it. She had killed a man they robbed in a motel in Colorado. He was a stupid man. He thought they were junkies and if he gave them money they would go away. He was surprised when she stuck her knife in his fat stomach. She would like to stab the chief of police and his two cops. She would save the chief for last. It was nothing personal. She would just like to do it. The other girl was waiting in the van and she and the boy were in the bedroom looking for the money. They were very quiet; they were quieter than the sea. She could hear the waves outside. But the man woke up. She was near the bed when she heard him move. Before he could get his feet on the floor she stabbed him. She stabbed him again while the boy grabbed the woman and put his hand over her mouth. The woman was on her stomach and he was sitting on her back and holding her arms behind her and she was moaning into his hand. He told Linda to look for something to tie her with. Linda said okay and reached across the man and stabbed her in the back. The boy ran out of the house but she kept stabbing till the moaning and jerking stopped.

Lying in the hammock Moissant loved her hands: going down his shirt that first night and combing the hair of his chest while her tongue wet his ear and she whispered; her hands taking off his clothes; her small soft hand stroking slow and patient until she could not close it. In the long nights he kneeled astride her legs and his hands caressed her body, like a child on the beach smoothing a figure made of sand. Under the high sun he was sleepy, was going, a dream starting, pines and fetid marsh breath and seawind in the dream; her smell; her breathing; he was swelling, then erect, and the dream was gone like fog burned away by the sun on his face. Then he slept.

Townies

THE CAMPUS SECURITY guard found her. She wore a parka and she lay on the footbridge over the pond. Her left cheek lay on the frozen snow. The college was a small one, he was the only guard on duty, and in winter he made his rounds in the car. But partly because he was sleepy in the heated car, and mostly because he wanted to get out of the car and walk in the cold dry air, wanted a pleasurable solitude within the imposed solitude of his job, he had gone to the bridge.

He was sixty-one years old, a tall broad man, but his shoulders slumped and he was wide in the hips and he walked with his toes pointed outward, with a long stride which appeared slow. His body, whether at rest or in motion, seemed the result of sixty-one years of erosion, as though all his life he had been acted upon and, with just enough struggle to keep going, he had conceded; fifty years earlier he would have sat quietly at the rear of a classroom, scraped dirt with his shoe on the periphery of a playground. In a way, he was the best man to find her. He was not excitable, he was not given to anger, he was not a man of action: when he realized the girl was dead he did not think immediately of what he ought to do, of what acts and words his uniform and wages required of him. He did not think of phoning the police. He knelt on the snow, so close to her that his knee touched her shoulder, and he stroked her cold cheek, her cold blonde hair.

He did not know her name. He had seen her about the campus. He believed she had died of an overdose of drugs or a mixture of drugs and liquor. This deepened his sorrow. Often when he thought of what young people were doing to themselves, he felt confused and sad, as though in the country he loved there were a civil war whose causes baffled him, whose victims seemed wounded and dead without reason. Especially the girls, and especially these girls. He had lived all his life in this town, a small city in northeastern Massachusetts; once there had been a shoe industry. Now that was over, only three factories were open, and the others sat empty along the bank of the Merrimack. Their closed windows and the dark empty rooms beyond them stared at the street, like the faces of the old and poor who on summer Sundays sat on the stoops of the old houses farther upriver and stared at the street, the river, the air before their eyes. He had worked in a factory, as a stitcher. When the factory closed he got a job driving a truck, delivering fresh loaves of bread to families in time for their breakfast. Then people stopped having their bread delivered. It was a change he did not understand. He had loved the smell of bread in the morning and its warmth in his hands. He did not know why the people he had delivered to would choose to buy bread in a supermarket. He did not believe that the pennies and nickels saved on one expense ever showed up in your pocket.

When they stopped eating fresh bread in the morning he was out of work for a while, but his children were grown and his wife did not worry, and then he got his last and strangest job. He was not an authorized constable, he carried no weapons, and he needed only one qualification other than the usual ones of punctuality and subservience: a willingness to work for very little money. He was so accustomed to all three that none of them required an act of will, not even a moment's pause while he made the decision to take and do the job. When he worked a daylight shift he spent some time ordering possible vandals off the campus: they were usually children on bicycles; sometimes they made him chase them away, and he did this in his long stride, watching the distance lengthen between him and the children, the bicycles. Mostly during the day he chatted with the maintenance men and students and some of the teachers; and he walked the campus, which was contained by an iron fence and four streets, and he looked at the trees. There were trees he recognized, and more that he did not. One of the maintenance men had told him that every kind of New England tree grew here. There was one with thick, low, spreading branches and, in the fall, dark red leaves; sometimes students sat on the branches.

The time he saw three girls in the tree he was fooled: they were pretty and they wore sweaters in the warm autumn afternoon. They looked like the girls he had grown up knowing about: the rich girls who came from all parts of the country to the school, and who were rarely seen in town. From time to time some of them walked the three blocks from the campus to the first row of stores where the commercial part of the town began. But most of them only walked the one block, to the corner where they waited for the bus to Boston. He had smelled them once, as a young man. It was a winter day. When he saw them waiting for the bus he crossed the street so he could walk near them. There were perhaps six of them. As he approached, he looked at their faces, their hair. They did not look at him. He walked by them. He could smell them and he could feel their eyes seeing him and not seeing him. Their smells were of perfume, cold fur, leather gloves, leather suitcases. Their voices had no accents he could recognize. They seemed the voices of mansions, resorts, travel. He was too conscious of himself to hear what they were saying. He knew it was idle talk; but its tone seemed peremptory; he would not have been surprised if one of them had suddenly given him a command. Then he was away from them. He smelled only the cold air now; he longed for their smells again: erotic, unattainable, a world that would never be open to him. But he did not think about its availability, any more than he would wish for an African safari. He knew people who hated them because they were rich. But he did not. In the late sixties more of them began appearing in town and they wore blue jeans and smoked on the street. In the early seventies, when the drinking age was lowered, he heard they were going to the bars at night, and some of them got into trouble with the local boys. Also, the college started accepting boys, and they lived in the dormitories with the girls. He wished all this were not so; but by then he wished much that was happening was not so.

When he saw the three girls in the tree with low spreading branches and red leaves, he stopped and looked across the lawn at them, stood for a moment that was redolent of his past, of the way he had always seen the college girls, and still tried to see them: lovely and nubile, existing in an ambience of benign royalty. Their sweaters and hair seemed bright as the autumn sky. He walked toward them, his hands in his back pockets. They watched him. Then he stood under the tree, his eyes level with their legs. They were all biting silenced giggles. He said it was a pretty day. Then the giggles came, shrill and relentless; they could have been monkeys in the tree. There was an impunity about the giggling that was different from the other graceful impunity they carried with them as they carried the checkbooks that were its source. He was accustomed to that. He looked at their faces, at their vacant eyes and flushed cheeks; then his own cheeks flushed with shame. It was marijuana. He lifted a hand in goodbye.

He was not angry. He walked with lowered eyes away from the giggling tree, walked impuissant and slow across the lawn and around the snack bar, toward the library; then he shifted direction and with raised eyes went toward the ginkgo tree near the chapel. There was no one around. He stood looking at the yellow leaves, then he moved around the tree and stopped to read again the bronze plaque he had first read and marvelled at his second day on the job. It said the tree was a gift of the class of 1941. He stood now as he had stood on that first day, in a reverie which refreshed his bruised heart, then healed it. He imagined the girls of 1941 standing in a circle as one of the maintenance men dug a hole and planted the small tree. The girls were pretty and hopeful and had sweethearts. He thought of them later in that year, in winter; perhaps skiing while the *Arizona* took the bombs. He was certain that some of them lost sweethearts in that war, which at first he had followed in the newspapers as he now followed the Red Sox and Patriots and Celtics and Bruins. Then he was drafted. They made him a truck driver and he saw England while the war was still on, and France when it was over. He was glad that he missed combat and when he returned he did not pretend to his wife and family and friends that he wished he had been shot at. Going over, he had worried about submarines; other than that, he had enjoyed his friends and England and France, and he had saved money. He still remembered it as a pleasurable interlude in his life. Looking at the ginkgo tree and the plaque he happily felt their presence like remembered music: the girls then, standing in a circle around the small tree on that spring day in 1941; those who were in love and would grieve; and he stood in the warmth of the afternoon staring at the yellow leaves strewn on the ground like deciduous sunshine.

So this last one was his strangest job: he was finally among them, not quite their servant like the cleaning women and not their protector either: an unarmed watchman and patrolman whose job con-

sisted mostly of being present, of strolling and chatting in daylight
and, when he drew the night shift, of driving or walking, depend-
ing on the weather, and of daydreaming and remembering and talking to himself. He enjoyed the job. He would not call it work, but
that did not bother him. He had long ago ceased believing in work:
the word and its connotation of fulfillment as a man. Life was cluttered with these ideas which he neither believed nor disputed. He
merely ignored them. He liked wandering about in this job, as he
had liked delivering bread and had liked the Army; only the stitching had been tedious. He liked coming home and drinking coffee in
the kitchen with his wife: the daily chatting which seemed eternal.
He liked his children and his grandchildren. He accepted the rest of
his life as a different man might accept commuting: a tolerable in-
convenience. He knew he was not lazy. That was another word he
did not believe in.

He kneeled on the snow and with his ungloved hand he touched
her cold blonde hair. In sorrow his flesh mingled like death-ash
with the pierced serenity of the night air and the trees on the banks
of the pond and the stars. He felt her spirit everywhere, fog-like
across the pond and the bridge, spreading and rising in silent weeping above him into the black visible night and the invisible space
beyond his ken and the cold silver truth of the stars.

On the bridge Mike slipped and cursed, catching himself on the
wooden guard rail, but still she did not look back. He was about to
speak her name but he did not: he knew if his voice was angry she
would not stop and if his voice was pleading she might stop and
even turn to wait for him but he could not bear to plead. He walked
faster. He had the singular focus that came from being drunk and
sad at the same time: he saw nothing but her parka and blonde hair.
All evening, as they drank, he had been waiting to lie with her in
her bright clean room. Now there would be no room. He caught up
with her and grabbed her arm and spun her around; both her feet
slipped but he held her up.

'You asshole,' she said, and he struck her with his fist, saw the
surprise and pain in her eyes, and she started to speak but he struck
her before she could; and when now she only moaned he swung
again and again, holding her up with his left hand, her parka
bunched and twisted in his grip; when he released her she fell forward. He kicked her side. He knew he should stop but he could

not. Kicking, he saw her naked in the bed in her room. She was slender. She moaned and gasped while they made love; sometimes she came so hard she cried. He stopped kicking. He knew she had died while he was kicking her. Something about the silence of the night, and the way her body yielded to his boot.

He looked around him: the frozen pond, the tall trees, the darkened library. He squatted down and looked at her red-splotched cheek. He lifted her head and turned it and lowered it to the snow. Her right cheek was untouched; now she looked asleep. In the mornings he usually woke first, hung over and hard, listening to students passing in the hall. Now on the snow she looked like that: in bed, on her pillow. Under the blanket he took her hand and put it around him and she woke and they smoked a joint; then she kneeled between his legs and he watched her hair going up and down.

He stood and walked off the bridge and around the library. His body was weak and sober and it weaved; he did not feel part of it, and he felt no need to hurry away from the campus and the bridge and Robin. What waited for him was home, and a two-mile walk to get there: the room he hated though he tried to believe he did not. For he lived there, his clothes hung there, most of all he slept there, the old vulnerable breathing of night and dreams; and if he allowed himself to hate it then he would have to hate his life too, and himself.

He walked without stealth across the campus, then up the road to town. He passed Timmy's, where he and Robin had drunk and where now the girls who would send him to prison were probably still drinking. He and Robin had sat in a booth on the restaurant side. She drank tequila sunrises and paid for those and for his Comfort and ginger, and she told him that all day she had been talking to people, and now she had to talk to him, her mind was blown, her father called her about her grades and he called the dean too so she had to go to the counselor's office and she was in there three hours, they talked about everything, they even got back to the year she was fifteen and she told the counselor she didn't remember much of it, that was her year on acid, and she had done a lot of balling, and she said she had never talked like that with anybody before, had never just sat down and *list*ed what she had done for the last four years, and the counselor told her in all that time she had never felt what she was doing or done what she felt. She was talking gently to Mike, but in her eyes she was already gone: back in her room; home in Darien; Bermuda at Easter; the year in Europe she had talked about before, the year her father would give her when she got out of school. He could not remember her loins, and he felt he could not remember himself either, that his life had begun a few minutes earlier in this booth. He watched her hands as she stirred her tequila sunrise and the grenadine rose from the bottom in a menstrual cloud, and she said the counselor had gotten her an appointment in town with a psychiatrist tomorrow, a woman psychiatrist, and she wanted to go, she wanted to talk again, because now she had admitted it, that she wasn't happy, hadn't been happy, had figured nobody ever could be.

Then he looked at her eyes. She liked to watch him when they made love, and sometimes he opened his eyes and saw on her face that eerie look of a woman making love: as if her eyes, while watching him, were turned inward as well, were indeed watching his thrusting from within her womb. Her eyes now were of the counselor's office, the psychiatrist's office tomorrow, they held no light for him; and in his mind, as she told him she had to stop dope and alcohol and balling, he saw the school: the old brick and the iron fence with its points like spears and the serene trees. All his life this town had been dying. His father had died with it, killing himself with one of the last things he owned: they did not have a garage so he drove the car into a woods and used the vacuum cleaner hose. She said she had never come, not with anybody all these years, she had always faked it; he finished his drink in a swallow and immediately wished he had not, for he wanted another but she didn't offer one and he only had three dollars which he knew now he would need for the rest of the night; then he refused to imagine the rest of the night. He smiled.

'Only with my finger,' she said.

'I hope it falls off.'

She slid out of the booth; his hand started to reach for her but he stopped it; she was saying something that didn't matter now, that he could not feel: her eyes were suddenly damp as standing she put on her parka, saying she had wanted to talk to him, she thought at least they could talk; then she walked out. He drank her tequila sunrise as he was getting out of the booth. Outside, he stood looking up the street; she was a block away, almost at the drugstore. Then she was gone around the bend in the street. He started after her, watching his boots on the shovelled sidewalk.

Now he walked on the bridge over the river and thought of her lying on the small one over the pond. The wind came blowing down freezing over the Merrimack; his moustache stiffened, and he lowered his head. But he did not hurry. Seeing Robin on the bridge over the pond he saw the dormitory beyond it, just a dormitory for them, rooms which they crowded with their things, but the best place he had ever slept in. The things that crowded their rooms were more than he had ever owned, yet he knew for the girls these were only selected and favorite or what they thought necessary things, only a transportable bit of what filled large rooms of huge houses at home. For four or five years now he had made his way into the dormitory; he met them at Timmy's and they took him back to the dormitory to drink and smoke dope and when the party dissolved one of them usually took him to bed.

One night in the fall before Robin he was at a party there and toward three in the morning nearly all the girls were gone and no one had given him a sign and there were only two girls left and the one college fag, a smooth-shaven, razor-cut boy who dressed better than the girls, went to Timmy's, and even to the bar side of it, the long, narrow room without booths or bar stools where only men drank; he wore a variety of costumes: heels and yellow and rust and gold and red, and drank sloe gin fizzes and smoked like a girl. And Mike, who rarely thought one way or another about fags but disliked them on sight, liked this one because he went into town like that and once a man poured a beer over his head, but he kept going and joking, his necklaces tapping on his chest as he swayed back and forth laughing. That night he came over and sat beside Mike just at the right time, when Mike had understood that the two remaining girls not only weren't interested in him, but they despised him, and he was thinking of the walk home to his room when the fag said he had some Colombian and Mike nodded and rose and left with him. In the room the fag touched him and Mike said twenty-five bucks and put it in his pocket, then removed the fag's fingers from his belt buckle and turned away and undressed. He would not let the fag kiss him but the rest was all right, a mouth was a mouth, except when he woke sober in the morning, woke early, earlier than he ever woke when he slept there with a girl. A presence woke him, as though a large bird had flown inches above his chest. He got up quickly and glanced at the sleeping fag, lying on his back, his bare, smooth shoulders and slender arms above the blanket, his face turned toward Mike, the mouth open, and Mike wanted to kill him or himself or both of them, looking away from the mouth which had consumed forever part of his soul, and with his back turned he dressed. Then quietly opening the door he was aware of his height and broad shoulders and he squared them as glaring he stepped into the corridor; but it was empty, and he got out of the dormitory without anyone seeing him and ate breakfast in town and at ten o'clock went to the employment office for his check.

Through the years he had stolen from them: usually cash from the girls he slept with, taking just enough so they would believe or make themselves believe that while they were drunk at Timmy's they had spent it. Twice he had stolen with the collusion of girls. One had gone ahead of him in the corridor, then down the stairs, as he rolled and carried a ten-speed bicycle. He rode it home and the next day sold it to three young men who rented a house down the street; they sold dope, and things other people stole, mostly things that kids stole, and Mike felt like a kid when he went to them and said he had a ten-speed. A year later, when a second girl helped him steal a stereo, he sold it at the same house. The girl was drunk and she went with him into the room one of her friends had left un-locked, and in the dark she got the speakers and asked if he wanted any records while he hushed her and took the amplifier and turn-table. They carried everything out to her Volvo. In the car he was relieved but only for a moment, only until she started the engine, then he thought of the street and the building where he lived, and by the time she turned on the heater he was trying to think of a way to keep her from taking him home.

All the time she was talking. It was the first time she had stolen anything. Or anything worth a lot of money. He made himself smile by thinking of selling her to the men in the house; he thought of her sitting amid the stereos and television sets and bicycles. Then he heard her say something. She had asked if he was going to sell his old set so he could get some bucks out of the night too. He said he'd give the old one to a friend, and when she asked for directions he pointed ahead in despair. He meant to get out at the corner but when she said Here? and slowed for the turn he was awash in the loss of control which he fought so often and overcame so little, though he knew most people couldn't tell by looking at him or even talking to him. She turned and climbed up the street, talking all the time, not about the street, the buildings, but about the stereo: or the stealing of it, and he knew from her voice she was repeating herself so she would not have to talk about what she saw. Or he felt she was. But that was not the worst. The worst was that he was so humiliated he could not trust what he felt, could not know if this dumb rich drunk girl was even aware of the street, and he knew there was no way out of this except to sleep and wake tomorrow in the bed that held his scent. He had been too long in that room (this was his third year), too long in the building: there were six apartments; families lived in the five larger ones; one family had a man: a pumper of gasoline, checker of oil and water, wiper of windshields. Mike thought of his apartment as a room, although there was a kitchen he rarely used, a bathroom, and a second room that for weeks at a time he did not enter. Some mornings when he woke he felt he had lived too long in his body. He smoked a joint in bed and showered and shaved and left the room, the building, the street of these buildings. Once free of the street he felt better: he liked feeling and smelling clean; he walked into town. The girl stopped the Volvo at another of his sighed directions and touched his thigh and said she would help him bring the stuff in. He said no and loaded everything in his arms and left her.

Robin had wanted to go to his room too and he had never let her and now for the first time grieving for her lost flesh, he wished he had taken her there. Saw her there at nights and on the weekends, the room—rooms: he saw even the second room—smelling of paint; saw buckets and brushes on newspaper awaiting her night and weekend hand, his hand too: the two of them painting while music played not from his tinny-sounding transistor but a stereo that was simply there in his apartment with the certainty of something casually purchased with cash neither from the employment office nor his occasional and tense forays into the world of jobs: dishwashing at Timmy's, the quick and harried waitresses bringing the trays of plates which he scraped and racked and hosed and slid into the washer, hot water in the hot kitchen wetting his clothes; he scrubbed the pots by hand and at the night's end he mopped the floor and the bartender sent him a bottle of beer; but he only worked there in summers, when the students were gone. He saw Robin painting the walls beside him, their brushstrokes as uniform as the beating of their hearts. He was approaching the bar next to the bus station. He did not like it because the band was too loud, and the people were losers, but he often went there anyway, because he could sit and drink and watch the losers dancing without having to make one gesture he had to think about, the way he did at Timmy's when he sat with the girls and was conscious of his shoulders and arms and hands, of his eyes and mouth as if he could see them, so that he smiled—and coolly, he knew—when girl after girl year after year touched his flesh and sometimes his heart and told him he was cool.

He went into the bar, feeling the bass drum beat as though it came from the floor and walls, and took the one untaken stool and ordered a shot of Comfort, out of habit checking his pocket although he knew he had three ones and some change. Everyone he saw was drunk, and the bartender was drinking. Vic was at the end of the bar, wearing a bandana on his head, earring on one ear, big fat arms on the bar; Mike nodded at him. He drank the shot and pushed the glass toward the bartender. His fingers trembled. He sipped the Comfort and lit a cigarette, cold sweat on his brow, and he thought he would have to go outside into the cold air or vomit.

He finished the shot then moved through the crowd to Vic and spoke close to his ear and the gold earring. 'I need some downs.' Vic wanted a dollar apiece. 'Come on,' Mike said. 'Two.' Vic's arm left the bar and he put two in Mike's hand; Mike gave him the dollar and left, out onto the cold street, heading uphill, swallowing, but his throat was dry and the second one lodged; he took a handful of snow from a mound at the base of a parking meter and ate it. He walked on the lee side of buildings now. He was dead with her. He lay on the bridge, his arm around her, his face in her hair. At the dormitory the night shift detectives would talk to the girls inside, out of the cold; they would sit in the big glassed-in room downstairs where drunk one night he had pissed on the carpet while Robin laughed before they went up to her room. The girls would speak his name. His name was in that room, back there in the dormitory; it was not walking up the hill in his clothing. He had two joints in his room and he would smoke those while he waited, lying dressed on his bed. When he heard their footsteps in the hall he would put on his jacket and open the door before they knocked and walk with them to the cruiser. He walked faster up the hill.

PART TWO

The Misogamist

I N THE SUMMER of 1944 Roy Hodges was back
from the Pacific. He was a staff sergeant, a drill
instructor at the Recruit Depot at San Diego.
He was twenty-six years old, and he was training eighteen-year-old
boys. He was also engaged to marry Sheila Russell, who was
twenty-six and had been waiting for eight years in Marshall, Texas,
to marry him. At eighteen, and still a virgin, her goodbye kiss was
sad, loving, and hopeful. She told him she would not go out with
other boys while he was gone. After boot camp he went home on
leave, and on the first night he took her virginity. She believed he
was giving his too; he had bought out of it with a middle-aged
whore when he was fifteen. He took her much more easily than he
had expected. Every night and sometimes the afternoons for three
weeks he made love with her, and she aroused in him an excitement
he had never felt before with a woman; nor did he ever feel it again.
In the evening she drank beer with him and learned to smoke his
cigarettes, and he liked that too. Then they drove in his father's
Ford out into the country, the woods. It was early spring and there
were no mosquitoes. Gently with her on the blanket he sometimes
remembered with a heart's grin the attacking mosquitoes as he lay
with Betty Jean Simpson in high school; with her, he had often
thought of Sheila at home, and thinking of that pure side of his life
had increased his passion for Betty Jean. Now, memory of Betty
Jean and the mosquitoes on his rump waxed his passion with
Sheila. And he finally felt in control of her: she was both his sweet,
auburn-haired brown-eyed girl and his lustful woman. When he
left her again, her goodbye kiss was erotic, fearful, and demanding.

He had told her, the night before leaving, that they would get married when his tour was up. She could tell her family and friends; he would write to his parents. Which he did: from sea duty, on a battleship. But most of the letter was about the sea. He had never in his life been out of sight of land: a sailor had told him the horizon was always twelve miles away; he wrote that to his parents, and told them to think of him seeing forty-eight miles of the Pacific by standing in one spot and turning in a circle. He wrote that he had won the heavyweight boxing championship in intramurals aboard ship; that in the final match he had won by jabbing and hooking the charging face of a slugging, body-punching sailor from Pittsburgh; that his commanding officer, a captain, had been a corporal in the Banana Wars, was tough and hard, and would throw you in the brig on bread and water if you looked at him wrong. He wrote of inspections, of gunnery, of Honolulu: the strange city and people and food.

His letters to Sheila were the same. He thought he should write love letters, write of their love on the blanket, but even while a sentence took shape in his mind it seemed false; the abstract words had little to do with what had occurred on the blanket; they had even less to do with how he felt about it. So finally he simply wrote that he loved and missed her. Both were true; but he did not know the extent of their truth.

He found it even more difficult to write of their future life together. Again, the words in his mind were abstract, for he could not imagine himself performing the concrete rituals of marriage. He did not know what work he would do as a civilian; he did not even want to know; sitting on his foot locker and feeling the roll of the sea, he could not imagine himself as a civilian in Marshall, Texas. And he could not see himself at night and on the weekends with Sheila. His days now were filled: in the normal pattern of the service, on some days he did very little, but because he did it in uniform it seemed worthwhile; on other days, when they practiced gunnery and he imagined actual combat, the work was intense. Either way, during the hours of his work he did not need Sheila, or anyone female. It was at night that he missed her, in the compartment smelling of male sweat and shoe polish and leather; that was when he wrote to her. When he was in port, on liberty, he did not miss her at all; he thought of her, usually after drinking and whoring, with paternal tenderness; and he sent her gifts, knowing they were junk, knowing he was incapable of buying gifts for a woman anyway, incapable of understanding their affinity for things which couldn't be used.

She wrote him love letters. They were not scented but they might as well have been; on their pages he felt the summer evening quiet of her front porch, heard the creaking of the chain that held the swing where she sat, where perhaps she had even written the letter; and he smelled her washed flesh and hair, and the lilac bush beside the porch. Reading these letters, touching them, sometimes after reading them just looking at each page as if they were pictures, he deeply loved her. He could have wept. He wanted to hold her. Yet he also felt, and with fear, the great division between them.

He was afraid because there was nothing wrong with Sheila. There was nothing he could hold against her, nothing he could point to and say: That's it; that's why I feel this way. She was pure in a way that excited his love: a good Methodist, she believed that making love with him was a sin. Yet she had sinned with him anyway, and he felt blessed. Betty Jean Simpson was the town punch: anyone who could move suitably as a boy in the world had a shot at her. The only element of challenge was finding a location where he thought she had never been, a fresh spot on the earth's surface, free of the memory of past and present boys; while at the same time the knowledge of those boys gave him advance acquittal in case she got pregnant. Sheila's sin was as secret as her parts were; each spot of earth and sheltering tree and concealing bush were new; as her breasts and loins were, eighteen years old and for the first time stroked and plunged into action. He would never forget that. (Nor would he ever make love with a virgin again, nor anyone who loved him, and when it was over with Sheila, when he had broken her heart, he wondered—this on the drill field one day at San Diego, while calling cadence to a marching platoon—if she had ever had an orgasm with him; saddened, he realized she had not, and he knew someone else would take her there, someone strong and gentle who could be for her what he could not, and that was almost enough to make him write to her again, to seek forgiveness and to return to her and nail down once and for all, with marriage, what he had started that first night he so easily unclothed her and shaped her into his sweet and sinful lover.) She was a cheerful girl. He had dated her for three years before joining the Marines, and he knew he had not been fooled. She was undemanding, acquiescent (a quality, strangely, that Betty Jean did not share, as though compensating for her round heels with trifling demands that were nevertheless rigid); there was nothing wrong with her.

It followed then, in his mind, that something was wrong with him: to prefer a life with men, broken periodically by forgettable transactions with whores. He began to believe that he was reaching a pivotal point in his life: either Sheila, who at times seemed to live in a fairy tale rather than in the world he knew; or whores, threats of VD, promises of nothing. Then he saw it wasn't that at all. In Marshall he would not miss the whores; he would long for the men. Now he knew what the pride in performing his duties and the immediate camaraderie of the Corps, as well as the deeper one—the sense that he belonged to a recognized group of men, past and present, dead and living—had been bringing him to: he had, as the troops said, found a home. He was a career man.

He wrote to her, asking how she felt about leaving Marshall and living with him on or near Marine bases until he retired. She answered his letter on the day she got it. Again her stationery in his fingers brought to him her smells, her lowered face as she talked to him, strolling with him. In a voice whose sweet compliance he could almost hear, she told him of course she would miss Marshall, she had never thought she would live any place else, but she loved him and would marry him and go with him wherever he had to go; and she looked forward to those new places.

His next leave was in summer and they made love with sweat and mosquitoes and he told her he must now work hard to get promoted so they could afford to be married. He did not name a rank. Now he could sense a brooding quality in her lovemaking, as though resigning herself to annual trysts granted by the Marine Corps which would someday grant the promotion and money that would allow them to live as they should; and he felt her trying to possess him. For the first time she asked what he did on liberty; she asked if he did this with other girls. He lied. He had lied about Betty Jean Simpson too, but in a different way: he had simply told her nothing about where he was going on a particular night. Now telling her a direct lie made him feel diminished as a man, and he held that against her. At the train station her goodbye kiss was both vulnerable and sternly possessive.

And so it went on: every year with a mingling of reluctance, fear, and passionate anticipation—all blurring his deeper and true feeling of love for her, his knowledge that for his own good he ought to marry her—he returned to Marshall. By the time she was twenty-two he was in the first year of his second enlistment, he was a corporal, and he had promised her that sergeant was the rank. He spoke to her father about it; he even spoke quite easily to her father, who had a small farm and believed in hard work and bad luck and little else, and who liked Roy's having man's work which was based on skill yet had nothing to do with rain or dry seasons or prices. In her father's eyes Roy saw neither suspicion nor misgivings, and he felt that his decision to wait until he made sergeant was that of a worldly, responsible man. Roy also suspected that Mr. Russell knew what he and Sheila did after they left the house for what they called a ride and a talk, and that further, Mr. Russell didn't care about it as long as he wasn't forced to.

Not so with Mrs. Russell: thin and nearly as wiry as her husband, beauty long gone from her strong face which had kept its humor and cheer in the eyes and their crinkled corners and the quick grin above the body which had waked so early and worked so hard for so long. She did not look at Roy with suspicion either; it was worse than that: at times, when her eyes met his, there was a flicker of pain: *Why did you do it to us?* Or that was the question and the pain he saw before she looked away or, more often, started talking and her eyes brightened again, as if the question had come against her will, like a sad, irrelevant memory while talking with a friend. *Why did you do it to us?* Not: Why have you taken my daughter's virginity and left her single? Not even: Why have you brought a secret sin between my daughter and me? But more than that, a vaster accusation, as if she represented in those moments—and, thankfully, they were sparse—all the women who lived on one side of the line he had drawn between them and the others: the forgotten sensations and names, the remembered faces and prices. And when she looked at him that way he felt that God and time, life and death, were on her side; that he was a puny and defenseless man who had committed a sin of Old Testament proportion, the kind of sin you never escaped from, no matter where you went, or how long you stayed there. So that at times, drinking and talking with Mr. Russell, sounding to himself like a reasonable, ambitious, and absolutely trustworthy man, he suddenly felt the judgmental presence of the mother and daughter in the room, as if in concert they had focused on him a knowing glare, and all his talk of money and promotion and career seemed no more than a boy's chatter about what he'd be when he grew up.

He was promoted to sergeant on the second of December, 1941. On the seventh he had still not written to tell her. He woke up that morning in a cheap two-room apartment in Los Angeles; woke tasting last night's beer and smelling traces of perfume and lovemaking. He had gone to the city with three friends, and had left them at a bar and walked home with the girl. She was not in bed with him. Then he remembered her name was Lisa. He wanted to make love to clear his hung-over head. He heard the radio in the kitchen, not music but a man's voice, and he imagined her making coffee and bringing him a cup, bringing him herself too, and he thought of that and then breakfast and the afternoon left to hitchhike back to the base. He took his wallet from the bedside table and was looking in it to see if there was another condom (there was) when she came to the door in an old blue robe, with her black hair unbrushed, last night's lipstick faint on her lips. She stood quietly in the doorway, looking at him, knowing she was about to tell him the most important news he had ever heard, and then she said: 'I think you better come to the kitchen. I think you better come hear what's on the radio.'

He didn't want to go; he was put off by her dramatics, and wanted her in bed. But looking at her face he suddenly knew with both fear and eagerness that somehow the news of the nation or even the world was affecting him; and since his only involvement with the world was as a Marine he knew by the time he reached the kitchen that, while he had been in bed with a strange girl, America had gotten into the war. He listened to the radio for perhaps thirty minutes, then he borrowed her leg-dulled razor and shaved and put on his uniform; for a moment he wanted to take Lisa to bed again, but as the desire struck him he tossed it aside as a foolish indulgence.

The man who picked him up was a Lutheran minister who was returning home from services and going only a few miles south of the city; but he drove Roy all the way to Camp Pendleton, called him Sergeant, wondered aloud about the damages to the fleet and if the Japs were going to keep on coming, to California; he spoke of coastal defense, of going into the Navy as a chaplain (he was thirty-six), and at the main gate he firmly shook Roy's hand, and said: 'Good luck, and God bless you, Sergeant.' Roy nearly smiled.

He thought of the man in uniform, the cross on his lapel. Roy had heard little of what the minister had said: on the drive south he had been thinking about his gear waiting for him, clean and ready, and trying to imagine what was happening in the barracks, and he knew he was late for something, but for what? What was the platoon doing? The company? He thought of them digging foxholes in the hills overlooking the beach; saw them marching to trucks which would drive them to ships. What happened when a war started? How did you finally get to where the war was? He could not imagine it. It was all too big.

Later that week he wrote his last lie to Sheila: told her his promotion had come through the day after the war started. He never saw her again. Exactly eight months after Pearl Harbor he followed Lieutenant DiMeo through the surf and across the beach at Guadalcanal. The Japanese were not there; that came two weeks later, farther inland.

In the summer of 1944, when he was certain as he could be that he would spend the rest of the war as a drill instructor, he applied for leave to get married, took some obscene harassment from the First Sergeant (and enjoyed it), and phoned Sheila, telling her to go ahead with the plans for the wedding. He felt no sense of duty. He wanted to hold her and tell her about the war. He had written about it, but not much: except for a few words his letters could have been written by any man doing work away from home. He had left out the details he now wanted to share with her because he had not wanted her to know them until he was with her.

The truth had not occurred to him: that because of newsreels and newspapers and magazines there was nothing he could tell her that would be as terrifying as what she had already imagined. She never wrote of this in her letters. Also, Marshall had its dead and its maimed (she never wrote of this either), and one—a victim of shell shock—who daily walked the streets, though his mind was permanently somewhere else; people treated him kindly, spoke to him as though he were sane; he liked to imitate the sound of a train whistle, did it often, and was very good at it. So Roy had protected her from nothing.

From nothing at all, so that when he did not get off the train the morning before the wedding she was heartbroken and humiliated (already thinking of the phone calls she would have to make), but she was not absolutely surprised. She did not phone the Recruit

Depot. That night her father got quietly drunk and finally said: 'I should have put a shotgun to his butt eight years ago and marched him down to the church.' Sheila moved to the sofa and sat beside him and held his hand to shut him up; she told him she was all right, it was better to learn this about Roy now than find it out later when they were married and maybe even had children. Though she was afraid he would start to mutter about seduction and damaged goods, she also felt loved because he knew, and she wished things were different between them and that she could take him out on the porch, away from her mother, and ask him how, all those years, from the very beginning, he had known. She promised herself that someday when she was older (and at this moment she knew she would leave Marshall soon, and would, yes, marry) she would take him aside, out in her backyard in Houston or Dallas (yes, it would have to be a city now, after this) and she would ask him how he had known. But she never did.

Yet out of that promise to herself came the vision of her future. A month later she moved to Houston and got a job as a dentist's receptionist. The dentist was single and was soon dating her. He was forty-two years old; she found that interesting, but little more. At one of his parties she met a geologist who had just returned to his job with an oil company after flying Corsairs from an aircraft carrier; his left arm was gone. At first when they made love and the stump moved above her right breast and shoulder she remembered Roy's arm: both arms on the earth in the woods. And sometimes she felt that the spirit of the arm extended from the stump and held her. When she told him, he said he could feel it too. Lying with him at night she listened to his war stories; a year later they drove to Marshall and got married.

On the night before he was supposed to pick up his leave papers and catch the train, Roy could not have predicted any of this. A half dozen sergeants took him out in San Diego. When they got drunk one of them joked about getting Roy laid. Roy blinked at him and was suddenly, drunkenly, depressed. He had forgotten why they were drinking. He had not forgotten the facts: that he was going on leave tomorrow, that he was going to Marshall, going to marry Sheila. But he had forgotten her presence. She seemed as far away as she had when he was younger, before the war. The friend who had suggested a whorehouse was watching him.

'Cheer up,' the friend said. The others looked at Roy, stopped talking.

'The troops,' Roy said. 'You've got to train the fucking troops.'

Someone nodded, motioned to the waitress, ordered Roy a shot. Roy didn't want it, but said nothing; then he did want it, waited with anticipation for it, felt his drunkenness taking him somewhere, somewhere he had been, somewhere he was going.

'You got to kick ass. At the Canal we weren't ready. Fucking Japs were ready.'

'Peleliu,' someone murmured, and Roy's shot came.

'We learned from them. We weren't ready.' He held the shot glass, looked at it; then he gulped it dry, seeing as clearly as the moment it happened the death of Lieutenant DiMeo walking into the jungle on Guadalcanal when they were still learning about the Japanese and camouflage; when DiMeo was ten feet from an anti-tank gun, looking directly at the brush that concealed it, they fired and took his head off. Roy saw himself on his belly firing into the brush, through the image of blood spurting out of DiMeo's body that twitched and seemed to try to speak; from that moment on he had been certain he would not leave Guadalcanal. When they left the island four months later he led the platoon up the landing net, onto the ship. At the top he looked down: the troops were spread beneath him; most were not halfway up the net; several stopped to rest after each climbing step. He climbed onto the deck and looked down at their helmets and the gear on their backs and their toiling arms and legs. He had not known until then how tired they were; then he realized they hadn't known either. 'We were ready in here,' he said, pointing to his heart. 'Not here.' He pointed to his head. 'We had to learn. When I write to—' He paused, waited, a moment's blank in his mind, the moment seeming to him longer, fearfully longer, until her name floated up to him out of some region of need for women, needs satisfied and needs not—'Sheila,' he said. 'When I write to her all I can write about is the troops. It's all I know.' He looked around at the six faces. 'It's all I fucking want to know. She answers the letters. She says, I'm glad your men are learning. But it's all I write to her about: the fucking troops. You know what I mean?'

He looked at the friend who wanted to go to a whorehouse.

'No,' the friend said.

'I mean I love the fucking troops. You got to train them. You got to put it in here—' again he touched his breast '—and it gets there through the ass end. That's all I write to her about. The fucking Corps. All I want to do is train troops and kick their ass and go out and drink with my Goddamn friends. I don't want a Goddamn house full of gear. I don't want to go home to that shit. If a man—' he picked up his empty shot glass, looked in it; someone ordered him another '—if a man could have his Goddamn quarters on the base, with his bunk and his gear squared away and go home to his woman—' He stopped again: the word woman drove Sheila's name from his mind, replaced the image of her in a San Diego kitchen with no image at all but merely with a nebulous and designated emotion; and he glimpsed the concrete details of his life as male and military, uniforms and gear and troops, and his needs for a woman had no surrounding details at all, they all ended in something abstract. He could not see himself in a house with one of them, could not see himself taking all but his noon meals with one of them, and could not imagine what he would do with one of them on ordinary Saturdays and the old useless Sundays: saw the two of them smoking cigarettes and listening to the radio; and the woman he saw was not Sheila, was not any woman at all, a face and body vague as the people in the far background of a newspaper photograph.

'Fuck it,' he said.

His curse was decisive. And he kept himself from feeling Sheila's pain by making her generic, placing her with all the good women who had no real part in his life, so that it wasn't Sheila he was rejecting but cohabitation, and in this brief and cathartic vision he was able to feel as guiltless and purposeful as a monk choosing prayers and a cell. Yet he wasn't happy either. He felt despair at his limitations, and he raised his glass in an unspoken toast to the grave forecast of loneliness, and repeated his curse.

Which followed him through the years, the years which began next morning when he reported in uniform to the burly First Sergeant who had Roy's leave papers waiting, along with a speech about women and marriage. Roy told him he was not going on leave, he was not getting married, and he wanted a platoon of recruits as soon as the next shitload of them came in. The First Sergeant glared at him; he did not like to show surprise but he knew it was in his face, so he exaggerated it, made it look like it wasn't surprise at all.

'What manner of coo-coo juice were you drinking last night, Hodges?'

'Most of San Diego.'

'And who called off this Texas altar-fuck?'

'I did.'

The First Sergeant leaned back in his chair.

'Sergeant Hodges, there are two holes a man doesn't want to get into. One of them he can't stay out of unless he's buried at sea, cremated, or set upon by a tribe of bone-licking cannibals. The other is the hole between the legs of a woman who's wearing the fuck-ring. Unless it has been placed on her finger by some other dumb son of a bitch who figured in order to fuck self-same lady he had to get a job and buy a house to do it in. I've had many adventures in the fuck-houses of others. You are a fortunate man: when you were seagoing I'm sure you heard many tales of woe from sailors who were unable to forgive the trespassers who entered their fuck-houses while the ship was out to sea. So I'm sure you have learned that the best duty in the Marine Corps is with the infantry, and the second best is to serve at a barracks on a naval base, so as to be available to those lonesome wives when the ships go do their merry shit at sea. I have no doubts that there are several U.S. Navy dependents who bear a resemblance to the First Sergeant who talks to you now, but who step on the toes of a sailor they call Daddy. This may also be true of certain Marine dependents. I have never known a woman who gave a fart whether she was married or not once it came upon her that what she wanted to do was fuck. But it could be that, as well-travelled as I am, my experience is still limited. For instance I have never fucked in the state of Nebraska, partly because I've heard it's considered a felony there. Then again, it could be I have only known bad women, because like a pointer I smell out the pheasant and ignore the dove. You will find that sailors have the worst wives of all military men. One reason is your average sailor is a dumb shit once he sets foot on land. They spend too much time on boats. They all turn into country hicks, doesn't matter where they came from to begin with. They get into port and they either believe everything they see, or they don't understand it; worse than that, they believe everything they hear. Which brings us to the next point: it's a rare sailor that gets more than six blocks from the pier. So what they do is meet the women that hang out in sailors' bars. There you have it. What they meet is semi-pro whores. I am right now, Sergeant Hodges—though not at the moment, since you can see I'm here at my desk about to tear up your leave papers and lend a helping hand in saving your young ass from bad watering hole number two—fucking the sweet wife of a gunner's mate, said gunner's mate stationed on a destroyer. I hope he comes back alive. She does not talk about him, nor has she told me his name. There is a color photograph of him in uniform; it sits on the bureau in the bedroom, which allows him to watch my ass-end doing its humble work on his wife. While I am thus at labor I do believe I think about him more than she does. Sergeant Hodges, I do not mean to piss you off when I say I assume you fucked this girl who lives and reigns in Marshall, Texas. It could even be that you were the first to do the old prone dance with her—' Roy nodded, and then was ashamed, and then he was sad, thinking of her eight years ago on the blanket in the woods. The phrase ran through his weary hung-over mind: *on the blanket in the woods.* 'Ah: a virgin. I have noticed that women can be compared to shooters. The virgin—and I have only had two of them, very long ago, and will never have another unless I come across some horny old nun—the virgin uses Kentucky windage. She moves her weapon this way and that, adjusting to the wind. And you are the wind. And the wind must go. But not to Nebraska, where it's frowned upon. I have no doubt the lady in Marshall is pretty, else you would not have spent such time and money crossing the state of Texas. So you can be assured that your place will soon be taken, and she'll be better at it this time around, and thus you will have two people who will be thankful to you. It behooves—'

'First Sergeant.'

'Speak.'

'Can I have the day off to get rid of this fucking hangover?'

'I recommend a shot of booze, a piece of ass, and a long sleep. Here—' He wrote on the note pad on his desk, tore the page out, and gave it to Roy.

'Her name is Meg. Tell her you're an old buddy of mine, just back from the wars. Don't let her get you out of the house, or she'll spend all your money.'

Roy neither liked nor understood the collusive look in the First

Sergeant's eyes, the softening of his mouth and jaw. But he put the paper in his pocket, borrowed a friend's car, and drove into town and to her apartment where, after coffee and pretense at talk, he spent the day in bed, from time to time looking at the gunner's mate watching from the bureau. Just after sundown he was lying on his back and she was licking his chest and belly, moving down, when she stopped and said: 'He'll ask about this too.'

'Who?'

'Johnny.'

It took him a moment to think of the First Sergeant as Johnny.

'What do you mean?'

'He likes to hear about it. While we're screwing he likes to hear about it with somebody else.'

'You tell him?'

'Yes.'

'You like to tell him?'

'Yes.'

'Jesus.'

But he was not really disturbed. Scornfully he thought of Sheila. Then Meg moved down again and he stroked her hair and thought of nothing. His curse of the night before had taken flesh, and he came in its mouth.

Two nights later he wrote to Sheila. He wrote that he loved his career and he had no place for a wife. It took him one page, and seeing his life so compressed saddened him. He dropped the page to the floor. On another page he told her how sorry he was, and how he hated himself. He thought of her standing at the train station, waiting after the last passenger had gone by. She would have been dressed up. He picked up the first letter and tore both of them in half and wadded them in his fist. Better to slash a wrist and send her a page soaked in his blood. The phone wouldn't do either. What he needed was to see her, to be there now without transition, to deliver to her some immortal touch that was neither erotic nor comforting but something new and final between them: to firmly and lovingly squeeze her hand and look into her eyes and then disappear, like a love-rooted ghost making its farewell.

At St. Croix

PETER JACKMAN and Jo Morrison were both divorced, and had been lovers since winter. She knew much about his marriage, as he did about hers, and at times it seemed to Peter that their love had grown only from shared pain. His ex-wife, Norma, had married and moved to Colorado last summer, and he had not seen David and Kathi since then. They were eleven and nine, and in June they were coming to Massachusetts to spend the summer with him. In May, Peter and Jo went to St. Croix to recover, as they said, from the winter. They did not mean simply the cold, but their nights tangled with the sorrow of divorce, with euphoric leaps away from it, with Peter's creeping out of the house while Jo's two girls slept, with his grieving for his children, and with both of them drinking too much, talking too much, needing too much.

The hotel at St. Croix was a crescent of separate buildings facing the sea. The beach was short and narrow, bounded by rocks that hid the rest of the coastline. About thirty yards out, a reef broke the surf, and the water came gently and foamless, and lapped at the beach. Peter could have walked to the reef without wetting his shoulders, but he stayed close to shore, swimming in water so shallow that sometimes his hands touched rocks and pebbles and sand. Jo was curious about him in that warmly possessive way that occurs when people become lovers before they are friends, and on the first day she asked him about the water. They were in lounge chairs near a palm tree on the beach, and she was watching his face. He looked beyond the reef at the blue sea and sky.

'I don't know. I've always been afraid of it.'

'What about the beach at home. You said you liked it.'

'I do. But I don't go out over my chest.'

'Maybe you just went for your children.'

'No. I love it. And this.' He waved a hand seaward. 'And body-surfing. The worst about that is when I turn my back. I don't like turning my back on the sea.'

'Let's leave Buck Island to the fish.'

She was smiling at him, and there was no disappointment in her face or voice.

'You'd enjoy it,' he said.

'It's not important.'

Each morning after breakfast he went alone to the hotel lobby and chose a postcard for David and Kathi from the racked pictures of the sea, beaches, a black fisherman squatting beside a dead shark on the wharf, scarlet-flowered trees, coconut palms, steep green hills, tall trees of the rain forest. He had not told them he was going to St. Croix with a woman, nor had he told them he was going alone, and on the postcards he wrote crowded notes about the island. On one he wrote that mongooses lived here but there were no snakes, so they ate lizards and frogs, and some of the young men killed them and soaked their tails in rum for two weeks, then wore them stiff like feathers in their hatbands. Then he realized that David would want a tail, so he tore up the card and threw it away, and began watching from taxi windows for a dead mongoose on the road. He also wrote that he wished they were with him, and next year he would wait until June, when they were out of school, and he would bring them here. He did not send them a picture of the hotel. The wound he had opened in himself when he left them had not healed, and it never would; now going to St. Croix was like leaving them again. Jo was glad to be away from her daughters for a week, so Peter did not talk to her about his children.

Always the trade winds were blowing across the island, and Peter only felt the heat when he walked on the lee side of a building. The breeze cooled the town of Christiansted too, where they went by taxi in late afternoons, and walked the narrow streets of tourist shops and restaurants, and looked at the boats in the harbor. On the third day, they went sailing at sunset on a boat owned by Don Jensen, a young blond man with a deep tan, who charged them twelve dollars and kept their paper cups filled with rum punch from the ice chest in the cabin, and told them he and his wife

had come from California six years ago, that she taught painting at a
private school on the island and, when the sun was low, he told
them if they were lucky they'd see the green ball when it sank
under the horizon, though he had rarely seen it. But he had seen
dust in the sky, blown from Africa, hanging red in the sunset. And
he asked if they were going to Buck Island. Peter and Jo were sitting on benches on opposite sides of the boat. Peter looked at the
glittering water near the sun and said: 'I'm afraid of it.'

'Can you swim?'

'Yes.'

'It's something you ought to see.'

'I know.'

'Nobody's ever drowned there. With the snorkel and fins, you
just can't. I even take nonswimmers: kids who just hold onto a float
and kick.'

'I want to see it. I don't want to get home, and then wish I had.'

'Are you sure?' Jo said.

'I think I'd like it when it's over.'

They watched the sun go down, did not see the green ball, then
sailed back to Christiansted in the twilight. That night Peter and Jo
got drinks from the hotel bar and took them to the beach and sat in
upright chairs. He watched the gentle white breakers at the reef,
and looked out at the dark sea, listened to it, smelled it. Next morning at breakfast he told the waitress where they were going, and she
said: 'I never go in the water. We have a saying: The sea has no back
door.' At eight-thirty he was on it, Don standing at the wheel next
to the cabin door and working the sail, the long boat heeling so that
when it rocked his way, to starboard, he could have touched the
water with his hand, and the spray smacked his face and bare
shoulders and chest, and when he looked up at Jo sitting on the port
bench he could see only the sky behind her; when the boat heeled
her way, he held onto his bench, and the sky was gone, and he was
looking past her face, down at the sea. She bowed her head and
cupped her hands to light a cigarette. When she straightened, Peter
shaped his lips in a kiss. She returned it. He tried to care whether
she was getting seasick or sunburned or was uncomfortable in the
sea-spray, but he could not: his effort seemed physical, as though
he were trying to push an interior part of his body out of himself
and across the boat to Jo. With a slapping of sail Don brought the
boat about and it steadied and now when it rocked, Peter could see

both sky and water behind Jo. The spray was not hitting them. He half turned and watched the shore of St. Croix and the hills rising up from it, dirt roads climbing them and disappearing into green swells of trees. A tern hovered near the boat. Beyond Jo, toward the open sea, two black fishermen sat in a small pink sailboat. Peter crossed the boat, his feet spread and body swaying, and took one of Jo's cigarettes, his first since leaving home. She smiled and pressed his hand. He went back to the bench and watched the horizon and thought of shopping this afternoon for David and Kathi, then drinking at the roofed veranda of the Paris Café, where the breeze came with scents of cooking and sweet flowers.

He looked ahead of the boat at Buck Island, and sailboats anchored around a boatless surface that he knew covered the reef. The island was a mile long, and steep and narrow, and stood now between them and the open sea. On this side of it the water and wind were calm. Beyond the uneven curve of anchored boats, people were swimming the trail, a waving line of them with snorkels sticking out of the water; most wore shirts to protect their backs from the sun. While Don dropped the anchor, Peter found children swimming in the line. He looked into the water beside the boat and saw the sand bottom. Don came up from the cabin, carrying masks and snorkels and fins.

'It's about a hundred yards, there and back. Maybe a little more. How are you?'

'All right, I think.'

'Keep letting me know.'

Don gave them fins and, when they had put them on, he showed them how to use the mask and snorkel. Peter took a snorkel from him and put it in his mouth and breathed through it, then took the mask and looked at the green island and up at the sky, then pulled the mask over the snorkel tube and his face, and went to the ladder, feeling nothing that he could recognize of himself, feeling only the fins on his feet, and the mask over his nose and eyes, and the mouthpiece against his gums and teeth.

Don told them to swim near the boat until they were used to the snorkel, then he went down the ladder. Jo went next, and Peter looked at Don treading water, then watched her climbing down; when she pushed away from the ladder he turned and backed onto it, and down: legs into the water, then his waist, and when his feet were beneath the last rung he still worked down the ladder with his hands until his arms were in the water, then he turned, swimming a breast stroke, his face in it now, his breathing loud in the tube, and he looked through the mask at the sand bottom and the anchor resting on it. When he saw to his left the keel and white hull of the boat, he jerked his head from the water and swam overhand to the ladder and grasped it with one hand while he took the snorkel from his mouth. Then Don and Jo were on either side of him, snorkels twisted away from their lips. He shook his head at Don.

'It's worse than I thought,' he said.

'I was watching you. You looked all right.'

'No. I can't do it.'

Jo moved to Don's side, treading.

'I panicked a little at first,' she said. 'You just have to get used to breathing.'

'No. You two go on, and I'll wait on the boat. I'll drink beer in the sun.'

Their faces were tender, encouraging.

'I've got some floats aboard,' Don said. 'What about trying that?'

'Me and the kids who can't swim. All right.'

He moved one hand from the ladder until Don climbed past him, then he held on with both again.

'I wish you'd go without me,' he said to Jo.

'I wouldn't want to think of you alone on the boat.'

'If you knew how I felt in the water you'd rather think of me alone on the boat.'

'We could just go back.'

He shook his head, and moved a hand from the ladder as Don came down with a small white float. Peter blew into the snorkel, placed it in his mouth, and took the float. Kicking, he stretched out behind it, and lowered his face into the water, into the sound of his breath moving through the tube past his ear; he looked once at the sand bottom, then raised his head and took out the mouthpiece. Don was beside him. He knew Jo was behind him, but he felt only water there.

'That's it. I drink beer.'

'How about this: you just hold onto the float and I'll pull you.'

Now Jo was with them.

'That's a lot of trouble, just so I can see some fish and a reef.'

'It's easy. I just hold the strap.'

'Everybody's so kind around here, I don't have much choice. You won't let go?'

'No. Just relax and look. You'll be glad you saw it.'

Peter grasped the corners of the float and watched Don's kicking legs which were his only hold on air, on earth, on returning to the day itself; and he concentrated on the act of breathing: in the tube it sounded as though it would stop and he would not be able to start it again; he emptied and filled his lungs with a sense that he was breathing life into the Peter Jackman who had vanished somewhere in the water behind him. He had no picture of himself in the water. He floated without thoughts or dreams, and when he entered the trail he saw the coral reef, and growing things waving like tall grass in the wind; he saw fish pause and dart; fish that were black, golden, scarlet, silver; fish in schools, fish alone, and he could not remember anything he saw. He recognized one fish as it swam into a tiny cave and three breaths later he could not remember its name and shape and color. Scattered along the trail were signs, driven into the bottom. They welcomed him to Buck Island National Park, quizzed him on the shapes of fish drawn on a signboard, told him what was growing near a sign . . . He found that he could remember the words longer than he could a fish or plant or part of the reef. He read each sign, and as he moved away from one he tried to hold its words in his mind; then the words were gone, and all he knew was the fluid snore of his breath, and the water: as though he were fathoms deep, he could not imagine the sky, nor the sun on his back; his mind was the sea bottom, and was covered too with that blue-green dispersal of his soul.

Then he saw only water and sand. He watched Don's legs, and waited for the reef again; he looked for fish, for signs, but the water now was empty and boundless and he wanted to look up but he did not, for he knew he would see miles of water to the horizon, and his breathing would stop. Then he saw a white hull. He was moving toward it, and the legs were gone; he looked up at the boat and sky, took the snorkel from his mouth, let go of the float, and grabbed the ladder. He did not look behind him. He climbed and stepped over the side and pulled off the mask and sat on the bench and took off the fins before Jo's hands, then masked face, appeared on the ladder. She was smiling. He looked at the deck. He watched the black fins on her feet as she crossed it, then she stood over him, smelling of the sea, and placed her hands on his cheeks. Don came over the side, carrying the float.

'You seemed all right,' he said. 'How was it?'

'Bad.'

Jo lifted his face.

'You didn't like any of it?'

'I didn't see any of it.' He looked at Don. 'You know something? I didn't even know you had turned and headed back. Not till you let me go at the boat.'

'You'd better have that beer now. Jo?'

'Please.'

He went down into the cabin.

'I want you to tell me about the fish,' Peter said.

'But you saw them.'

'No I didn't.'

'Maybe you'd better tell me about that.'

'I want you to tell me about the fish,' he said.

On the ride back he drank beer and smoked her cigarettes and listened to her talking about the fish and the reef. For a while her voice sounded as it did on those nights when they fought and, the fight ended, they talked about other things, past their wounds and over the space between them. He did not watch her face. St. Croix was beyond her, and he looked at the sky touching the hills, and listened to Jo and Don talking about the reef. But he could not remember it. Sometimes he looked over his shoulder at the horizon and the dark blue swelling sea.

That night, after Jo was asleep, he dressed and crept out of the room and went to the beach. Lying sunburned in a chair he shuddered as the sea came at him over the reef, and he looked beyond the breakers at the endless dark surface of it, and watched the lights and silhouette of a passing ship, fixed on it as though on a piece of solid and arid earth, and remembered the summer evening four years ago when he and Ryan, both drunk, had left their wives and children in the last of the charcoal smoke on Ryan's sundeck and had rowed an aluminum boat in a twilight fog out to the middle of the lake where they could drink beer and complain about marriage, and Ryan had stood in the bow to piss, and the boat had turned over; Peter hit the water swimming to the shore he could not see. He heard Ryan calling him back to the boat but he swam on into the fog, and when he tired he four times lowered his legs to nothing but water, and finally the evergreens appeared above the fog; he swam until he was in reeds and touching mud, then he crawled out of the water and lay on mud until Ryan came in, kicking alongside the overturned boat. When he and Norma and David and Kathi got home and he stepped into the shower and was enclosed by water he started to scream.

Yet in the summer of 1960 he was a Marine lieutenant at Camp Pendleton, California. One July afternoon his company boarded landing crafts and went a mile out to sea and then, wearing life jackets, floated to shore. Peter and his platoon were in one boat. He waited while his men, barefoot and free of helmets, cartridge belts, and weapons, climbed over the side and dropped into the sea. Then Peter went over and, floating on his back, he paddled and kicked into the cluster of his troops. Slowly, bantering, they formed a line parallel to the coast. With their heads toward shore, they started floating in on their backs. Peter kept watching them, counting them, twenty to his right, twenty-one to his left. He looked past their faces and green wet uniforms and orange jackets at the bobbing lines of the other platoons on his flanks. Sometimes he looked at his feet trailing white as soap in the water, then out beyond the landing crafts at the horizon. Always he saw himself as his troops did: calm, smiling, talking to them; their eyes drew him out of the narrow space where he floated, as though he were spread over the breadth of forty-one men.

Wind blew the palm leaves behind his chair. The ship's lights were fading; its silhouette started to blend with the sea and sky; then it was gone, and he saw Kathi one night two years ago, perhaps a month after he had left them. She was seven, and it was Wednesday night, the night he was with them during the week; they ate at a restaurant and planned their weekend and when he drove them home she said, as she always did that first year, 'Do you want to come in?' And he did, and drank one cup of coffee with Norma, and they both talked to Kathi and David. But when he got his coat from the hall and went back to the kitchen Kathi was gone. He went from room to room, not calling her name, unable to call her name, until he found her in the den lying face down on the couch. She was not crying. He went to her, and leaning forward petted her long red hair; then he lifted her to his chest, held her while her arms went suddenly and tightly around his neck. Then she kissed him. Her lips on his were soft, cool, parted like a woman's.

Now, for the first time since going into the water that morning, he felt the scattered parts of his soul returning, as if they were in the salt air he breathed, filling his lungs, coursing with his blood. Behind his eyes the dark sea and sky were transformed: the sky blue and cloudless with a low hot sun, the sea the cold blue Atlantic off the coast at home, waves coming high and breaking with a crack and a roar, and he was between Kathi and David, holding their hands; they walked out against the surf and beyond it and let go of each other and waited for a wave, watched it coming, then dived in front of it as it broke, rode it in until their bodies scraped sand. Then they walked out again, but now sand shifted under their feet, water rushed seaward against their legs, then she was gone, her hand slipping out of his quick squeeze, she was tumbling and rolling out to sea, and he dived through a breaking wave and swam toward her face, her hair, her hands clutching air and water; swam out and held her against him, spoke to her as he kicked and stroked back through the waves, into the rush of surf, then he stood and walked toward David waiting in foam, and he spoke to her again, pressing her flesh against his. Lying in the chair on the beach at St. Croix, he received that vision with a certainty as incarnate as his sunburned flesh. He looked up at the stars. He was waiting for June: their faces at the airport, their voices in the car, their bodies with his in the sea.

The Pitcher

for Philip

THEY CHEERED AND clapped when he and Lucky Ferris came out of the dugout, and when the cheering and clapping settled to sporadic shouts he had already stopped hearing it, because he was feeling the pitches in his right arm and watching them the way he always did in the first few minutes of his warm-up. Some nights the fast ball was fat or the curve hung or the ball stayed up around Lucky's head where even the hitters in this Class C league would hit it hard. It was a mystery that frightened him. He threw the first hard one and watched it streak and rise into Lucky's mitt; and the next one; and the next one; then he wasn't watching the ball anymore, as though it had the power to betray him. He wasn't watching anything except Lucky's target, hardly conscious of that either, or of anything else but the rhythm of his high-kicking wind-up, and the ball not thrown but released out of all his motion; and now he felt himself approaching that moment he could not achieve alone: a moment that each time was granted to him. Then it came: the ball was part of him, as if his arm stretched sixty feet six inches to Lucky's mitt and slammed the ball into leather and sponge and Lucky's hand. Or he was part of the ball.

Now all he had to do for the rest of the night was concentrate on prolonging that moment. He had trained himself to do that, and while people talked about his speed and curve and change of pace and control, he knew that without his concentration they would be only separate and useless parts; and instead of nineteen and five on the year with an earned run average of two point one five and two hundred and six strikeouts, going for his twentieth win on the last day of the season, his first year in professional ball, three months short of his twentieth birthday, he'd be five and nineteen and on his way home to nothing. He was going for the pennant too, one half game behind the New Iberia Pelicans who had come to town four nights ago with a game and a half lead, and the Bulls beat them Friday and Saturday, lost Sunday, so that now on Monday in this small Louisiana town, Billy's name was on the front page of the local paper alongside the news of the war that had started in Korea a little over a month ago. He was ready. He caught Lucky's throw, nodded to him, and walked with head down toward the dugout and the cheers growing louder behind it, looking down at the bright grass, holding the ball loosely in his hand.

He spoke to no one. He went to the far end of the dugout that they left empty for him when he was pitching. He was too young to ask for that, but he was good enough to get it without asking; they gave it to him early in the year, when they saw he needed it, this young pitcher Billy Wells who talked and joked and yelled at the field and the other dugout for nine innings of the three nights he didn't pitch, but on his pitching night sat quietly, looking neither relaxed nor tense, and only spoke when politeness required it. Always he was polite. Soon they made a space for him on the bench, where he sat now knowing he would be all right. He did not think about it, for he knew as the insomniac does that to give it words summons it up to dance; he knew that the pain he had brought with him to the park was still there; he even knew it would probably always be there; but for a good while now it was gone. It would lie in wait for him and strike him again when he was drained and had a heart full of room for it. But that was a long time from now, in the shower or back in the hotel, longer than the two and a half hours or whatever he would use pitching the game; longer than a clock could measure. Right now it seemed a great deal of his life would pass before the shower. When he trotted out to the mound they stood and cheered and, before he threw his first warm-up pitch, he tipped his cap.

He did not make love to Leslie the night before the game. All season, he had not made love to her on the night before he pitched. He did not believe, as some ballplayers did, that it hurt you the next day. *It's why they call it the box score anyway*, Hap Thomas had said on the bus one night after going hitless; *I left me at least two base hits in that whorehouse last night*. Like most ballplayers in the Evangeline League, Thomas had been finished for a long time: a thirty-six-year-old outfielder who had played three seasons—not consecutively—in Triple A ball, when he was in his twenties. Billy didn't make love the night before a game because he still wasn't used to night baseball; he still had the same ritual that he'd had in San Antonio, playing high school and American Legion ball: he drank a glass of buttermilk then went to bed, where for an hour or more he imagined tomorrow's game, although it seemed the game already existed somewhere in the night beyond his window and was imagining him. When finally he slept, the game was still there with him, and in the morning he woke to it, remembered pitching somewhere between daydream and nightdream; and until time for the game he felt like a shadow cast by the memory and the morning's light, a shadow that extended from his pillow to the locker room, when he took off the clothes which had not felt like his all day and put on the uniform which in his mind he had been wearing since he went to bed the night before. In high school, his classes interfered with those days of being a shadow. He felt that he was not so much going to classes as bumping into them on his way to the field. But in summer when he played American Legion ball, there was nothing to bump into, there was only the morning's wait which wasn't really waiting because waiting was watching time, watching it win usually, while on those mornings he joined time and flowed with it, so that sitting before the breakfast his mother cooked for him he felt he was in motion toward the mound.

And he had played a full season less one game of pro ball and still had not been able to convince his mind and body that the night before a game was far too early to enter the rhythm and concentration that would work for him when he actually had the ball in his hand. Perhaps his mind and body weren't the ones who needed convincing; perhaps he was right when he thought he was not imagining the games, but they were imagining him: benevolent and slow-witted angels who had followed him to take care of him, who couldn't understand they could rest now, lie quietly the night before, because they and Billy had all next day to spend with each other. If he had known Leslie was hurt he could have told her, as simply as a man saying he was beset by the swollen agony of mumps, that he could not make love on those nights, and it wasn't because he preferred thinking about tomorrow's game, but because those angels had followed him all the way to Lafayette, Louisiana. Perhaps he and Leslie could even have laughed about it, for finally it was funny, as funny as the story about Billy's Uncle Johnny whose two hounds had jumped the fence and faithfully tracked or followed him to a bedroom a few blocks from his house, and bayed outside the window: a bedroom Uncle Johnny wasn't supposed to be in, and more trouble than that, because to get there he had left a bedroom he wasn't supposed to leave.

Lafayette was funny too: a lowland of bayous and swamps and Cajuns. The Cajuns were good fans. They were so good that in early season Billy felt like he was barnstorming in some strange country, where everybody loved the Americans and decided to love baseball too since the Americans were playing it for them. They knew the game, but often when they yelled about it, they yelled in French, and when they yelled in English it sounded like a Frenchman's English. This came from the colored section too. The stands did not extend far beyond third and first base, and where the first base stands ended there was a space of about fifty feet and, after that, shoved against each other, were two sections of folding wooden bleachers. The Negroes filled them, hardly noticed beyond the fifty feet of air and trampled earth. They were not too far down the right field line: sometimes when Billy ran out a ground ball he ended his sprint close enough to the bleachers to hear the Negroes calling to him in French, or in the English that sounded like French.

Two Cajuns played for the Bulls. The team's full name was the Lafayette Brahma Bulls, and when the fans said all of it, they said Bremabulls. The owner was a rancher who raised these bulls, and one of his prizes was a huge and dangerous-looking hump-necked bull whose grey coat was nearly white; it was named Huey for their governor who was shot and killed in the state capitol building. Huey was led to home plate for opening day ceremonies, and after that he attended every game in a pen in foul territory against the right field fence. During batting practice the left handers tried to pull the ball into the pen. Nobody hit him, but when the owner heard about it he had the bull brought to the park when batting practice was over. By then the stands were filling. Huey was brought in a truck that entered through a gate behind the colored bleachers, and the Negroes would turn and look behind them at the bull going by. The two men in the truck wore straw cowboy hats.

So did the owner, Charlie Breaux. When the Cajuns said his first and last names together they weren't his name anymore. And since it was the Cajun third baseman, E. J. Primeaux, a wiry thirty-year-old who owned a small grocery store which his wife ran during the season, who first introduced Billy to the owner, Billy had believed for the first few days after reporting to the club that he pitched for a man named Mr. Chollibro.

One night someone did hit Huey: during a game, with two outs, a high fly ball that Hap Thomas could have reached for and caught; he was there in plenty of time, glancing down at the pen's fence as he moved with the flight of the ball, was waiting safe from collision beside the pen, looking now from the ball to Huey who stood just on the other side of the fence, watching him; Hap stuck his arm out over the fence and Huey's head; then he looked at Huey again and withdrew his arm and stepped back to watch the ball strike Huey's head with a sound the fans heard behind third base. The ball bounced up and out and Hap barehanded it as Huey trotted once around the pen. Hap ran toward the dugout, holding the ball up, until he reached the first base umpire who was alternately signalling safe and pointing Hap back to right field. Then Hap flipped him the ball and, grinning, raised both arms to the fans behind the first base line, kept them raised to the Negroes as he ran past their bleachers and back to Huey's pen, taking off his cap as he approached the fence where Huey stood again watching, waved his cap once over the fence and horns, then trotted to his position, thumped his glove twice, then lowered it to his knee, and his bare hand to the other, and crouched. The fans were still laughing and cheering and calling to Hap and Huey and Chollibro when two pitches later the batter popped up to Caldwell at short.

In the dugout Primeaux said: 'Hap, I seen many a outfielder miss a fly ball because he's wall-shy, but that's the first time I ever seen one miss because he's *bull*-horn shy.' And Hap said: 'In this league? That's nothing. No doubt about it, one of these nights I'll go out to right field and get bit by a cottonmouth so big he'll chop my leg in two.' 'Or get hit by lightning,' Shep Caldwell said. In June lightning had struck a centerfielder for the Abbeville Athletics; struck the metal peak of his cap and exited into the earth through his spikes. When the Bulls heard the announcement over their public address system, their own sky was cloudy and there were distant flashes; perhaps they had even seen the flash that killed

Tommy Lyons thirty miles away. The announcement came between innings when the Bulls were coming to bat; the players and fans stood for a minute of silent prayer. Billy was sitting beside Hap. Hap went to the cooler and came back with a paper cup and sat looking at it but not drinking, then said: 'He broke a leg, Lyons did. I played in the Pacific Coast League with him one year. Forty-one. He was hitting three-thirty; thirty-something home runs; stole about forty bases. Late in the season he broke his leg sliding. He never got his hitting back. Nobody knew why. Tommy didn't know why. He went to spring training with the Yankees, then back to the Pacific Coast League, and he kept going down. I was drafted by then, and next time I saw him was two years ago when he came to Abbeville. We had a beer one night and I told him he was headed for the major leagues when he broke his leg. No doubt about it. He said he knew that. And he still didn't understand it. Lost something: swing; timing. Jesus, he used to hit the ball. Now they fried him in front of a bunch of assholes in Abbeville. How's that for shit.' For the rest of the game most of the players watched their sky; those who didn't were refusing to. They would not know until next day about the metal peak on Lyons's cap; but two innings after the announcement, Lucky went into the locker room and cut his off. When he came back to the dugout holding the blue cap and looking at the hole where the peak had been, Shep said: 'Hell, Lucky, it never strikes twice.' Lucky said: 'That's because it don't have to,' and sat down, stroking the hole.

Lafayette was only a town on the way to Detroit, to the Tigers; unless he got drafted, which he refused to think about, and thought about daily when he read of the war. Already the Tiger scout had watched Billy pitch three games and talked to him after each one, told him all he needed was time, seasoning; told him to stay in shape in the off-season; told him next year he would go to Flint, Michigan, to Class A ball. He was the only one on the club who had a chance for the major leagues, though Billy Joe Baron would probably go up, but not very far; he was a good first baseman and very fast, led the league in stolen bases, but he had to struggle and beat out drag bunts and ground balls to keep his average in the two-nineties and low three hundreds, and he would not go higher than Class A unless they outlawed the curve ball. The others would stay with the Bulls, or a team like the Bulls. And now Leslie was staying in this little town that she wasn't supposed to see as a town to live in longer than a season, and staying too in the little furnished house they were renting, with its rusted screen doors and its yard that ended in the back at a woods which farther on became a swamp, so that Billy never went off the back porch at night and if he peered through the dark at the grass long enough he was sure he saw cottonmouths.

She came into the kitchen that morning of the final game, late morning after a late breakfast so he would eat only twice before pitching, when he was already—or still, from the night before—concentrating on his twentieth win; and the pennant too. He wanted that: wanted to be the pitcher who had come to a third-place club and after one season had ridden away from a pennant winner. She came into the kitchen and looked at him more seriously than he'd ever seen her, and said: 'Billy, it's a terrible day to tell you this but you said today was the day I should pack.'

He looked at her from his long distance then focussed in closer, forced himself to hear what she was saying, felt like he was even forcing himself to see her in three dimensions instead of two, and said: 'What's the matter, baby?'

'I'm not going.'

'Not going where?'

'San Antonio. Flint. I'm staying here.'

Her perspiring face looked so afraid and sorry for him and determined all at once that he knew he was finished, that he didn't even know what was happening but there would never be enough words he could say. Her eyes were brimming with tears, and he knew they were for herself, for having come to this moment in the kitchen, so far from everything she could have known and predicted; deep in her eyes, as visible as stars, was the hard light of something else, and he knew that she had hated him too, and he imagined her hating him for days while he was on the road: saw her standing in this kitchen and staring out the screen door at the lawn and woods, hating him. Then the picture completed itself: a man, his back to Billy, stood beside her and put his arm around her waist.

'Leslie?' and he had to clear his throat, clear his voice of the fear in it: 'Baby, have you been playing around?'

She looked at him for such a long time that he was both afraid of what she would say, and afraid she wouldn't speak at all.

'I'm in love, Billy.'

Then she turned and went to the back door, hugging her breasts and staring through the screen. He gripped the corners of the table, pushed his chair back, started to rise, but did not; there was nothing to stand for. He rubbed his eyes, then briskly shook his head.

'It wasn't just that you were on the road so much. I was ready for that. I used to tell myself it'd be exciting a lot of the time, especially in the big leagues. And I'd tell myself in ten years it'd be over anyway, some women have to—'

'*Ten?*' Thinking of the running he did, in the outfield on the days he wasn't pitching, and every day at home between seasons, having known long ago that his arm was a gift and it would last until one spring when it couldn't do the work anymore, would become for the first time since it started throwing a baseball just an ordinary arm; and what he could and must do was keep his lungs and legs strong so they wouldn't give out before it did. He surprised himself: he had not known that, while his wife was leaving him, he could proudly and defensively think of pitching in his early thirties. He had a glimpse of the way she saw him, and he was frightened and ashamed.

'All right: fifteen,' she said. 'Some women are married to sailors and soldiers and it's longer. It wasn't the road trips. It was when you were home: you weren't here. You weren't here, with me.'

'I was here all day. Six, seven hours at the park at night. I don't know what that means.'

'It means I'm not what you want.'

'How can you tell me what I want?'

'You want to be better than Walter Johnson.'

From his angle he saw very little of her face. He waited. But this time she didn't speak.

'Leslie, can't a man try to be the best at what he's got to do and still love his wife?' Then he stood: 'Goddamnit who *is* he?'

'George Lemoine,' she said through the screen.

'George Lemoine. Who's George Lemoine?'

'The dentist I went to.'

'What dentist you went to?'

She turned and looked at his face and down the length of his arms to his fists, then sat at the opposite end of the table.

'When I lost the filling. In June.'

'*June?*'

'We didn't start then.' Her face was slightly lowered, but her eyes were raised to his, and there was another light in them: she was ashamed but not remorseful, and her voice had the unmistakable tone of a woman in love; they were never so serious as this, never so threatening, and he was assaulted by images of Leslie making love with another man. 'He went to the games alone. Sometimes we talked down at the concession stand. We−' Now she looked down, hid her eyes from him, and he felt shut out forever from the mysteries of her heart.

All his life he had been confident. In his teens his confidence and hope were concrete: the baseball season at hand, the season ahead, professional ball, the major leagues. But even as a child he had been confident and hopeful, in an abstract way. He had barely suffered at all, and he had survived that without becoming either callous or naive. He was not without compassion when his life involved him with the homely, the clumsy, the losers. He simply considered himself lucky. Now his body felt like someone else's, weak and trembling. His urge was to lie down.

'And all those times on the road I never went near a whorehouse.'

'It's not the same.'

He was looking at the beige wall over the sink, but he felt that her eyes were lowered still. He was about to ask what she meant, but then he knew.

'So I guess when I go out to the mound tonight he'll be moving in, is that right?'

Now he looked at her, and when she lifted her face, it had changed: she was only vulnerable.

'He has to get a divorce first. He has a wife and two kids.'

'Wait a minute. *Wait* a minute. He's got a wife and two *kids?* How *old* is this son of a bitch?'

'Thirty-four.'

'God*damn* it Leslie! How dumb can you be? He's getting what he wants from you, what makes you think he won't be smart enough to leave it at that? God*damn.*'

'I believe him.'

'You believe him. A dentist anyhow. How can you be married to a ballplayer and fall for a dentist anyhow? And what'll you do for money? You got that one figured out?'

'I don't need much. I'll get a job.'

'Well, you won't have much either, because I'm going over there and kill him.'

'Billy.' She stood, her face as admonitory as his mother's. 'He's got enough troubles. All summer I've been in trouble too. I've been sad and lonesome. That's the only way this could ever happen. You know that. All summer I've been feeling like I was running along-side the players' bus waving at you. Then he came along.'

'And picked you up.'

He glared at her until she blushed and lowered her eyes. Then he went to the bedroom to pack. But she had already done it: the suit-case and overnight bag stood at the foot of the bed. He picked them up and walked fast to the front door. Before he reached it she came out of the kitchen, and he stopped.

'Billy. I don't want you to be hurt; and I know you won't be for long. I hope someday you can forgive me. Maybe write and tell me how you're doing.'

His urge to drop the suitcase and overnight bag and hold her and ask her to change her mind was so great that he could only fight it with anger; and with the clarity of anger he saw a truth which got him out the door.

'You want it all, don't you? Well, forget it. You just settle for what you chose.'

Scornfully he scanned the walls of the living room, then Leslie from feet to head; then he left, out into the sun and the hot still air, and drove into town and registered at a hotel. The old desk clerk recognized him and looked puzzled but quickly hid it and said: 'Y'all going to beat them New Iberia boys tonight?'

'Damn right.'

The natural thing to do now was go to Lemoine's office, walk in while he was looking in somebody's mouth: *It's me you son of a bitch*, and work him over with the left hand, cancel his afternoon for him, send him off to another dentist. What he had to do was unnatural. And as he climbed the stairs to his room he thought there was much about his profession that was unnatural. In the room he turned off the air conditioning and opened the windows, because he didn't want his arm to be in the cool air, then lay on the bed and closed his eyes and began pitching to the batting order. He knew them all perfectly; but he did not trust that sort of perfection, for it was too much like confidence, which was too much like complacency. So he started with Vidrine, the lead-off man. Left-handed. Went with the pitch, hit to all fields; good drag-bunter but only fair speed and Primeaux would be crowding him at third; choke-hitter, usually got a piece of the ball, but not that quick with the bat either; couldn't hit good speed. Fastballs low and tight. Change on him. Good base-runner but he had to get a jump. Just hold him close to the bag. Then Billy stopped thinking about Vidrine on base. Thing was to concentrate now on seeing his stance and the high-cocked bat and the inside of the plate and Lucky's glove. He pushed aside the image of Vidrine crouching in a lead off first, and at the same time he pushed from his mind Leslie in the kitchen telling him; he saw Vidrine at the plate and, beyond him, he saw Leslie going away. She had been sitting in the box seat but now she walked alone down the ramp. Poor little Texas girl. She even sounded like a small town in Texas: Leslie Wells. Then she was gone.

The home run came with one out and nobody on in the top of the third inning after he had retired the first seven batters. Rick Stanley hit it, the eighth man in the order, a good-field no-hit third baseman in his mid-twenties. He had been in the minors for seven years and looked like it: though trimly built, and the best third baseman Billy had ever seen, he had a look about him of age, of resignation, of having been forced—when he was too young to bear it well—to compromise what he wanted with what he could do. At the plate he looked afraid, and early in the season Billy thought Stanley had been beaned and wasn't able to forget it. Later he realized it wasn't fear of beaning, not fear at all, but the strain of living so long with what he knew. It showed in the field too. Not during a play, but when it was over and Stanley threw the ball to the pitcher and returned to his position, his face looking as though it were adjusting itself to the truth he had forgotten when he backhanded the ball over the bag and turned and set and threw his mitt-popping peg to first; his face then was intense, reflexive as his legs and hands and arm; then the play was over and his face settled again into the resignation that was still new enough to be terrible. It spread downward to his shoulders and then to the rest of him and he looked old again. Billy wished he had seen Stanley play third when he was younger and still believed there was a patch of dirt and a bag and a foul line waiting for him in the major leagues.

One of Billy's rules was never to let up on the bottom of the batting order, because when one of them got a hit it hurt more. The pitch to Stanley was a good one. Like many players, Stanley was a poor hitter because he could not consistently be a good hitter; he was only a good hitter for one swing out of every twelve or so; the other swings had changed his life for him. The occasional good one gave the fans, and Stanley too by now, a surprise that always remained a surprise and so never engendered hope. His home run was a matter of numbers and time, for on this one pitch his concentration and timing and swing all flowed together, making him for that instant the hitter of his destroyed dream. It would happen again, in other ball parks, in other seasons; and if Stanley had been able to cause it instead of having it happen to him, he would be in the major leagues.

Billy's first pitch to him was a fast ball, waist high, inside corner. Stanley took it for a strike, with that look on his face. Lucky called for the same pitch. Billy nodded and played with the rosin bag to keep Stanley waiting longer; then Stanley stepped out of the box and scooped up dust and rubbed it on his hands and the bat handle; when he moved to the plate again he looked just as tense and Billy threw the fast ball; Stanley swung late and under it. Lucky called for the curve, the pitch that was sweet tonight, and Billy went right into the wind-up, figuring Stanley was tied up tightly now, best time to throw a pitch into all that: he watched the ball go in fast and groin-high, then fall to the left, and it would have cut the outside corner of the plate just above Stanley's knees; but it was gone. Stanley not only hit it so solidly that Billy knew it was gone before looking, but he got around on it, pulled it, and when Billy found it in the left-centerfield sky it was still climbing above James running from left and LeBlanc from center. At the top of its arc, there was something final about its floodlit surface against the real sky, dark up there above the lighted one they played under.

He turned his back to the plate. He never watched a home run hitter cross it. He looked out at LeBlanc in center; then he looked at Harry Burke at second, old Harry, the manager, forty-one years old and he could still cover the ground, mostly through cunning; make the pivot—how many double plays had he turned in his life?—and when somebody took him out with a slide Billy waited for the cracking sound, not just of bone but the whole body, like a dried tree limb. Hap told him not to worry, old Harry was made of oiled leather. His face looked as if it had already outlived two bodies like the one it commanded now. Never higher than Triple A, and that was long ago; when the Bulls hired him and then the fans loved him he moved his family to Lafayette and made it his home, and between seasons worked for an insurance company, easy money for him, because he went to see men and they drank coffee and talked baseball. He had the gentlest eyes Billy had ever seen on a man. Now Harry trotted over to him.

'We got twenty-one outs to get that back for you.'

'The little bastard hit that pitch.'

'Somebody did. Did you get a close look at him?'

Billy shook his head and went to the rubber. He walked the fat pitcher Talieferro on four pitches and Vidrine on six, and Lucky came to the mound. They called him Lucky because he wasn't.

'One run's one thing,' Lucky said. 'Let's don't make it three.'

'The way y'all are swinging tonight, one's as good as nine.' For the first time since he stepped onto the field, Leslie that morning rose up from wherever he had locked her, and struck him.

'Hey,' Lucky said. 'Hey, it's early.'

'Can't y'all hit that fat son of a bitch?'

'We'll hit him. Now you going to pitch or cry?'

He threw Jackson a curve ball and got a double play around the horn, Primeaux to Harry to Baron, who did a split stretching and got Jackson by a half stride.

He went to his end of the bench and watched Talieferro, who for some reason pronounced his name Tolliver: a young big left-handed pitcher with the kind of belly that belonged on a much older man, in bars on weekend afternoons; he had pitched four years at the local college, this was his first season of pro ball, he was sixteen and nine and usually lost only when his control was off. He did not want to be a professional ballplayer. He had a job with an oil company at the end of the season, and was only pitching and eating his way through a Louisiana summer. Billy watched Lucky adjust his peakless cap and dust his hands and step to the plate, and he pushed Leslie back down, for she was about to burst out of him and explode in his face. He looked down at the toe plate on his right shoe, and began working the next inning, the middle of the order, starting with their big hitter, the centerfielder Remy Gauthreaux, who was finished too, thirty years old, but smart and dangerous

and he'd knock a mistake out of the park. Low and away to Gauthreaux. Lucky popped out to Stanley in foul territory and came back
to the dugout shaking his head.

Billy could sense it in all the hitters in the dugout, and see it
when they went to the plate: Talieferro was on, and they were off.
It could be anything: the pennant game, when every move counted;
the last game of the season, so the will to be a ballplayer was losing
to that other part of them which insisted that when they woke tomorrow nothing they felt tonight would be true; they would drive
home to the jobs and other lives that waited for them; most would
go to places where people had not even heard of the team, the
league. All of that would apply to the Pelicans too; it could be that
none of it applied to Talieferro: that rarely feeling much of anything
except digestion, hunger, and gorging, he had no conflict between
what he felt now and would start feeling tomorrow. And it could be
that he simply had his best stuff tonight, that he was throwing
nearly every pitch the way Stanley had swung that one time.

Billy went to the on-deck circle and kneeled and watched Harry
at the plate, then looked out at Simmons, their big first baseman:
followed Gauthreaux in the order, a power hitter but struck out
about a hundred times a year: keep him off balance, in and out, and
throw the fast one right into his power, and right past him too.
Harry, choking high on the bat, fouled off everything close to the
plate then grounded out to short, and Billy handed his jacket to the
batboy and went through cheers to the plate. When he stepped in
Talieferro didn't look at him, so Billy stepped out and stared until
he did, then dug in and cocked the bat, a good hitter so he had
played right field in high school and American Legion when he
wasn't pitching. He watched the slow, easy fatman's wind-up and
the fast ball coming out of it: swung for the fence and popped it to
second, sprinting down the line and crossing the bag before the ball
came down. When he turned he saw Talieferro already walking in,
almost at the third base line. Harry brought Billy's glove out to the
mound and patted his rump.

'I thought you were running all the way to Flint.'

In the next three innings he pitched to nine men. He ended the
fifth by striking out Stanley on curve balls; and when Talieferro led
off the sixth Billy threw a fast ball at his belly that made him spin
away and fall into the dust. Between innings he forced himself to
believe in the hope of numbers: the zeros and the one on the

scoreboard in right center, the inning number, the outs remaining for the Bulls; watched them starting to hit, but only one an inning, and nobody as far as second base. He sat sweating under his jacket and in his mind pitched to the next three Pelicans, then the next three just to be sure, although he didn't believe he would face six of them next inning, or any inning, and he thought of eighteen then fifteen then twelve outs to get the one run, the only one he needed, because if it came to that, Talieferro would tire first. When Primeaux struck out leading off the sixth, Billy looked at Hap at the other end of the bench, and he wanted to be down there with him. He leaned forward and stared at his shoes. Then the inning was over and he gave in to the truth he had known anyway since that white vision of loss just before the ball fell.

Gauthreaux started the seventh with a single to right, doing what he almost never did: laid off pulling and went with the outside pitch. Billy worked Simmons low and got the double play he needed, then he struck out the catcher Lantrip, and trotted off the field with his string still going, thirteen batters since the one-out walk to Vidrine in the third. He got the next six. Three of them grounded out, and the other three struck out on the curve, Billy watching it break under the shiny blur of the bat as it would in Flint and wherever after that and Detroit too: his leg kicking and body wheeling and arm whipping around in rhythm again with his history which had begun with a baseball and a friend to throw it to, and had excluded all else, or nearly all else, and had included the rest somewhere alongside him, almost out of his vision (once between innings he allowed himself to think about Leslie, just long enough to forgive her); his history was his future too and the two of them together were twenty-five years at most until the time when the pitches that created him would lose their speed, hang at the plate, become hits in other men's lives instead of the heart of his; they would discard him then, the pitches would. But he loved them for that too, and right now they made his breath singular out of the entire world, so singular that there was no other world: the war would not call him because it couldn't know his name; and he would refuse the grief that lurked behind him. He watched the final curve going inside, then breaking down and over, and Lucky's mitt popped and the umpire twisted and roared and pointed his right fist to the sky.

He ran to the dugout, tipping his cap to the yelling Cajuns, and sat between Hap and Lucky until Baron flied out to end the game. After the showers and goodbyes he drove to the hotel and got his still-packed bags and paid the night clerk and started home, out of the lush flatland of marsh and trees, toward Texas. Her space on the front seat was filled as with voice and touch. He turned on the radio. He was not sleepy, and he was driving straight through to San Antonio.

Waiting

J UANITA CREEHAN was a waitress in a piano bar
near Camp Pendleton, California. She had
been a widow for twelve years, and her most
intense memory of her marriage was an imagined one: Patrick's
death in the Chosin Reservoir. After Starkey got back from Korea,
he and Mary came to her apartment, and he told Juanita how it
happened: they were attacking a hill, and when they cleared it they
went down to the road and heard that Patrick had caught it. Starkey went over to the second platoon to look at him.

'What did they do to him?' Juanita said.

'They wrapped him in a shelter half and put him in a truck.'

She thought of the road of frozen mud and snow; she had never
seen snow but now when it fell or lay white in her mind it was
always death. Many nights she drank and talked with Starkey and
Mary, and she asked Starkey for more details of the Reservoir, and
sometimes she disliked him for being alive, or disliked Mary for
having him alive. She had been tolerant of Mary's infidelity while
Starkey was gone, for she understood her loneliness and dread; but
now she could not forgive her, and often she looked quickly into
Mary's eyes, and knew that her look was unforgiving. Years later,
when she heard they were divorced, she was both pleased and angry. At the end of those nights of listening to Starkey, she went to
bed and saw the hills and sky, and howitzers and trucks and troops
on the road. She saw Patrick lying in the snow while the platoon
moved up the hill; she saw them wrap him in the shelter half and
lift him to the bed of the truck.

Some nights she descended further into the images. First she saw

Patrick walking. He was the platoon sergeant, twenty-six years old. He walked on the side of the road, watching his troops and the hills. He had lost weight, was thinner than ever (my little bantam rooster, she had called him), his cheeks were sunken, and on them was a thin red beard. She no longer felt her own body. She was inside his: she felt the weight of helmet and rifle and parka; the cold feet; and the will to keep the body going, to believe that each step took him and his men closer to the sea. Through his green eyes and fever-warmth she looked up the road: a howitzer bounced behind a truck; Lieutenant Dobson, walking ahead on the road, wore a parka hood under his helmet; she could see none of his flesh as he looked once up at the sky. She heard boots on the hard earth, the breathing and coughing of troops, saw their breath-plumes in the air. She scanned the hills on both sides of the road, looked down at her boots moving toward the sea; glanced to her left at the files of young troops, then looked to the right again, at a snow-covered hill without trees, and then her chest and belly were struck and she was suddenly ill: she felt not pain but nausea, and a sense of futility at living this long and walking this far as her body seemed to melt into the snow . . .

On a summer night in 1962, for the first time in her life, she woke with a man and had to remember his name. She lay beside the strange weight of his body and listened to his breath, then remembered who he was: Roy Hodges, a sergeant major, who last night had talked with her when she brought his drinks, and the rest of the time he watched her, and when she went to the restroom she looked at her tan face and blonde hair; near the end of the evening he asked if he could take her home; she said she had a car but he could follow her, she'd like to have a drink, and they drank vodka at her kitchen table. Now she did not want to touch him, or wake him and tell him to go. She got up, found her clothes on the floor and dressed; quietly she opened a drawer and took a sweater and put it on her shoulders like a cape. Her purse was in the kitchen. She found it in the dark, on the floor beside her chair, and went out of the apartment and crossed the cool damp grass to her car. With the windshield wipers sweeping dew, she drove down a hill and through town to the beach. She locked her purse in the car and sat on loose sand and watched the sea. Black waves broke with a white slap, then a roar. She sat huddled in the cool air.

Then she walked. To her left the sea was loud and dark, and she thought of Vicente Torrez with the pistol in his lap: a slender Mexican boy who in high school had teased her about being named Juanita, when she had no Mexican blood. Blonde gringita, he called her, and his eyes looked curiously at her, as if her name were an invitation to him, but he didn't know how to answer it. Five years after high school, while she was married to Patrick, she read in the paper that he had shot himself. There was no photograph, so she read the story to know if this were the same Vicente, and she wanted it to be him. He had been a cab driver in San Diego, and had lived alone. The second and final paragraph told of the year he was graduated from the high school in San Diego, and listed his survivors: his parents, brothers, sisters. So it was Vicente, with the tight pants and teasing face and that question in his eyes: Could you be my girl? Love me? Someone she once knew had sat alone in his apartment and shot himself; yet her feeling was so close to erotic that she was frightened. Patrick came home in late afternoon and she watched through the window as he walked uniformed across the lawn (it was winter: he was wearing green) and when he came inside she held him and told him and then she was crying, seeing Vicente sitting in a dirty and disorderly room, sitting on the edge of his bed and reaching that moment when he wanted more than anything else not to be Vicente, and crying into Patrick's chest she said: 'I wonder if he knew somebody would cry; I wonder if he wouldn't have done it; if that would have seen him through till tomorrow—' The word tomorrow stayed in her heart. She saw it in her mind, its letters printed across the black and white image of Vicente sitting on the bed with the pistol, and she loosened Patrick's tie and began to unbutton his green blouse.

She was looking out at the sea as she walked, and she stepped into a shallow pool left by the tide; the water covered her sandalled feet and was cool and she stood in it. Then she stepped out and walked on. For a year after Patrick was killed she took sleeping pills. She remembered lying in bed and waiting for the pill to work, and the first signals in her fingers, her hands: the slow-coming dullness, and she would touch her face, its skin faintly tingling, going numb, then she was aware only of the shallow sound and peaceful act of her slow breathing.

Juanita Jody Noury Creehan. Her mother had named her, given her a choice that would not change her initials if later she called herself Jody. Her mother's maiden name had been Miller. She looked up at the sky: it was clear, stars and a quarter-moon. Noury Creehan: both names from men. She stepped out of her sandals, toe against heel, toe against heel, heart beating as though unclothing for yet another man, remembering the confessions when she was in high school, remembering tenderly as if she were mother to herself as a young girl. Petting: always she called it that, whispering through lattice and veil, because that was the word the priests used in the confessional and when they came to the Saturday morning catechism classes for talks with the junior and senior girls; and the word the nuns used too on Saturday mornings, black-robed and looking never-petted themselves, so the word seemed strange on their tongues. The priests looked as if they had petted, or some of them did, probably only because they were men, they had hands and faces she liked to watch, voices she liked to hear.

Petting, for the bared and handled and suckled breasts, her blouse unbuttoned, and her pants off and skirt pulled up for the finger; the boys' pants on and unzipped as they gasped, thick warmth on her hand, white faint thumping on the dashboard. She confessed her own finger too, and while petting was a vague word and kept her secrets, masturbation was stark and hid nothing, exposed her in the confessional like the woman in the photograph that Ruth had shown her: a Mexican woman of about thirty, sitting naked in an armchair, legs spread, hand on her mound, and her face caught forever in passion real or posed.

Then finally in high school it was Billy Campbell in the spring of her junior year, quick-coming Billy dropping the Trojan out of the car window, the last of her guilt dropping with it, so that after one more confession she knew she had kneeled and whispered to a priest for the last time. Young and hot and pretty, she could not imagine committing any sin that was not sexual. When she was thirty there was no one to tell that sometimes she could not bear knowing what she knew: that no one would help her, not ever again. That was the year she gained weight and changed sizes and did not replace her black dress, though she liked herself in black, liked her blonde hair touching it. She began selecting colors which in the store were merely colors; but when she thought of them on her body and bed, they seemed to hold possibilities: sheets and pillowcases of yellow and pink and pale blue, and all her underwear was pastel, so she could start each day by stepping into color. Many of those days she spent at the beach, body-surfing and swimming beyond the breakers and sleeping in the sun, or walking there in cool months. Once a bartender told her that waitresses and bartenders should have a month off every year and go to a cabin in the mountains and not smile once. Just to relax the facial muscles, he said; maybe they go, like pitchers' arms. Her days were short, for she slept late, and her evenings long; and most days she was relieved when it was time to go to work, to the costume-smile and chatter that some nights she brought home with a gentle man, and next day she had that warmth to remember as she lay on the beach.

She unbuttoned and unzipped her skirt, let it fall to the sand; pulled down her pants and stepped out of them. She took off the sweater and blouse and shivering dropped them, then reached around for the clasp of her brassiere. She walked across wet sand, into the rushing touch of sea. She walked through a breaking wave, sand moving under her feet, current pulling and pushing her farther out, and she walked with it and stood breast-deep, watching the surface coming from the lighter dome of the sky. A black swell rose toward her and curled, foam skimming its crest like quick smoke; she turned to the beach, watched the wave over her shoulder: breaking it took her with head down and outstretched arms pointing, eyes open to dark and fast white foam, then she scraped sand with breasts and feet, belly and thighs, and lay breathing salt-taste as water hissed away from her legs. She stood and crossed the beach, toward her clothes.

He was sleeping. In the dark she undressed and left her clothes on the floor and took a nightgown to the bathroom. She showered and washed her hair and when she went to the bedroom he said: 'Do you always get up when it's still night?'

'I couldn't sleep.'

She got into bed; he placed a hand on her leg and she shifted away and he did not touch her again.

'In three months I'll be thirty-nine.'

'Thirty-nine's not bad.'

'I was born in the afternoon. They didn't have any others.'

'What time is it?'

'Almost five.'

'It's going to be a long day.'

'Not for me. I'll sleep.'

'Night worker.'

'They were Catholics, but they probably used something anyway. Maybe I was a diaphragm baby. I feel like one a lot of the time.'

'What's that supposed to mean?'

'Like I sneaked into the movie and I'm waiting for the usher to come get me.'

'Tell him to shove off.'

'Not this usher.'

'You talking about dying?'

'No.'

'What then?'

'I don't know. But he's one shit of an usher.'

She believed she could not sleep until he left. But when she closed her eyes she felt it coming in her legs and arms and breath, and gratefully she yielded to it: near-dreaming, she saw herself standing naked in the dark waves. One struck her breast and she wheeled slow and graceful, salt water black in her eyes and lovely in her mouth, hair touching sand as she turned then rose and floated in swift tenderness out to sea.

PART THREE

Delivering

JIMMY WOKE BEFORE the alarm, his parents'
sounds coming back to him as he had known
they would when finally three hours ago he
knew he was about to sleep: their last fight in the kitchen, and Chris
sleeping through it on the top bunk, grinding his teeth. It was
nearly five now, the room sunlit; in the dark while they fought
Jimmy had waited for the sound of his father's slap, and when it
came he felt like he was slapping her and he waited for it again,
wished for it again, but there was only the one clap of hand on face.
Soon after that, she drove away.

Now he was ashamed of the slap. He reached down to his morning hardness which always he had brought to the bathroom so she
wouldn't see the stain; he stopped once to turn off the alarm when
he remembered it was about to ring into his quick breath. Then he
stood and gently shook Chris's shoulder. He could smell the ocean.
He shook Chris harder: twelve years old and chubby and still
clumsy about some things. Maybe somebody else was Chris's
father. No. He would stay with what he heard last night; he would
not start making up more. Somewhere his mother was naked with
that son of a bitch, and he squeezed Chris's shoulder and said:
'Wake up.' Besides, their faces looked alike: his and Chris's and his
father's. Everybody said that. Chris stared at him.

'Come with me.'

'You're crazy.'

'I need you to.'

'You didn't say anything last night.'

'Come on.'

'You buying the doughnuts?'

'After we swim.'

In the cool room they dressed for the warm sun, in cut-off jeans and T-shirts and sneakers, and went quietly down the hall, past the closed door where Jimmy stopped and waited until he could hear his father's breath. Last night after she left, his father cried in the kitchen. Chris stood in the doorway, looking into the kitchen; Jimmy looked over his head at the table, the beer cans, his father's bent and hers straight, the ashtray filled, ashes on the table and, on the counter near the sink, bent cans and a Seagram's Seven bottle.

'Holy shit,' Chris said.

'You'd sleep through World War III.'

He got two glasses from the cupboard, reaching over the cans and bottle, holding his breath against their smell; he looked at the two glasses in the sink, her lipstick on the rim of one, and Chris said: 'What's the matter?'

'Makes me sick to smell booze in the morning.'

Chris poured the orange juice and they drank with their backs to the table. Jimmy picked up her Winston pack. Empty. Shit. He took a Pall Mall. He had learned to smoke by watching her, had started three years ago by stealing hers. He was twelve then. Would he and Chris see her alone now, or would they have to go visit her at that son of a bitch's house, wherever it was? They went out the back door and around to the front porch where the stacked papers waited, folded and tied, sixty-two of them, and a note on top saying Mr. Thompson didn't get his paper yesterday. 'It's his Goddamn dog,' he said, and cut the string and gave Chris a handful of rubber bands. Chris rolled and banded the papers while Jimmy stood on the lawn, smoking; he looked up the road at the small houses, yellow and brown and grey, all of them quiet with sleeping families, and the tall woods beyond them and, across the road, houses whose back lawns ended at the salt marsh that spread out to the northeast where the breeze came from. When he heard the rolling papers stop, he turned to Chris sitting on the porch and looking at him.

'Where's the car?'

'Mom took it.'

'This early?'

He flicked the cigarette toward the road and kneeled on the porch and started rolling.

'Where'd she go so early?'

'Late. Let's go.'

He trotted around the lawn and pushed up the garage door and went around the pickup; he did not look at Chris until he had unlocked the chain and pulled it from around the post, coiled it under his bicycle seat, and locked it there. His hands were ink-stained.

'You can leave your chain. We'll use mine at the beach.'

He took the canvas sack from its nail on the post and hung it from his right side, its strap over his left shoulder, and walked his bicycle past the truck and out into the sun. At the front porch he stuffed the papers into the sack. Then he looked at Chris.

'We're not late,' Chris said.

'She left late. Late last night.' He pushed down his kickstand. 'Hold on. Let's get these papers out.'

'She left?'

'Don't you start crying on me. Goddamnit, don't.'

Chris looked down at his handlebar.

'They had a fight,' Jimmy said.

'Then she'll be back.'

'Not this time. She's fucking somebody.'

Chris looked up, shaking his head. Shaking it, he said: 'No.'

'You want to hear about it or you just going to stand there and tell me I didn't hear what I heard.'

'Okay, tell me.'

'Shit. I was going to tell you at the beach. Wait, okay?'

'Sixty-two papers?'

'You know she's gone. Isn't that enough for a while?' He kicked up his stand. 'Look. We've hardly ever lived with both of them. It'll be like Pop's aboard ship. Only it'll be her.'

'That's not true.'

'What's not.'

'About hardly ever living with both of them.'

'It almost is. Let's go.'

Slowly across the grass, then onto the road, pumping hard, shifting gears, heading into the breeze and sun, listening for cars to their rear, sometimes looking over his shoulder at the road and Chris's face, the sack bumping his right thigh and sliding forward but he kept shoving it back, keeping the rhythm of his pedalling and his throws: the easy ones to the left, a smooth motion across his chest like second to first, snapping the paper hard and watching it drop on the lawn; except for the people who didn't always pay on time or who bitched at him, and he hit their porches or front doors, a good hard sound in the morning quiet. He liked throwing to his right better. The first week or so he had cheated, had angled his bicycle toward the houses and thrown overhand; but then he stopped that, and rode straight, leaning back and throwing to his right, sometimes having to stop and leave his bicycle and get a paper from under a bush or a parked car in the driveway, but soon he was hitting the grass just before the porch, unless it was a house that had a door or wall shot coming, and he could do that with velocity too. Second to short. He finished his road by scaring himself, hitting Reilly's big front window instead of the wall beside it, and it shook but didn't break and when he turned his bicycle and headed back he grinned at Chris, who still looked like someone had just punched him in the mouth.

He went left up a climbing road past a pine grove, out of its shade into the warmth on his face: a long road short on customers, twelve of them scattered, and he rode faster, thinking of Chris behind him, pink-cheeked, breathing hard. Ahead on the right he saw Thompson's collie waiting on the lawn, and he pulled out a paper and pushed the sack behind his leg, then rose from the seat pumping toward the house, sitting as he left the road and bounced on earth and grass: he threw the paper thumping against the open jaws, his front tire grazing the yelping dog as it scrambled away, and he lightly hand-braked for his turn then sped out to the road again. He threw two more to his left and started up a long steep hill for the last of the route: the road cut through woods, in shade now, standing, the bicycle slowing as the hill steepened near the hardest house of all: the Claytons' at the top of the hill, a pale green house with a deep front lawn: riding on the shoulder, holding a paper against the handlebar, standing, his legs hot and tight, then at the top he sat to throw, the bicycle slowing, leaning, and with his left hand he moved the front wheel from side to side while he twisted to his right and cocked his arm and threw; he stood on the pedals and gained balance and speed before the paper landed sliding on the walk. The road wound past trees and fifteen customers and twice that many houses. He finished quickly. Then he got off his bicycle, sweating, and folded the sack and put it in his orange nylon saddlebag, and they started back, Chris riding beside him.

From one house near the road he smelled bacon. At another he saw a woman at the kitchen window, her head down, and he looked away. Some of the papers were inside now. At Clayton's house he let the hill take him down into the shade to flat land and, Chris behind him now, he rode past the wide green and brown salt marsh, its grass leaning with the breeze that was cool and sea-tanged on his face, moving the hair at his ears. There were no houses. A fruit and vegetable stand, then the bridge over the tidal stream: a quick blue flow, the tide coming in from the channel and cove beyond a bend to the north, so he could not see them, but he knew how the cove looked this early, with green and orange charter boats tied at the wharves. An hour from now, the people would come. He and Chris and his father went a few afternoons each summer, with sandwiches and soft drinks and beer in the ice chest, and his father drank steadily but only a six-pack the whole after-noon, and they stood abreast at the rail, always near the bow, the boat anchored a mile or two out, and on lucky days filled a plastic bag with mackerel slapping tails till they died, and on unlucky ones he still loved the gentle rocking of the boat and the blue sea and the sun warmly and slowly burning him. Twice in late summer they had bottom-fished and pulled up cusks from three hundred feet, tired arm turning the reel, cusk breaking the surface with eyes pushed outward and guts in its mouth. His mother had gone once. She had not complained, had pretended to like it, but next time she told them it was too much sun, too smelly, too long. Had she been with that son of a bitch when they went fishing again? The boats headed in at five and his father inserted a cleaning board into a slot in the gunwale and handed them slick cool mackerel and he and Chris cleaned them and threw their guts and heads to the sea gulls that hovered and cried and dived until the boat reached the wharf. Sometimes they could make a gull come down and take a head from their fingers.

They rode past beach cottages and up a one-block street to the long dune that hid the sea, chained their bicycles to a telephone pole, and sprinted over loose sand and up the dune; then walking, looking at the empty beach and sea and breakers, stopping to take off sneakers and shirts, Jimmy stuffing his three bills into a sneaker, then running onto wet hard sand, into the surf cold on his feet and ankles, Chris beside him, and they both shouted at once, at the cold but to the sea as well, and ran until the water pushed at their hips

and they walked out toward the sea and low sun, his feet hurting in
the cold. A wave came and they turned their backs to it and he
watched over his shoulder as it rose; when it broke they dived and
he was riding it fast, swallowing water, and in that instant of old
sea-panic he saw his father crying; he opened his eyes to the sting,
his arms stretched before him, hands joined, then he was lying on
the sand and the wave was gone and he stood shouting: 'All *right*.'
They ran back into the sea and body-surfed until they were too
cold, then walked stiffly up to higher sand. He lay on his back
beside his clothes, looked at the sky; soon people would come with
blankets and ice chests. Chris lay beside him. He shut his eyes.

'I was listening to the ball game when they came home. With the
ear plug. They won, three to two. Lee went all the way. Rice drove
in two with a double—' Bright field and uniforms under the lights
in Oakland, him there too while he lay on his bunk, watching Lee
working fast, Remy going to his left and diving to knock it down,
on his knees for the throw in time when they came in talking past
the door and down the hall to the kitchen— 'They talked low for a
long time; that's when they were drinking whiskey and mostly I
just heard Pop getting ice, then I don't know why but after a while I
knew it was trouble, all that ice and quiet talk and when they popped cans I figured they'd finished the whiskey and they were still
talking that way so I started listening. She had already told him.
That's what they were talking about. Maybe she told him at the
Chief's Club. She was talking nice to him—'

'What did she say?'

'She said—shit—' He opened his eyes to the blue sky, closed them
again, pressed his legs into the warm sand, listened to the surf. 'She
said I've tried to stop seeing him. She said Don't you believe I've
tried? You think I want to hurt you? You know what it's like. I can't
stop. I've tried and I can't. I wish I'd never met him. But I can't
keep lying and sneaking around. And Pop said Bullshit: you mean
you can't keep living here when you want to be fucking him. They
didn't say anything for a minute and they popped two more cans,
then she said You're right. But maybe I don't have to leave. Maybe
if you'd just let me go to him when I wanted to. That's when he
started yelling at her. They went at it for a long time, and I thought
you'd wake up. I turned the game up loud as I could take it but it
was already the ninth, then it was over, and I couldn't stop hearing
them anyway. She said Jason would never say those things to her,

that's all I know about that son of a bitch, his name is Jason and he's a civilian somewhere and she started yelling about all the times Pop was aboard ship he must have had a lot of women and who did he think he was anyway and she'd miss you and me and it broke her heart how much she'd miss you and me but she had to get out from under his shit, and he was yelling about she was probably fucking every day he was at sea for the whole twenty years and she said You'll never know you bastard you can just think about it for another twenty. That's when he slapped her.'

'Good.'

'Then she cried a little, not much, then they drank some more beer and talked quiet again. He was trying to make up to her, saying he was sorry he hit her and she said it was her fault, she shouldn't have said that, and she hadn't fucked anybody till Jason—'

'She said that?'

'What.'

'Fuck.'

'Yes. She was talking nice to him again, like he was a little kid, then she went to their room and packed a suitcase and he went to the front door with her, and I couldn't hear what they said. She went outside and he did too and after she drove off he came back to the kitchen and drank beer.' He raised his head and looked past his feet at a sea gull bobbing on the water beyond the breakers. 'Then he cried for a while. Then he went to bed.'

'He did?'

'Yes.'

'I've never heard him cry.'

'Me neither.'

'Why didn't you wake me up?'

'What for?'

'I don't know. I wish you had.'

'I did. This morning.'

'What's going to happen?'

'I guess she'll visit us or something.'

'What if they send Pop to sea again and we have to go live with her and that guy?'

'Don't be an asshole. He's retiring and he's going to buy that boat and we'll fish like bastards. I'm going to catch a big fucking tuna and sell it to the Japanese and buy you some weights.'

He squeezed Chris's bicep and rose, pulling him up. Chris turned his face, looking up the beach. Jimmy stepped in front of him, still holding his arm.

'Look: I heard Pop cry last night. For a long time. Loud. That's all the fucking crying I want to hear. Now let's take another wave and get some doughnuts.'

They ran into the surf, wading coldly to the wave that rose until there was no horizon, no sea, only the sky beyond it.

Dottie from tenth grade was working the counter, small and summer-brown.

'Wakefield boys are here,' Jimmy said. 'Six honey dip to go.'

He only knew her from math and talking in the halls, but the way she smiled at him, if it were any other morning, he would stay and talk, and any other day he would ask her to meet him in town tonight and go on some of the rides, squeeze her on the roller coaster, eat pizza and egg rolls at the stands, get somebody to buy them a six-pack, take it to the beach. He told her she was foxy, and got a Kool from her. Cars were on the roads now, but so many that they were slow and safe, and he and Chris rode side by side on the shoulder; Chris held the doughnut bag against the handlebar and ate while Jimmy smoked, then he reached over for the bag and ate his three. When they got near the house it looked quiet. They chained their bicycles in the garage and crept into the kitchen and past the closed door, to the bathroom. In the shower he pinched Chris's gut and said: 'No shit, we got to work on that.'

They put on gym shorts and sneakers and took their gloves and ball to the backyard.

'When we get warmed up I'm going to throw at your face, okay?'

'Okay.'

'You're still scared of it there and you're ducking and you'll get hurt that way.'

The new baseball smooth in his hand and bright in the sun, smacking in Chris's glove, coming back at him, squeezed high in the pocket and webbing; then he heard the back door and held the ball and watched his father walking out of the shade into the light. He squinted at his father's stocky body and sunburned face and arms, his rumpled hair, and motioned to Chris and heard him trotting on the grass. He was nearly as tall as his father, barely had to tilt his head to look into his eyes. He breathed the smell of last night's booze, this morning's sleep.

'I heard you guys last night,' he said. 'I already told him.'

His father's eyes shifted to Chris, then back.

'She'll come by tomorrow, take you boys to lunch.' He scratched his rump, looked over his shoulder at the house, then at Jimmy. 'Maybe later we'll go eat some lobsters. Have a talk.'

'We could cook them here,' Chris said.

'Sure. Steamers too. Okay: I'll be out in a minute.'

They watched him walk back to the house, then Jimmy touched Chris, gently pushed him, and he trotted across the lawn. They threw fly balls and grounders and one-hop throws from the outfield and straight ones to their bare chests, calling to each other, Jimmy listening to the quiet house too, seeing it darker in there, cooler, his father's closet where in a corner behind blue and khaki uniforms the shotgun leaned. He said, 'Here we go,' and threw at Chris's throat, then face, and heard the back door; his breath quickened, and he threw hard: the ball grazed the top of Chris's glove and struck his forehead and he bent over, his bare hand rubbing above his eye, then he was crying deeply and Jimmy turned to his running father, wearing his old glove, hair wet and combed, smelling of after-shave lotion, and said: 'He's all right, Pop. He's all right.'

The Winter Father

for Pat

THE JACKMAN'S marriage had been adulterous and violent, but in its last days, they became a couple again, as they might have if one of them were slowly dying. They wept together, looked into each other's eyes without guile, distrust, or hatred, and they planned Peter's time with the children. On his last night at home, he and Norma, tenderly, without a word, made love. Next evening, when he got home from Boston, they called David and Kathi in from the snow and brought them to the kitchen.

David was eight, slender, with light brown hair nearly to his shoulders, a face that was still pretty; he seemed always hungry, and Peter liked watching him eat. Kathi was six, had long red hair and a face that Peter had fallen in love with, a face that had once been pierced by glass the shape of a long dagger blade. In early spring a year ago: he still had not taken the storm windows off the screen doors; he was bringing his lunch to the patio, he did not know Kathi was following him, and holding his plate and mug he had pushed the door open with his shoulder, stepped outside, heard the crash and her scream, and turned to see her gripping then pulling the long shard from her cheek. She got it out before he reached her. He picked her up and pressed his handkerchief to the wound, midway between her eye and throat, and held her as he phoned his doctor who said he would meet them at the hospital and do the stitching himself because it was cosmetic and that beautiful face should not be touched by residents. Norma was not at home. Kathi lay on the car seat beside him and he held his handkerchief on her cheek, and in the hospital he held her hands while she lay on the table. The doctor said it would only take about four stitches and it would be better without anesthetic, because sometimes that puffed the skin, and he wanted to fit the cut together perfectly, for the scar; he told this very gently to Kathi, and he said as she grew, the scar would move down her face and finally would be under her jaw. Then she and Peter squeezed each other's hands as the doctor stitched and she gritted her teeth and stared at pain.

She was like that when he and Norma told them. It was David who suddenly cried, begged them not to get a divorce, and then fled to his room and would not come out, would not help Peter load his car, and only emerged from the house as Peter was driving away: a small running shape in the dark, charging the car, picking up something and throwing it, missing, crying *You bum You bum You bum . . .*

Drunk that night in his apartment whose rent he had paid and keys received yesterday morning before last night's grave lovemaking with Norma, he gained through the blur of bourbon an intense focus on his children's faces as he and Norma spoke: We fight too much, we've tried to live together but can't; you'll see, you'll be better off too, you'll be with Daddy for dinner on Wednesday nights, and on Saturdays and Sundays you'll do things with him. In his kitchen he watched their faces.

Next day he went to the radio station. After the news at noon he was on; often, as the records played, he imagined his children last night, while he and Norma were talking, and after he was gone. Perhaps she took them out to dinner, let them stay up late, flanking her on the couch in front of the television. When he talked he listened to his voice: it sounded as it did every weekday afternoon. At four he was finished. In the parking lot he felt as though, with stooped shoulders, he were limping. He started the forty-minute drive northward, for the first time in twelve years going home to empty rooms. When he reached the town where he lived he stopped at a small store and bought two lamb chops and a package of frozen peas. *I will take one thing at a time,* he told himself. Crossing the sidewalk to his car, in that short space, he felt the limp again, the stooped shoulders. He wondered if he looked like a man who had survived an accident which had killed others.

That was on a Thursday. When he woke Saturday morning, his first thought was a wish: that Norma would phone and tell him they were sick, and he should wait to see them Wednesday. He amended his wish, lay waiting for his own body to let him know it was sick, out for the weekend. In late morning he drove to their coastal town; he had moved fifteen miles inland. Already the snow-ploughed streets and country roads leading to their house felt like parts of his body: intestines, lung, heart-fiber lying from his door to theirs. When they were born he had smoked in the waiting room with the others. Now he was giving birth: stirruped, on his back, waves of pain. There would be no release, no cutting of the cord. Nor did he want it. He wanted to grow a cord.

Walking up their shovelled walk and ringing the doorbell, he felt at the same time like an inept salesman and a con man. He heard their voices, watched the door as though watching the sounds he heard, looking at the point where their faces would appear, but when the door opened he was looking at Norma's waist; then up to her face, lipsticked, her short brown hair soft from that morning's washing. For years she had not looked this way on a Saturday morning. Her eyes held him: the nest of pain was there, the shyness, the coiled anger; but there was another shimmer: she was taking a new marriage vow: This is the way we shall love our children now; watch how well I can do it. She smiled and said: 'Come in out of the cold and have a cup of coffee.'

In the living room he crouched to embrace the hesitant children. Only their faces were hesitant. In his arms they squeezed, pressed, kissed. David's hard arms absolved them both of Wednesday night. Through their hair Peter said pleasantly to Norma that he'd skip the coffee this time. Grabbing caps and unfurling coats, they left the house, holding hands to the car.

He showed them his apartment: they had never showered behind glass; they slid the doors back and forth. Sand washing down the drain, their flesh sunburned, a watermelon waiting in the refrigerator . . .

'This summer—'

They turned from the glass, looked up at him.

'When we go to the beach. We can come back here and shower.'

Their faces reflected his bright promise, and they followed him to the kitchen; on the counter were two cans of kidney beans, Jalapeño peppers, seasonings. Norma kept her seasonings in small jars, and two years ago when David was six and came home bullied and afraid of next day at school, Peter asked him if the boy was bigger than he was, and when David said 'A lot,' and showed him the boy's height with one hand, his breadth with two, Peter took the glass stopper from the cinnamon jar, tied it in a handkerchief corner, and struck his palm with it, so David would know how hard it was, would believe in it. Next morning David took it with him. On the schoolground, when the bully shoved him, he swung it up from his back pocket and down on the boy's forehead. The boy cried and went away. After school David found him on the sidewalk and hit his jaw with the weapon he had sat on all day, chased him two blocks swinging at his head, and came home with delighted eyes, no damp traces of yesterday's shame and fright, and Peter's own pain and rage turned to pride, then caution, and he spoke gently, told David to carry it for a week or so more, but not to use it unless the bully attacked; told him we must control our pleasure in giving pain.

Now reaching into the refrigerator he felt the children behind him; then he knew it was not them he felt, for in the bathroom when he spoke to their faces he had also felt a presence to his rear, watching, listening. It was the walls, it was fatherhood, it was himself. He was not an early drinker but he wanted an ale now; looked at the brown bottles long enough to fear and dislike his reason for wanting one, then he poured two glasses of apple cider and, for himself, cider and club soda. He sat at the table and watched David slice a Jalapeño over the beans, and said: 'Don't ever touch one of those and take a leak without washing your hands first.'

'Why?'

'I did it once. Think about it.'

'Wow.'

They talked of flavors as Kathi, with her eyes just above rim-level of the pot, her wrists in the steam, poured honey, and shook paprika, basil, parsley, Worcestershire, wine vinegar. In a bowl they mixed ground meat with a raw egg: jammed their hands into it, fingers touching; scooped and squeezed meat and onion and celery between their fingers; the kitchen smelled of bay leaf in the simmering beans, and then of broiling meat. They talked about the food as they ate, pressing thick hamburgers to fit their mouths, and only then Peter heard the white silence coming at them like afternoon snow. They cleaned the counter and table and what they had used; and they spoke briefly, quietly, they smoothly passed things; and when Peter turned off the faucet, all sound stopped, the

kitchen was multiplied by silence, the apartment's walls grew
longer, the floors wider, the ceilings higher. Peter walked the distance to his bedroom, looked at his watch, then quickly turned to
the morning paper's television listing, and called: 'Hey! *The Magni-
ficent Seven*'s coming on.'

'All *right*,' David said, and they hurried down the short hall, light
footsteps whose sounds he could name: Kathi's, David's, Kathi's.
He lay between them, bellies down, on the bed.

'Is this our third time or fourth?' Kathi said.

'I think our fourth. We saw it in a theater once.'

'I could see it every week,' David said.

'Except when Charles Bronson dies,' Kathi said. 'But I like when
the little kids put flowers on his grave. And when he spanks them.'

The winter sunlight beamed through the bedroom window, the
afternoon moving past him and his children. Driving them home he
imitated Yul Brynner, Eli Wallach, Charles Bronson; the children
praised his voices, laughed, and in front of their house they kissed
him and asked what they were going to do tomorrow. He said he
didn't know yet; he would call in the morning, and he watched
them go up the walk between snow as high as Kathi's waist. At the
door they turned and waved; he tapped the horn twice, and drove
away.

That night he could not sleep. He read *Macbeth*, woke propped
against the pillows, the bedside lamp on, the small book at his side.
He put it on the table, turned out the light, moved the pillows
down, and slept. Next afternoon he took David and Kathi to a
movie.

He did not bring them to his apartment again, unless they were on
the way to another place, and their time in the apartment was purposeful and short: Saturday morning cartoons, then lunch before
going to a movie or museum. Early in the week he began reading
the movie section of the paper, looking for matinees. Every
weekend they went to a movie, and sometimes two, in their towns
and other small towns and in Boston. On the third Saturday he
took them to a PG movie which was bloody and erotic enough to
make him feel ashamed and irresponsible as he sat between his children in the theater. Driving home, he asked them about the movie
until he believed it had not frightened them, or made them curious
about bodies and urges they did not yet have. After that, he saw all

PG movies before taking them, and he was angry at mothers who left their children at the theater and picked them up when the movie was over; and left him to listen to their children exclaiming at death, laughing at love; and often they roamed the aisles going to the concession stand, and distracted him from this weekly entertainment which he suspected he waited for and enjoyed more than David and Kathi. He had not been an indiscriminate moviegoer since he was a child. Now what had started as a duty was pleasurable, relaxing. He knew that beneath this lay a base of cowardice. But he told himself it would pass. A time would come when he and Kathi and David could sit in his living room, talking like three friends who had known each other for eight and six years.

Most of his listeners on weekday afternoons were women. Between love songs he began talking to them about movie ratings. He said not to trust them. He asked what they felt about violence and sex in movies, whether or not they were bad for children. He told them he didn't know; that many of the fairy tales and all the comic books of his boyhood were violent; and so were the westerns and serials on Saturday afternoons. But there was no blood. And he chided the women about letting their children go to the movies alone.

He got letters and read them in his apartment at night. Some thanked him for his advice about ratings. Many told him it was all right for him to talk, he wasn't with the kids every afternoon after school and all weekends and holidays and summer; the management of the theater was responsible for quiet and order during the movies; they were showing the movies to attract children and they were glad to take the money. The children came home happy and did not complain about other children being noisy. Maybe he should stop going to matinees, should leave his kids there and pick them up when it was over. *It's almost what I'm doing*, he thought; and he stopped talking about movies to the afternoon women.

He found a sledding hill: steep and long, and at its base a large frozen pond. David and Kathi went with him to buy his sled, and with a thermos of hot chocolate they drove to the hill near his apartment. Parked cars lined the road, and children and some parents were on the hill's broad top. Red-faced children climbed back, pulling their sleds with ropes. Peter sledded first; he knew the ice on the pond was safe, but he was beginning to handle fatherhood as he did guns: always as if they were loaded, when he knew they were not. There was a satisfaction in preventing even dangers which did not exist.

The snow was hard and slick, rushed beneath him; he went over a bump, rose from the sled, nearly lost it, slammed down on it, legs outstretched, gloved hands steering around the next bump but not the next one suddenly rising toward his face, and he pressed against the sled, hugged the wood-shock to his chest, yelled with delight at children moving slowly upward, hit the edge of the pond and sledded straight out, looking at the evergreens on its far bank. The sled stopped near the middle of the pond; he stood and waved to the top of the hill, squinting at sun and bright snow, then two silhouettes waved back and he saw Kathi's long red hair. Holding the sled's rope he walked on ice, moving to his left as David started down and Kathi stood waiting, leaning on her sled. He told himself he was a fool: had lived winters with his children, yet this was the first sled he had bought for himself; sometimes he had gone with them because they asked him to, and he had used their sleds. But he had never found a sledding hill. He had driven past them, seen the small figures on their crests and slopes, but no more. Watching David swerve around a bump and Kathi, at the top, pushing her sled, then dropping onto it, he forgave himself; there was still time; already it had begun.

But on that first afternoon of sledding he made a mistake: within an hour his feet were painfully cold, his trousers wet and his legs cold; David and Kathi wore snow pants. Beneath his parka he was sweating. Then he knew they felt the same, yet they would sled as long as he did, because of the point and edges of divorce that pierced and cut all their time together.

'I'm freezing,' he said. 'I can't move my toes.'

'Me too,' David said.

'Let's go down one more time,' Kathi said.

Then he took them home. It was only three o'clock.

After that he took them sledding on weekend mornings. They brought clothes with them, and after sledding they went to his apartment and showered. They loved the glass doors. On the first day they argued about who would shower first, until Peter flipped a coin and David won and Peter said Kathi would have the first

shower next time and they would take turns that way. They showered long and when Peter's turn came the water was barely warm
and he was quickly in and out. Then in dry clothes they ate lunch
and went to a movie.

Or to another place, and one night drinking bourbon in his living
room, lights off so he could watch the snow falling, the yellowed,
gentle swirl at the corner streetlight, the quick flakes at his window,
banking on the sill, and across the street the grey-white motion
lowering the sky and making the evergreens look distant, he
thought of owning a huge building to save divorced fathers. Free
admission. A place of swimming pool, badminton and tennis
courts, movie theaters, restaurants, soda fountains, batting cages, a
zoo, an art gallery, a circus, aquarium, science museum, hundreds
of restrooms, two always in sight, everything in the tender charge
of women trained in first aid and Montessori, no uniforms, their
only style warmth and cheer. A father could spend entire days
there, weekend after weekend, so in winter there would not be all
this planning and driving. He had made his cowardice urbane,
mobile, and sophisticated; but perhaps at its essence cowardice
knows it is apparent: he believed David and Kathi knew that their
afternoons at the aquarium, the Museum of Fine Arts, the Science
Museum, were houses Peter had built, where they could be together as they were before, with one difference: there was always
entertainment.

Frenetic as they were, he preferred weekends to the Wednesday
nights when they ate together. At first he thought it was shyness.
Yet they talked easily, often about their work, theirs at school, his
as a disc jockey. When he was not with the children he spent much
time thinking about what they said to each other. And he saw that,
in his eight years as a father, he had been attentive, respectful,
amusing; he had taught and disciplined. But no: not now: when
they were too loud in the car or they fought, he held onto his anger,
his heart buffetted with it, and spoke calmly, as though to another
man's children, for he was afraid that if he scolded as he had before,
the day would be spoiled, they would not have the evening at
home, the sleeping in the same house, to heal them; and they might
not want to go with him next day or two nights from now or two
days. During their eight and six years with him, he had shown
them love, and made them laugh. But now he knew that he had

remained a secret from them. What did they know about him? What did he know about them?

He would tell them about his loneliness, and what he had learned about himself. When he wasn't with them, he was lonely all the time, except while he was running or working, and sometimes at the station he felt it waiting for him in the parking lot, on the highway, in his apartment. He thought much about it, like an athletic man considering a sprained ligament, changing his exercises to include it. He separated his days into parts, thought about each one, and learned that all of them were not bad. When the alarm woke him in the winter dark, the new day and waiting night were the grey of the room, and they pressed down on him, fetid repetitions bent on smothering his spirit before he rose from the bed. But he got up quickly, made the bed while the sheets still held his warmth, and once in the kitchen with coffee and newspaper he moved into the first part of the day: bacon smell and solemn disc jockeys with classical music, an hour or more at the kitchen table, as near-peaceful as he dared hope for; and was grateful for too, as it went with him to the living room, to the chair at the southeast window where, pausing to watch traffic and look at the snow and winter branches of elms and maples in the park across the street, he sat in sun-warmth and entered the cadence of Shakespeare. In mid-morning, he Vaselined his face and genitals and, wearing layers of nylon, he ran two and a half miles down the road which, at his corner, was a town road of close houses but soon was climbing and dropping past farms and meadows; at the crest of a hill, where he could see the curves of trees on the banks of the Merrimack, he turned and ran back.

The second part began with ignition and seat belt, driving forty minutes on the highway, no buildings or billboards, low icicled cliffs and long white hills, and fields and woods in the angled winter sun, and in the silent car he received his afternoon self: heard the music he had chosen, popular music he would not listen to at home but had come to accept and barely listen to at work, heard his voice in mime and jest and remark, often merry, sometimes showing off and knowing it, but not much, no more than he had earned. That part of his day behind glass and microphone, with its comfort drawn from combining the familiar with the spontaneous, took him to four o'clock.

The next four hours, he learned, were not only the time he had to prepare for, but also the lair of his loneliness, the source of every quick chill of loss, each sudden whisper of dread and futility: for if he could spend them with a woman he loved, drink and cook and eat with her while day changed to night (though now, in winter, night came as he drove home), he and this woman huddled in the light and warmth of living room and kitchen, gin and meat, then his days until four and nights after eight would demand less from him of will, give more to him of hopeful direction. After dinner he listened to jazz and read fiction or watched an old movie on television until, without lust or even the need of a sleeping woman beside him, he went to bed: a blessing, but a disturbing one. He had assumed, as a husband and then an adulterous one, that his need for a woman was as carnal as it was spiritual. But now celibacy was easy; when he imagined a woman, she was drinking with him, eating dinner. So his most intense and perhaps his only need for a woman was then; and all the reasons for the end of his marriage became distant, blurred, and he wondered if the only reason he was alone now was a misogyny he had never recognized: that he did not even want a woman except at the day's end, and had borne all the other hours of woman-presence only to have her comfort as the clock's hands moved through their worst angles of the day.

Planning to tell all this to David and Kathi, knowing he would need gin to do it, he was frightened, already shy as if they sat with him now in the living room. A good sign: if he were afraid, then it took courage; if it took courage, then it must be right. He drank more bourbon than he thought he did, and went to bed excited by intimacy and love.

He slept off everything. In the morning he woke so amused at himself that, if he had not been alone, he would have laughed aloud. He imagined telling his children, over egg rolls and martinis and Shirley Temples, about his loneliness and his rituals to combat it. And *that* would be his new fatherhood, smelling of duck sauce and hot mustard and gin. Swallowing aspirins and orange juice, he saw clearly why he and the children were uncomfortable together, especially at Wednesday night dinners: when he lived with them, their talk had usually dealt with the immediate (I don't like playing with Cindy anymore; she's too bossy. I wish it would snow; it's no use being cold if it doesn't snow); they spoke at dinner and breakfast and, during holidays and summer, at lunch; in the car and stores while running errands; on the summer lawn while he prepared charcoal; and in their beds when he went to tell them goodnight; most of the time their talk was deep only because it was affectionate and tribal, sounds made between creatures sharing the same blood. Now their talk was the same, but it did not feel the same. They talked in his car and in places he took them, and the car and each place would not let them forget they were there because of divorce.

So their talk had felt evasive, fragile, contrived, and his drunken answer last night had been more talk: courageous, painful, honest. *My God*, he thought, as in a light snow that morning he ran out of his hangover, into lucidity. *I was going to have a Goddamn therapy session with my own children.* Breathing the smell of new snow and winter air he thought of this fool Peter Jackman, swallowing his bite of pork fried rice, and saying: And what do you feel at school? About the divorce, I mean. Are you ashamed around the other kids? He thought of the useless reopening and sometimes celebrating of wounds he and Norma had done with the marriage counselor, a pleasant and smart woman, but what could she do when all she had to work with was wounds? After each session he and Norma had driven home, usually mute, always in despair. Then, running faster, he imagined a house where he lived and the children came on Friday nights and stayed all weekend, played with their friends during the day, came and left the house as they needed, for food, drink, bathroom, diversion, and at night they relaxed together as a family; saw himself reading as they painted and drew at the kitchen table . . .

That night they ate dinner at a seafood restaurant thirty minutes from their town. When he drove them home he stayed outside their house for a while, the three of them sitting in front for warmth; they talked about summer and no school and no heavy clothes and no getting up early when it was still dark outside. He told them it was his favorite season too because of baseball and the sea. Next morning when he got into his car, the inside of his windshield was iced. He used the small plastic scraper from his glove compartment. As he scraped the middle and right side, he realized the grey ice curling and falling from the glass was the frozen breath of his children.

At a bar in the town where his children lived, he met a woman. This was on a Saturday night, after he had taken them home from the Museum of Fine Arts. They had liked Monet and Cézanne, had shown him light and color they thought were pretty. He told them Cézanne's *The Turn in the Road* was his favorite, that every time he came here he stood looking at it and he wanted to be walking up that road, toward the houses. But all afternoon he had known they were restless. They had not sledded that morning. Peter had gone out drinking the night before, with his only married friend who could leave his wife at home without paying even a subtle price, and he had slept through the time for sledding, had apologized when they phoned and woke him, and on the drive to the museum had told them he and Sibley (whom they knew as a friend of their mother too) had been having fun and had lost track of time until the bar closed. So perhaps they wanted to be outdoors. Or perhaps it was the old resonance of place again, the walls and ceiling of the museum, even the paintings telling them: You are here because your father left home.

He went to the bar for a sandwich, and stayed. Years ago he had come here often, on the way home from work, or at night with Norma. It was a neighborhood bar then, where professional fishermen and lobstermen and other men who worked with their hands drank, and sometimes brought their wives. Then someone from Boston bought it, put photographs and drawings of fishing and pleasure boats on the walls, built a kitchen which turned out quiche and crêpes, hired young women to tend the bar, and musicians to play folk and bluegrass. The old customers left. The new ones were couples and people trying to be a couple for at least the night, and that is why Peter stayed after eating his sandwich.

Within an hour she came in and sat at the bar, one empty chair away from him: a woman in her late twenties, dark eyes and light brown hair. Soon they were talking. He liked her because she smiled a lot. He also liked her drink: Jack Daniel's on the rocks. Her name was Mary Ann; her last name kept eluding him. She was a market researcher, and like many people Peter knew, she seemed to dismiss her work, though she was apparently good at it; her vocation was recreation: she skied down and across; backpacked; skated; camped; ran and swam. He began to imagine doing things with her, and he felt more insidious than if he were imagining passion: he saw her leading him and Kathi and David up a mountain trail. He told her he spent much of his life prone or sitting, except for a daily five-mile run, a habit from the Marine Corps (she gave him the sneer and he said: Come on, that was a long time ago, it was peacetime, it was fun), and he ran now for the same reasons everyone else did, or at least everyone he knew who ran: the catharsis, which kept his body feeling good, and his mind more or less sane. He said he had not slept in a tent since the Marines; probably because of the Marines. He said he wished he did as many things as she did, and he told her why. Some time in his bed during the night, she said: 'They probably did like the paintings. At least you're not taking them to all those movies now.'

'We still go about once a week.'

'Did you know Lennie's has free matinees for children? On Sunday afternoons?'

'No.'

'I have a divorced friend; she takes her kids almost every Sunday.'

'Why don't we go tomorrow?'

'With your kids?'

'If you don't mind.'

'Sure. I like kids. I'd like to have one of my own, without a husband.'

As he kissed her belly he imagined her helping him pitch the large tent he would buy, the four of them on a weekend of cold brook and trees on a mountainside, a fire, bacon in the skillet . . .

In the morning he scrambled their eggs, then phoned Norma. He had a general dislike of telephones: talking to his own hand gripping plastic, pacing, looking about the room; the timing of hanging up was tricky. Nearly all these conversations left him feeling as disconnected as the phone itself. But talking with Norma was different: he marvelled at how easy it was. The distance and disembodiment he felt on the phone with others were good here. He and Norma had hurt each other deeply, and their bodies had absorbed the pain: it was the stomach that tightened, the hands that shook, the breast that swelled then shrivelled. Now fleshless they could talk by phone, even with warmth, perhaps alive from the time when their bodies were at ease together. He thought of having a huge house where he could live with his family, seeing Norma only at meals, shared for the children, he and Norma talking to David and Kathi; their own talk would be on extension phones in their separate wings: they would discuss the children, and details of running the house. This was of course the way they had finally lived, without the separate wings, the phones. And one of their justifications as they talked of divorce was that the children would be harmed, growing up in a house with parents who did not love each other, who rarely touched, and then by accident. There had been moments near the end when, brushing against each other in the kitchen, one of them would say: Sorry. Now as Mary Ann Brighi (he had waked knowing her last name) spread jam on toast, he phoned.

'I met this woman last night.'

Mary Ann smiled; Norma's voice did.

'It's about time. I was worried about your arm going.'

'What about you?'

'I'm doing all right.'

'Do you bring them home?'

'It's not them, and I get a sitter.'

'But he comes to the house? To take you out?'

'Peter?'

'What.'

'What are we talking about?'

'I was wondering what the kids would think if Mary Ann came along this afternoon.'

'What they'll think is Mary Ann's coming along this afternoon.'

'You're sure that's all?'

'Unless you fuck in front of them.'

He turned his face from Mary Ann, but she had already seen his blush; he looked at her smiling with toast crumbs on her teeth. He wished he were married and lovemaking were simple. But after cleaning the kitchen he felt passion again, though not much; in his mind he was introducing the children to Mary Ann. He would make sure he talked to them, did not leave them out while he talked to her. He was making love while he thought this; he hoped they would like her; again he saw them hiking up a trail through pines, stopping for Kathi and David to rest; a sudden bounding deer; the camp beside the stream; he thanked his member for doing its work down there while the rest of him was in the mountains in New Hampshire.

As he walked with David and Kathi he held their hands; they were looking at her face watching them from the car window.

'She's a new friend of mine,' he said. 'Just a friend. She wants to show us this night club where children can go on Sunday afternoons.'

From the back seat they shook hands, peered at her, glanced at Peter, their eyes making him feel that like adults they could sense when people were lovers; he adjusted the rearview mirror, watched their faces, decided he was seeing jumbled and vulnerable curiosity: Who was she? Would she marry their father? Would they like her? Would their mother be sad? And the night club confused them.

'Isn't that where people go drink?' Kathi said.

'It's afternoon too,' David said.

Not for Peter; the sky was grey, the time was grey, dark was coming, and all at once he felt utterly without will; all the strength he had drawn on to be with his children left him like one long spurt of arterial blood: all his time with his children was grey, with night coming; it would always be; nothing would change: like three people cursed in an old myth they would forever be thirty-three and eight and six, in this car on slick or salted roads, going from one place to another. He disapproved of but understood those divorced fathers who fled to live in a different pain far away. Beneath his despair, he saw himself and his children sledding under a lovely blue sky, heard them laughing in movies, watching in awe like love a circling blue shark in the aquarium's tank; but these seemed beyond recapture.

He entered the highway going south, and that quick transition of hands and head and eyes as he moved into fast traffic snapped him out of himself, into the sound of Mary Ann's voice: with none of the rising and falling rhythm of nursery talk, she was telling them, as if speaking to a young man and woman she had just met, about Lennie's. How Lennie believed children should hear good music, not just the stuff on the radio. She talked about jazz. She hummed some phrases of 'Somewhere Over the Rainbow,' then improvised. They would hear Gerry Mulligan today, she said, and as she talked about the different saxophones, Peter looked in the mirror at their listening faces.

'And Lennie has a cook from Tijuana in Mexico,' Mary Ann said. 'She makes the best chili around.'

Walking into Lennie's with a pretty woman and his two healthy and pretty children, he did not feel like a divorced father looking for something to do; always in other places he was certain he looked that way, and often he felt guilty when talking with waitresses. He paid the cover charge for himself and Mary Ann and she said: All right, but I buy the first two rounds, and he led her and the children to a table near the bandstand. He placed the children between him and Mary Ann. Bourbon, Cokes, bowls of chili. The room was filling and Peter saw that at most tables there were children with parents, usually one parent, usually a father. He watched his children listening to Mulligan. His fingers tapped the table with the drummer. He looked warmly at Mary Ann's profile until she turned and smiled at him.

Often Mulligan talked to the children, explained how his saxophone worked; his voice was cheerful, joking, never serious, as he talked about the guitar and bass and piano and drums. He clowned laughter from the children in the dark. Kathi and David turned to each other and Peter to share their laughter. During the music they listened intently. Their hands tapped the table. They grinned at Peter and Mary Ann. At intermission Mulligan said he wanted to meet the children. While his group went to the dressing room he sat on the edge of the bandstand and waved the children forward. Kathi and David talked about going. Each would go if the other would. They took napkins for autographs and, holding hands, walked between tables and joined the children standing around Mulligan. When it was their turn he talked to them, signed their napkins, kissed their foreheads. They hurried back to Peter.

'He's *neat*,' Kathi said.

'What did you talk about?'

'He asked our names,' David said.

'And if we liked winter out here.'

'And if we played an instrument.'

'What kind of music we liked.'

'What did you tell him?'

'Jazz like his.'

The second set ended at nearly seven; bourbon-high, Peter drove carefully, listening to Mary Ann and the children talking about Mulligan and his music and warmth. Then David and Kathi were gone, running up the sidewalk to tell Norma, and show their autographed napkins, and Peter followed Mary Ann's directions to her apartment.

'I've been in the same clothes since last night,' she said.

In her apartment, as unkempt as his, they showered together, hurried damp-haired and chilled to her bed.

'This is the happiest day I've had since the marriage ended,' he said.

But when he went home and was alone in his bed, he saw his

cowardice again. All the warmth of his day left him, and he lay in the dark, knowing that he should have been wily enough to understand that the afternoon's sweetness and ease meant he had escaped: had put together a family for the day. That afternoon Kathi had spilled a Coke; before Peter noticed, Mary Ann was cleaning the table with cocktail napkins, smiling at Kathi, talking to her under the music, lifting a hand to the waitress.

Next night he took Mary Ann to dinner and, driving to her apartment, it seemed to him that since the end of his marriage, dinner had become disproportionate: alone at home it was a task he forced himself to do, with his children it was a fragile rite, and with old friends who alternately fed him and Norma he felt vaguely criminal. Now he must once again face his failures over a plate of food. He and Mary Ann had slept little the past two nights, and at the restaurant she told him she had worked hard all day, yet she looked fresh and strong, while he was too tired to imagine making love after dinner. With his second martini, he said: 'I used you yesterday. With my kids.'

'There's a better word.'

'All right: needed.'

'I knew that.'

'You did?'

'We had fun.'

'I can't do it anymore.'

'Don't be so hard on yourself. You probably spend more time with them now than when you lived together.'

'I do. So does Norma. But that's not it. It's how much I wanted your help, and started hoping for it. Next Sunday. And in summer: the sort of stuff you do, camping and hiking; when we talked about it Saturday night —'

'I knew that too. I thought it was sweet.'

He leaned back in his chair, sipped his drink. Tonight he would break his martini rule, have a third before dinner. He loved women who knew and forgave his motives before he knew and confessed them.

But he would not take her with the children again. He was with her often; she wanted a lover, she said, not love, not what it still did to men and women. He did not tell her he thought they were using each other in a way that might have been cynical, if it were not so frightening. He simply followed her, became one of those who make love with their friends. But she was his only woman friend, and he did not know how many men shared her. When she told him she would not be home this night or that weekend, he held his questions. He held onto his heart too, and forced himself to make her a part of the times when he was alone. He had married young, and life to him was surrounded by the sounds and touches of a family. Now in this foreign land he felt so vulnerably strange that at times it seemed near madness as he gave Mary Ann a function in his time, ranking somewhere among his running and his work.

When the children asked about her, he said they were still friends. Once Kathi asked why she never came to Lennie's anymore, and he said her work kept her pretty busy and she had other friends she did things with, and he liked being alone with them anyway. But then he was afraid the children thought she had not liked them; so, twice a month, he brought Mary Ann to Lennie's.

He and the children went every Sunday. And that was how the cold months passed, beginning with the New Year, because Peter and Norma had waited until after Christmas to end the marriage: the movies and sledding, museums and aquarium, the restaurants; always they were on the road, and whenever he looked at his car he thought of the children. How many conversations while looking through the windshield? How many times had the doors slammed shut and they re-entered or left his life? Winter ended slowly. April was cold and in May Peter and the children still wore sweaters or windbreakers, and on two weekends there was rain, and everything they did together was indoors. But when the month ended, Peter thought it was not the weather but the patterns of winter that had kept them driving from place to place.

Then it was June and they were out of school and Peter took his vacation. Norma worked, and by nine in the morning he and Kathi and David were driving to the sea. They took a large blanket and tucked its corners into the sand so it wouldn't flap in the wind, and they lay oiled in the sun. On the first day they talked of winter, how they could feel the sun warming their ribs, as they had watched it warming the earth during the long thaw. It was a beach with gentle currents and a gradual slope out to sea but Peter told them, as he had every summer, about undertow: that if ever they were caught in one, they must not swim against it; they must let it take them out and then they must swim parallel to the beach until the current shifted and they could swim back in with it. He could not imagine his children being calm enough to do that, for he was afraid of water and only enjoyed body-surfing near the beach, but he told them anyway. Then he said it would not happen because he would always test the current first.

In those first two weeks the three of them ran into the water and body-surfed only a few minutes, for it was too cold still, and they had to leave it until their flesh was warm again. They would not be able to stay in long until July. Peter showed them the different colors of summer, told them why on humid days the sky and ocean were paler blue, and on dry days they were darker, more beautiful, and the trees they passed on the roads to the beach were brighter green. He bought a whiffle ball and bat and kept them in the trunk of his car and they played at the beach. The children dug holes, made castles, Peter watched, slept, and in late morning he ran. From a large thermos they drank lemonade or juice; and they ate lunch all day, the children grazing on fruit and the sandwiches he had made before his breakfast. Then he took them to his apartment for showers, and they helped carry in the ice chest and thermos and blanket and their knapsack of clothes. Kathi and David still took turns showering first, and they stayed in longer, but now in summer the water was still hot when his turn came. Then he drove them home to Norma, his skin red and pleasantly burning; then tan.

When his vacation ended they spent all sunny weekends at the sea, and even grey days that were warm. The children became braver about the cold, and forced him to go in with them and body-surf. But they could stay longer than he could, and he left to lie on the blanket and watch them, to make sure they stayed in shallow water. He made them promise to wait on the beach while he ran. He went in the water to cool his body from the sun, but mostly he lay on the blanket, reading, and watching the children wading out to the breakers and riding them in. Kathi and David did not always stay together. One left to walk the beach alone. Another played with strangers, or children who were there most days too. One built a castle. Another body-surfed. And, often, one would come to the blanket and drink and take a sandwich from the ice chest, would sit eating and drinking beside Peter, offer him a bite, a swallow. And on all those beach days Peter's shyness and apprehension were gone. It's the sea, he said to Mary Ann one night.

And it was: for on that day, a long Saturday at the beach, when he had all day felt peace and father-love and sun and salt water, he had understood why now in summer he and his children were as he had yearned for them to be in winter: they were no longer confined to car or buildings to remind them why they were there. The long beach and the sea were their lawn; the blanket their home; the ice chest and thermos their kitchen. They lived as a family again. While he ran and David dug in the sand until he reached water and Kathi looked for pretty shells for her room, the blanket waited for them. It was the place they wandered back to: for food, for drink, for rest, their talk as casual as between children and father arriving, through separate doors, at the kitchen sink for water, the refrigerator for an orange. Then one left for the surf; another slept in the sun, lips stained with grape juice. He had wanted to tell the children about it, but it was too much to tell, and the beach was no place for such talk anyway, and he also guessed they knew. So that afternoon when they were all lying on the blanket, on their backs, the children flanking him, he simply said: 'Divorced kids go to the beach more than married ones.'

'Why?' Kathi said.

'Because married people do chores and errands on weekends. No kid-days.'

'I love the beach,' David said.

'So do I,' Peter said.

He looked at Kathi.

'You don't like it, huh?'

She took her arm from her eyes and looked at him. His urge was to turn away. She looked at him for a long time; her eyes were too tender, too wise, and he wished she could have learned both later, and differently; in her eyes he saw the car in winter, heard its doors closing and closing, their talk and the sounds of heater and engine and tires on the road, and the places the car took them. Then she held his hand, and closed her eyes.

'I wish it was summer all year round,' she said.

He watched her face, rosy tan now, lightly freckled; her small scar was already lower. Holding her hand, he reached over for David's, and closed his eyes against the sun. His legs touched theirs. After a while he heard them sleeping. Then he slept.

Finding a Girl
in America

Sorrow is one of the vibrations that prove the fact of living.
Antoine de Saint Exupéry, *Wind, Sand and Stars*

for Suzanne and Nicole

O N AN OCTOBER night, lying in bed with a nine-
teen-year-old girl and tequila and grapefruit
juice, thirty-five-year-old Hank Allison gets the
story. They lie naked, under the sheet and one light blanket, their
shoulders propped by pillows so they can drink. Lori's body is
long; Hank is not a tall man, and she is perhaps a half inch taller;
when she wears high-heeled boots and lowers her face to kiss him,
he tells her she is like a swan bending to eat. Knowing he is foolish,
he still wishes she were shorter; he has joked with Jack Linhart
about this, and once Jack told him: *Hell with it: just stick out that big
chest of yours and swagger down the road with that pretty girl.* Hank
never wishes he were taller.

Tonight they have gone to Boston for a movie and dinner, and at
the Casa Romero, their favorite restaurant, they started with mar-
garitas but as they ate appetizers of Jalapeño and grilled cheese on
tortillas, of baked cheese and sausage, they became cheerful about
the movie and food and what they would order next, and switched
to shots of tequila chased with Superior. They ate a lot and left the
restaurant high though not drunk; then Hank bought a six-pack of
San Miguel for the forty-five minute drive home, enough for one
cassette of Willie Nelson and part of one by Kristofferson, Hank
doing most of the talking, while a sober part of himself told him not
to, reminded him that he must always control his talking with Lori;
for he loves her and he knows that with him, as with everyone else,

she feels and thinks much that she cannot say. He guesses her mother has something to do with this, a talk-crackling woman who keeps her husband and three daughters generally quiet, who is good-looking and knows it and works at it, and is a flirt and, Hank believes from the bare evidence Lori so often murmurs in his bed, more than that. But he does not work hard at discovering why it is so difficult for Lori to give the world, even him, her heart in words. He believes some mysterious balance of power exists between lovers, and if he ever fully understands the bonds that tie her tongue, and if he tells her about them, tries to help her cut them, he will no longer be her lover. He settles for the virtues he sees in her, and waits for her to see them herself. Often she talks of her childhood; she cannot remember her father ever kissing or hugging her; she loves him, and she knows he loves her too. He just does not touch.

Until they got back to his apartment and took salty dogs to bed, Hank believed they would make love. He thought of her long body under him. But, his heart ready, his member was dull, numb, its small capacity for drink long passed. So Hank parted her legs and lowered his face: when she came he felt he had too: the best way to share a woman's orgasm, the only way to use all his senses: looking over the mound at her face between breasts, touching with hands and tongue, the lovely taste and smell, and he heard not only her moan-breaths but his tongue on her, and her hands' soft timpani against his face.

Now he lies peacefully against the pillows; the drinks on his desk beside the bed are still half-full, and he hands one to Lori. Sometimes he takes a drag from her cigarette, though he remembers this is the way to undo his quitting nine years ago when he faced how long it took him to write, and how long he would have to live to write the ten novels he had set as his goal. He is nearly finished the second draft of his third. Lori is talking about Monica. Something in her voice alerts him. She and Lori were friends. Perhaps he is going to learn something new; perhaps Monica was unfaithful while she was still here, when she was his student and they were furtive lovers, as he and Lori are now. He catches a small alcoholic slip Lori makes: No, I can't, she says, in the midst of a sentence which seems to need no restraint.

'You can't what?'

'Nothing.'

'Tell me.'

'I promised Monica I wouldn't.'

'When I tell a friend a secret, I know he'll tell his wife or woman. That's the way it is.'

'It'll hurt you.'

'How can anything about Monica hurt me? I haven't seen her in over a year.'

'It will.'

'It can't. Not now.'

'You remember when she came down that weekend? Last October? You cooked dinner for the three of us.'

'Shrimp scampi. We got drunk on hot sake.'

'Before dinner she and I went to the liquor store. She kept talking about this guy she'd met in art class.'

'Tommy.'

'She didn't say it. But I knew she was screwing him then. I could tell she wanted me to know. It was her eyes. The way she'd smile. And I got pissed at her but I didn't say anything. I loved her and I'd never had a friend who had two lovers at once and I thought she was a bitch. I was starting to love you too, and I hated knowing she was going to hurt you, and I couldn't see why she even came to spend the weekend with you.'

'So she was screwing him before she told me it was over. Well, I should have known. She talked about him enough: his drawings anyway.'

'That wasn't it. She was pregnant. She found out after she broke up with you.' He has never heard Lori's voice so plaintive except when she speaks of her parents. 'You know how Monica is. She went hysterical; she phoned me at school every night, she phoned her parents, she went to three doctors. Two in Maine and one in New York. They all placed it at the same time: it was yours. By that time she was two months pregnant. Her father took her in and they had it done.'

An image comes to Hank: he sees his daughter, Sharon, thirteen, breast-points under her sweater: she is standing in his kitchen, hair dark and long; she is chopping celery at the counter for their weekly meal. He pulls Lori's cheek to his chest and strokes her hair.

'I'm all right,' he says. 'I had to know. I know if I didn't know I'd never know I didn't know; but I hate not knowing. I don't want to die not knowing everything about my life. You had to tell me. Who else would? You know I have to know. I'm all right. Shit. Shit that bitch. I could have—it would have been born in spring—I would have had all summer off—I could have taken it. I can raise a kid— I'm no Goddamn—I have to piss—'

He leaves the bed so quickly that he feels, barely, her head drop as his chest jerks from beneath it. He hurries down the hall, stands pissing, then as suddenly and uncontrollably as vomiting he is crying; and as with vomiting he has no self, he is only the helpless and weak host of these sounds and jerks and tears, and he places both palms on the wall in front of him, standing, moaning; the tears stop, his chest heaves, he groans, then tears come again as from some place so deep inside him that it has never been touched, even by pain. Lori stands naked beside him. She is trying to pull his arm from its push against the wall; she is trying to hold him and is crying too and saying something but he can only hear her comforting tone like wind-sough in trees that grew in a peaceful place he left long ago. Finally he turns to her, he will let her hold him and do what she needs to do; yet when he faces her tall firm body, still in October her summer tan lingering above and between breasts and loins, he swings his fists, pulling short each punch, pulling them enough so she does not even back away, nor lift an arm to protect herself; left right left right, short hooked blows at her womb and he hears himself saying No no no—He does not know whether he is yelling or mumbling. He only knows he is sounds and tears and death-sorrow and strong quick arms striking the air in front of Lori's womb.

Then it stops; his arms go to her shoulders, he sags, and she turns him and walks him back down the hall, her left arm around his waist, her right hand holding his arm around her shoulders. He lies in bed and she asks if he wants a drink; he says he'd better not. She gets into bed, and holds his face to her breast.

'Seven months,' he says. 'That's all she had to give it. Then I could have taken it. You think I couldn't do that?'

'I know you could.'

'It would be hard. Sometimes it would be terrible. I wasn't swinging at you.'

'I know.'

'It was just the womb.'

'Monica's?'

'I don't know.'

That night he dreams: it is summer, the lovely summers when he does not teach, does not have to hurry his writing and running before classes, and in the afternoons he picks up Sharon and sometimes a friend or two of hers and they go to Seabrook beach in New Hampshire; usually Jack and Terry Linhart are there with their daughter and son, and all of them put their blankets side by side and talk and doze and go into the sea, the long cooling afternoons whose passage is marked only by the slow arc of the sun, time's symbol giving timelessness instead. His dream does not begin with those details but with that tone: the blue peaceful days he teaches to earn, wakes in the dark winter mornings to write, then runs in snow and cold wind and over ice. The dream comes to him with an empty beach: he feels other people there but does not see them, only a stretch of sand down to the sea, and he and Sharon are lying on a blanket. They are talking to each other. She is on his right. Then he rolls slightly to his left to look down at the fetus beside him; he is not startled by it; he seems to have known it is there, has been there as long as he and Sharon. The dream tells him it is a girl; he loves her, loves watching her sleep curled on her side: he looks at the disproportionate head, the small arms and legs. But he is troubled. She is bright pink, as if just boiled, and he realizes he should have put lotion on her. She sleeps peacefully and he wonders if she will be all right sleeping there while he and Sharon go into the surf. He knows he will bring her every afternoon to the beach and she will sleep pink and curled beside him and Sharon and, nameless, she will not grow. His love for her becomes so tender that it changes to grief as he looks at her flesh in the sun's heat.

The dream does not wake him. But late next morning, when he does wake, it is there, as vivid as if he is having it again. He sees and feels it before he feels his headache, his hung-over dry mouth, his need to piss; before he smells the cigarette butts on the desk beside him, and the tequila traces in the glasses by the ashtray. Before he is aware of Lori's weight and smell in bed. Quietly he rises and goes to the bathroom then sneaks back into bed, not kindness but because he does not want Lori awake, and he lies with his dream. His heart needs to cry but his body cannot, it is emptied, and again he thinks it is like vomiting: the drunken nights when he suddenly wakes from a dream of nausea and goes quickly to the toilet, kneeling, gripping its seat, hanging on through the last dry heaves, then

waking in the morning still sick, red splotches beside his eyes where
the violence of his puking has broken vessels, and feeling that next
moment he would be at the toilet again, but there is nothing left to
disgorge and he simply lies in bed for hours.

But this will not pass. He will have to think. His employers at
the college and his editor and publisher believe his vocations have to
do with thinking. They are wrong. He rarely thinks. He works on
instincts and trying to articulate them. What his instincts tell him
now is that he'd better lie quietly and wait: today is Sunday and
this afternoon he and Lori are taking Sharon for a walk on Plum
Island. He lies there and imagines the three of them on the dunes
until he senses Lori waking.

She knows what he likes when he wakes hung over and, without
a word, she begins licking and caressing his nipples; his breath
quickens, he feels the hung-over lust whose need is so strong it is
near-desperate, as though only its climax can return him from the
lethargy of his body, the spaces in his brain, and he needs it the
way others need hair of the dog. Lori knows as well as he does that
his need is insular, masturbatory; knows that she is ministering to
him, her lips and fingers and now her mouth medicinal. But she
likes it too. Yet this morning even in her soft mouth he remains soft
until finally he takes her arms and gently pulls her up, rolls her onto
her back, and kneels between her calves. When it is over he is still
soft, and his lust is gone too.

'It wasn't tequila,' he says. 'This morning.'

'I know.'

Then he tells her his dream.

The day, when they finally leave his apartment, is crisp enough for
sweaters and windbreakers, the air dry, the sky deep blue, and
most of the trees still have their leaves dying in bright red and
orange and yellow. It has taken them two hours to get out of the
apartment: first Hank went to the bathroom, leaving a stench that
shamed him, then he lay in bed while Lori went; and because he
was trying to focus on anything to keep the dream away, he figured
out why his girl friends, even on a crapulent morning like this one,
never left a bad smell. Always they waited in bed, let him go first;
then they went, bringing their boxes and bottles, and after sitting
on the seat he had warmed they showered long and when they were
finished, he entered a steamy room that smelled of woman: clean,

powdered, whatever else they did in there. Very simple, and thoughtful too: let him go first so he would not have to wait with aching bowels while they went through the process of smell-changing; and they relied on him, going first, not to shower and shave and make them wait. It was sweetly vulpine and endearing and on another morning he would have smiled.

While he showered, Lori dressed and put on bacon. At breakfast he talked about last night's movie, about the day as it looked through the window near the table, about Plum Island's winter erosion, about the omelette, about anything, and Lori watched him with her soft brown eyes, and he knew she knew and was helpless, and he wished she didn't hurt that way, he knew the pain of being helpless with a lover, but there was nothing he could do except wish they both weren't helpless.

Driving the car, he is in love with Sharon, needs to see her, listen to her voice, touch her as they walk on the beach. At the house, Lori waits in the car, for she is shy about going in; she and Edith have talked outside, either because Edith was in the yard when they arrived or she walked with Hank and Sharon to the car and leaned over to talk to Lori at the window. Edith divorced him, and he has told Lori that she feels no jealousy or pain, but still Lori is uncomfortable. Hank understands this. He would feel the same. What he does not understand is why Lori loves him, and he prefers not to try, for he is afraid he will find no reason strong enough for him to rely on.

It is not the age of his body that makes him wonder. In the past three or four years, love handles and a bald spot have appeared, and all his running has no effect on the love handles, and he knows they are here to stay, and the bald spot will spread like a tonsure. But it isn't that. It's the fettered way he is thirty-five. When Monica left him, she flared after a night of silence when her eyes in turn glowered and sulked; she said, as they were finishing their last drinks in the bar near her college in Maine: *I want out. You worry about your writing first, your daughter second, money third, and I'm last.* All evening he had known something was coming. But he had never been broken up with so cleanly, precisely, succinctly. At once he was calm. He simply watched Monica's face. She was taut with fury. He was not. He was not even sad yet. He watched her, and waited for whatever he was going to say. He had no idea what it would be. He was simply repeating her words in his mind. Then he said:

You're right. Why should you put up with that shit? Her fury was still there. Perhaps she wanted a fight. Yet all he felt was forgiveness for her, and futility because he had loved a woman so young.

Then he felt something else: that his forgiveness and futility were familiar, coming from foreknowledge, as if on that first night he took her to dinner in Boston and they ate soft-shelled crabs and his heart began to warm and rise, he had known it would end; that at the most he would get love's year. It ended with the four sentences in the bar, his two the last, and they drove quietly to her apartment near the campus; at the door he embraced her more tightly than he had intended, because holding her he saw images of death, hers and his years from now, neither knowing of the death of the first, the odds bad that it would be him since he had fifteen years on her and was a man. Then he gave her a gentle closed-lip kiss, and was walking back to his car before she could speak.

He put Waylon Jennings in the deck, and on the two-hour moonlit drive home he longed for a beer and did not cry. When he got to his apartment he drank a six-pack with bourbon and did cry and nearly phoned her; all that kept him from it was his will to keep their last scene together sculpted forever with him, Hank Allison Goddamnit, showing only dignity and strength and tenderness. She had seen him as he was now, on nights when writing or money or guilt and sorrow about Sharon or, often enough, all three punched him around the walls of his apartment, and he counterpunched with one hand holding a beer, the other a bourbon on the rocks. But she had never seen him like this because of her. So each time he went to the kitchen to get another beer or more bourbon and looked at the phone on the wall, he remembered how he was and what he said when she told him in the bar, and how he was at the door, and turned, sometimes lunged, away from the phone.

He drank in his bedroom, at his desk but with his back to it, and he listened to Dylan, the angry songs about women, the volume low because he rented the upstairs of a house whose owners were a retired couple sleeping beneath him, and he started his cure: he focused on every one of her flaws, and with booze and will and Dylan's hurt and angry encouragement, he multiplied them by emotion until they grew so out of proportion that he could no longer see what he had loved about her. He relived her quick temper and screaming rage, so loud and long that some nights he was afraid she was going mad, and always he had to command her to stop, squeeze her arms, tell her she would wake the couple downstairs; and her crying, never vulnerably, never seeming to need comfort, more a variation of her rage and nearly as loud, as she twisted from him and fled from room to room until again he had to hold and command; and the source of these rages and tears never defined so he could try to deal with them, these sources always just a little concrete but mostly abstract so on those nights he felt the impotence of believing she already was mad; and his impotence brought with it a detachment which in turn opened him up to shades of despair: he imagined her ten years from now, when her life would be more complicated and difficult, when it would attack her more often, with more strength. Listening to 'Positively Fourth Street' he sipped the smooth Jack Daniel's and chased it with the foamy bite of beer and thought if she had stayed with him she would have so drained his energy that, after spending his nights as a shrink and a lion-tamer, he would wake peaceless and weary to face his morning's work. He recalled her mischievous face as, in front of his friends, in bars or at the beach, she pinched his love handles or kissed his bald spot. This usually did not bother him because he was in good condition, and she smoked heavily and could not run half a mile, was slender only because she was made that way, and she was young, and she dieted. And he guessed she was doing this for herself rather than to him; testing herself; actually touching his signs of age to see if she really wanted a man fifteen years older, with an ex-wife, a twelve-year-old daughter, and child support.

Beneath the teasing, though, something was in her eyes: something feral, and at times as she smiled and teased he looked into her eyes and felt a stir of fear which had nothing to do with her fingers squeezing his flesh, her lips smacking his crown. It was more like the detached fear he had once, looking at a Russell's viper in a zoo, the snake coiled asleep behind glass, and Hank read the typed card on the cage, about this lethargic snake and how one of its kind finally got Russell and his name.

He went to the kitchen, did not even look at the phone as he passed it. He was thinking of the snake, and one night Jack saying that after the one bit Russell, he wrote down the effects of the poison as it killed him; and Jack said: *You know, maybe he studied those bastards so long that finally he had to go all the way, know it all, and he just reached down and touched it* . . . In the dark bedroom which to-morrow would still be a bedroom, a dreary and hung-over place, not a study as it became most mornings, he listened to 'Just Like a Woman' and thought *Maybe that's what I was doing, waiting for that bitch to give me the venom, end it between us, between me and all of them, between me and—* He stopped. It was time to finish the drinks, swallow aspirins and vitamin B and go to bed, for—had he completed the sentence in his mind—it would have concluded with some euphemism for suicide. He went to bed hating Monica; it was a satisfying hatred; it felt like the completion of a long-planned revenge.

He woke with relief, nearly happiness, nearly strength. He knew, for today, that was enough: last night's cure had worked. As it had with every young girl who left him since his divorce. They all left. One night he told Jack: *I think I'll get a fire escape up to my window, so they can just climb out while I'm taking a piss.* When Edith sent him away, he did not have a cure.

Five years ago, when all his pleas and arguments and bargains and accusations lay on the living room floor between them (he actually felt he was stepping on his own words as he paced while she sat watching), and he knew that she really wanted him to leave, he believed it was because he had been unfaithful. So his grief was coupled with injustice, for she had had lovers too; and even as Hank talked that night her newest and, she said, her last lover so long as she was married, was dying early of cancer: Joe Ritchie, an ex-priest who taught philosophy at the college where Hank worked.

When he moved to his apartment he was too sad to be angry at Edith. He tried to be. Alone at night, and while running, and watching movies, he told himself that he and Edith had lived equally. Or almost. True, he had a head start on her, had student girl friends before she caught him because he was with a woman more demanding: a woman not only his own age but rich and from Paris, idling for six months with friends in Boston; a woman who laughed at him when he worried about Edith catching him. Now, at thirty-five, with eight years' distance, he saw how foolish he had been, for she was a woman of no substance: her idea of a good day was to sleep late, buy things at Bonwit Teller or Ann Taylor, and make love with Hank in the afternoon. He was young enough to be excited by her accent, so that he heard its sound more than what it said. He saw her in Boston, on Saturday afternoons, on Tuesdays and Thursdays when he was supposed to be in his office at school, he got careless, and he got caught.

When it happened he realized he had always known that some-day it would: that he could not have lived uncaught his entire life, or until he outgrew his crushes that so quickly turned to passion not only for the body, for that lovely first penetration into new yielding flesh, but for the woman's soul too, a passion to know as much of her as he could before they parted (they were students; parting was graduation) and went on with their lives. Sometimes for weeks, even months, he would not notice a particular girl in class. Because while he was teaching he was aware mostly of himself: this was only partly vanity; more, it was his love of teaching, his fear of failing, so that before every class he had stage-fright, had to spend a few minutes in silence in his office or walking about the campus, letting his apprehension and passion grow inside him until, entering the classroom, those were all he felt. When he began to speak about a novel or story, it was as though another man were talking, and Hank listening. He taught three afternoons a week, had many bad days when he became confused, lost the students, and seeing their listless faces, his apprehension overcame his passion and he fearfully waited, still talking, for the fifty minutes to pass. At a week's end, if he had had two good days out of three, he was satisfied. He knew that hardly anyone hit three for three in this work. On his best days he listened to Hank the teacher talking, and he tried to follow the ideas coming from his mouth, ideas he often didn't know he had until he heard them. So, usually, he did not notice a certain girl until she said something in class, something that halted him, made him look at her and think about what she had said. Or, while he was talking, his face sweeping the class, the windows, the ceiling, his hands busy with a pen or keys or coins, his face would suddenly stop, held by a girl whose eyes were fixed on his; sometimes he would stop speaking for a moment, lose the idea he was working on, as he looked at her. Then he would turn away, toss his keys or coin or pen in the air, catch the idea again as he caught the tossed object, and speak. Soon he would be talking to her on the campus.

In his thirties, he understood what those crushes, while he was married, had been. His profession was one of intimacy, but usually it went only from him to the faces sitting in the room. Any student who listened could know as much about him as all his friends, except those two or three truly deep ones. His crushes were rope bridges, built in haste between him and the girl. It was a need not only to give her more of what attracted her in the classroom, but to receive from her, to know her; and with the beginning of that, talking on the campus sidewalks or in his office, came the passion to know all of her. The ones he chose (or, he realized in his thirties, the ones who chose him) were girls who would have been known as promiscuous when he was in college; or even now in the seventies if they were salesclerks or cashiers and at night went to those bars where the young men who had gone to work instead of college drank and waited. But they were educated, affluent, and well-travelled; they wore denim to class, but he knew that what hung in their dormitory closets and in their closets at home cost at least half of his year's salary. He never saw those clothes until he was divorced at thirty and started taking the girls to Boston for the evening; and then he rarely saw the same dress or skirt and blouse twice; only a favorite sweater, a warm coat. While married, his lovemaking was in his car, and what he quiveringly pulled from their thighs was denim. They all took the pill, they all had what they called a healthy attitude toward sex, which meant they knew the affair with Hank, as deep and tender as it might be, so that it certainly felt like love (and, for all Hank knew, it probably was) would end with the school year in May, would resume (if she and Hank felt like it) in the fall, and would certainly end on Commencement Day.

So they made it easy for him. He was a man who planned most days of his life. In the morning he wrote; then he ran, then he taught; then he was a husband and father. He tried to keep them all separated, and most days it worked, and he felt like three or four different men. When the affairs started, he made time for them as well. After class or instead of office hours he drove through town where the girl was walking. She entered his car as though he had offered her a ride. Even when they left town and drove north she would sit near her door until he turned onto the dirt road leading to the woods. Going back he stayed on the highway, skirted the town, approached the school from the south, and let her out several blocks away. Then he went home and hugged and kissed Sharon and Edith, and holding their bodies in the warmth of his house, he felt love only for them.

But with Jeanne in Boston he had to lie too much about where he was going and where he had been, and finally when Edith asked him one night: *Are you having an affair with that phony French bitch?* he said: *Yes.* He and Edith had met Jeanne when someone brought her to their Christmas party; Edith had not seen her since, but in

April, when she asked him, he did not even wonder how she knew. He was afraid, but he was also relieved. That may have been why he didn't ask how she knew. Because it didn't matter: Edith was dealing with what she believed was an affair with a specific woman. To Hank, his admission of that one was an admission of all of them.

He was surprised that he felt relief. Then he believed he understood it: he had been deluding himself with his scheduled adulteries, as if a girl on his car seat in the woods were time in the classroom or at his desk; the years of lies to himself and Edith had been a detraction from the man he wanted and sometimes saw himself to be. So, once cornered, he held his ground and told her. It broke her heart. He wanted to comfort her, to make fraudulent promises, but he would not. He told her he loved her and wanted to live with no one else. But he would not become like most people he knew. They were afraid; and old, twenty years early. They bought houses, spoke often of mortgages, repairs, children's ailments, and the weight of their bodies. As he talked she wiped from her eyes the dregs of her first heavy weeping. His own eyes were damp because of hers, and more: because of the impotence he felt, the old male-burden of having to be strong for both of them at once, to give her the assurance of his love so she could hear as a friend what he was saying: that he was what he was, that he had to be loved that way, that he could not limit the roads of his life until they narrowed down to one, leading from home to campus. She screamed at him: *You're a writer too! Isn't that enough for one man?* He said: *No. There's never enough. I don't want to have to say no to anything, not ever—* It was the most fearful moment of his marriage until the night over three years later when she told him he had to leave her and Sharon. He felt closer to her than he ever had before, now that all the lies were gone. And he knew he might lose her, right there in that April kitchen; he was sure of her love, but he was sure of her strength too. Yet he would not retreat into lies: he had to win.

He did. She stayed with him. Every night there was talk, and always there was pain. But she stayed. He built a case against monogamy, spoke of it as an abstraction with subtle and insidious roots in the economy: passion leashed so that lovers would need houses and things to put in them. He knew he was using his long apprenticeship to words, not to find truths, but to confuse and win his wife. He spoke of monogamy as unnatural. *The heart is too big for it*, he said. *Yours too.*

In May she started an affair with Jack Linhart, who no longer loved his wife Terry; or believed he no longer loved her. Hank knew: their faces, their voices, and when they were in the same room he could feel the passion and collusion between them as surely as he could smell a baking ham. He controlled his pain and jealousy, his moments of anger at Jack; he remembered the April night in the kitchen. He kept his silence and waited until the summer night Edith told him she was Jack's lover. He was gentle with her. He knew now that, within the marriage he needed and loved, he was free.

That summer he watched her. He had been her only lover till now; he watched the worry about what they were doing to their marriage leave her face, watched her face in its moments of girlish mischief, of vanity, of sensuality that brightened her eyes and shaped her lips, these moments coming unpredictably: as they ate dinner with Sharon, paused at the cheese counter in the supermarket . . . Toward the end of the summer he made love twice with Terry, on successive nights, because he liked her, because she was pretty, because she was unhappy, and because he felt he had earned it. That ended everything. Terry told Jack about Hank. Then, desperate and drunk, Jack told Terry about Edith, said he wanted a divorce, and when Terry grieved he could not leave her: all of this in about twelve hours, and within twenty-four Edith and Terry had lunch together, and next afternoon Hank and Jack went running, and that evening, with the help of gin and their long friendship, they all gathered and charcoaled steaks. When the Linharts went home, Hank and Edith stood on the front lawn till the car turned a corner and was gone. Then Edith put her arm around his waist. *We're better off*, she said: *they're still unhappy*. He felt he was being held with all her strength; that strength he had feared last April; he was proud to be loved by her and, with some shame, he was proud of himself, for bringing her this far. That fall they both had new lovers.

When three years later she told him to leave and he tried to believe the injustice of it, he could not. For a long time he did not understand why. Then one night it came to him: he remembered her arm around his waist that summer night, and the pride he had felt, and then he knew why his tallying of her affairs meant nothing. She had not made him leave her life because he was unfaithful; she had made him leave because she was; because he had changed her. So she had made him leave because—and this struck him so hard, standing in his bedroom, he needed suddenly to lie down—he was Hank Allison.

On the morning after Monica jettisoned him, he woke with the images he had brought to bed. He had no memory, as he might have without last night's treatment, of anything about her that was intelligent or kind or witty or tender. Instead of losing a good woman, he had been saved from a bad one. He knew all this was like Novocain while the dentist drilled; but no matter. For what he had to face now was not the loss of Monica; he had to face, once again, what to do about loss itself. He put a banana, wheat germ, a raw egg, and buttermilk in the blender. He brought the drink downstairs and sat on the front steps, in the autumn sunlight. It was a Saturday, and Sharon wanted to see a movie that afternoon. Good: nearly two hours of distraction; he would like the movie, whatever it was. Before picking up Sharon he must plan his night, be sure he did not spend it alone in his apartment. If he called the Linharts and told them about Monica, they would invite him to dinner, stay up drinking with him as long as he wanted. He touched the steps. *It's these steps*, he thought. He looked up and down the street lined with old houses and old trees. *This street. This town. How the fuck can I beat geography?* A small town, and a dead one. The bright women went to other places. The ones he taught with were married. So he was left with either students or the women he knew casually in town, women he had tried talking to in bars—secretaries, waitresses, florists, beauticians—and he had enjoyed their company, but no matter how pretty and good-natured they were, how could he spend much time with a woman who thought Chekhov was something boys did in their beds at night? He remembered a night last summer drinking with Jack at a bar that was usually lined with girls, and he said: *Look at her: she's pretty, she looks sweet, she's nicely dressed, but look at that face: nothing there. Not one thought in her head.* And Jack said: *Sure she's got thoughts: thirty-eight ninety-five . . . size nine . . . partly cloudy.* Sharon was twelve. He would not move away until she was at least eighteen. He was with her every weekend, and they cooked at his apartment one night during the week. When his second book was published, an old friend offered him a job in Boston: he had thought about the bigger school, more parties with more women, even graduate students, as solemn as they were. But he would not leave Sharon. And when she was eighteen, he would be forty, twice the age of most of his students, and having lived on temporary love for six years, one limping, bloodstained son of a bitch. And if he moved then, who would want what was left of him?

He stood and climbed the stairs to his apartment and phoned the Linharts. Jack answered. When Hank told him, he said to come to dinner; early, as soon as he took Sharon home.

'Maybe I'll invite Lori,' Hank said.

'Why not.'

'I mean, she's just a friend. But maybe she'll keep the night from turning into a wake.'

'Bring her. Just be careful. You fall in love faster than I can fry an egg. What is it with these Goddamn girls anyway? Are they afraid of something permanent? Is that it?'

'Old buddy, I think there's something about me that just scares shit out of them. Something they just can't handle.'

You were all the way across the room, Monica said as soon as he came, before he had even collapsed on her, to nestle his cheek beside hers. So instead he rolled away and marvelled that she knew, that Goddamnit they always knew: his soul *had* been across the room; he had felt it against the wall behind him, opposite the foot of the bed, thinking, watching him and Monica, waiting for them to finish. Because of that, finishing had taken him a long time: erect and eager, his cock seemed attached not to his flesh but to that pondering soul back there; and since it did not seem his flesh, it did not seem to be inside Monica's either: there was a mingling of his hardness and her softness and liquid heat, but it had nothing to do with who he was for those minutes, or for who she was either. He knew it was an occupational hazard. Then, because of why it had just happened on that early Friday evening in winter when she was still his student, had two hours ago been in his class, had then walked to his apartment in cold twilight, he laughed. He had not expected to laugh, he knew it was a mistake, but he could not stop. A warning tried to stop him, to whisper *hush* to the laughter, a warning that knew not only the perils with a woman at a time like this, but the worse peril of being so confident in a woman's love that he could believe she would love his laughter now too, and his reason for it. She got out of bed and went to the bathroom and then the kitchen and when she came back she had a glass of Dry Sack—one glass, not two—and even that sign could not make him serious, for he was caught in the comic precision of what had just happened. She pulled on leotards, slipped into a sweater that she left unbuttoned, and brought a cigarette to bed where she lay beside him, not touching, and the space between them and the sound of her breathing felt to Hank not quite angry yet, not quite subdued either.

'You were right,' he said. He was still smiling. 'I *was* across the room. I can't help it. I was all right until we started; then while we were making love I thought about what I was working on today. I didn't want to. I never want to after I stop for the day. And I wanted to ask you about it but I figured we'd better finish first—'

'Oh good, Hank: oh good.'

'I know, I know. But I was working on a scene about a girl who's only made love once, say a few months ago, and then one night she makes love twice to this guy and again in the morning, and I wanted to know if I was right. In the scene her pussy is sore next day; after the three times. Is that accurate?'

'Yes. You son of a bitch.'

'Now wait a minute. None of this was on purpose. You think I want my Goddamn head to start writing whenever it decides to? It's not like being un*kind*, for Christ's sake. You think surgeons and lawyers and whatever don't go through this too? Shit: you came, didn't you?'

'I could do that alone.'

'Well, what am I supposed to fucking *do*?'

He got out of bed and went for the bottle of sherry and brought it back with another glass; but at the doorway to his room, looking at her leotarded legs, the stretch of belly and chest and the inner swell of breasts exposed by the sweater, at her wide grim mouth concentrating on smoking, and her grey eyes looking at the ceiling, he stopped and stayed at the threshold. He said softly: 'Baby, what am I supposed to do? I don't believe in all this special crap about writers, you know that. We're just like everybody else. *Every*body gets distracted by their work, or whatever.'

He cut himself off: he had been about to say *Housewives too*, but the word was too dangerous and, though he believed that vocation one of the hardest and most distracting of all, believed if he were one he could never relax enough to make unhindered love, he kept quiet. Monica would not be able to hear what he said; she would hear only the word *housewife*, would slip into jargon, think of labels, roles, would not be soothed. She did not look at him. She said: 'You could try harder. You could concentrate more. You could even pretend, so I wouldn't feel like I was getting fucked by a dildo.' She was often profane, but this took him by surprise; he felt slapped. 'And you could shut up about it. And not laugh about it. And you could Goddamn not ask me your fucking questions when you stop laughing. I want a lover, not a Papermate.'

The line pleased him, even cheered him a little, and he almost told her so; but again he heard his own warnings, and stopped.

'Look,' he said, 'let's go to Boston. To Casa Romero and have a hell of a dinner.'

She stayed on his bed long enough to finish the cigarette; she occupied herself with it, held it above her face between drags and studied it as though it were worthy of concentration; watched her exhaled smoke plume and spread toward the ceiling; for all he knew (he still stood naked in the doorway) she was thinking, perhaps even about them. But he doubted it. For a girl so young, she had a lot of poses; when did they start learning them, for Christ's sake? When they still wrote their ages with one digit? She exhaled the last drag with a sigh, put the cigarette out slowly, watching its jabs against the ashtray as if this were her last one before giving them up; then quickly she put on her skirt, buttoned her sweater, pulled on her boots, slung her suede jacket over her shoulder, and walked toward him as if he were a swinging door. He turned sideways; passing, she touched neither him nor the doorjamb. *Awfully slender*, he thought. He followed her down the short hall; stood at the doorway and watched her going down the stairs; he hoped his semen was dripping into the crotch of her leotards, just to remind her that everything can't be walked away from. 'Theatrical bitch,' he said to her back, and shut the door.

Which six hours later he opened when she knocked and woke him. She was crying. Her kiss smelled of vermouth. She had been drinking with her roommate. She missed him. She was sorry. She loved him. He took her to bed with fear and sadness which were more distracting than this afternoon's thinking; he pretended passion and tenderness; he urged his cock *Come on come you bastard*, while all the time he felt defeat with this woman, felt it as surely as if it stood embodied behind him, with a raised sword. Some night, some day, the sword would arc swiftly down; all he could do was

hang on to the good times with Monica while he waited for the
blade.

Monica did, though, give him Lori. They were friends from summers in Maine, where Lori lived, and Monica's parents, from Man-
hattan, had a summer house. The girls met when Lori was fifteen
and Monica sixteen. It was Monica who convinced Lori to enroll in
the college, and to take Hank's courses. Then Monica transferred to
Maine after her freshman year, because she didn't like her art
teachers; but Lori came to the college anyway and saw Monica on
the weekends when she drove down and stayed with Hank. He
liked Lori on those weekends, he liked seeing her in his class, and
some week nights they walked to town and drank beer; a few people
probably thought they were lovers, but Hank was only afraid of
gossip that was true, so he and Lori went to Timmy's, where students drank. And the night after Monica left him, he picked her up
at the dormitory, for dinner at the Linharts. They did not become
lovers until over a month later and, when they did, Hank realized it
was the first time since Edith that he had made love with a woman
who was already his good friend. So their transition lacked the fear
and euphoria that people called romance. For Hank, it felt comfort-
able and safe, as though he had loved her for a long and good time.

Still, with Lori, he was careful: so careful that at times he
thought all the will and control it demanded of him was finally the
core of love; that for the first time he knew how to go about it. He
watched her shyness, listened to it, loved it, and did not try to cure
it. While he did this, he felt his love for her growing deeper, becoming a part of who he was in the world.

She was his fourth young girl since divorce. Each had lasted a
year or more; with each he had been monogamous; and they had
left him. None but Monica had told him why, in words he could
understand. The other two had cried and talked about needing
space. When the first left him he was sad, but he was all right. The
loss of the second frightened him. That was when he saw his trap.
Drinking with Jack, he could smile about it: for what had been
spice in his married twenties was now his sustenance. Certainly, he
told Jack, when he was married he had fallen in love with his girl
friends, or at least had the feeling of being in love, had said the
words, had the poignant times when he and the girl held each other

and spoke, in the warm spring, of the end that was coming to them on the school calendar. But all those affairs had simply given him emotions which he had believed marriage, by its nature, could not give.

For the first time in his life he felt a disadvantage with women. Too often, as he looked at a young face in his apartment or across a restaurant table, he knew he had nothing to offer this girl with her waiting trust fund, this girl who had seen more of the world than he ever would; he imagined her moving all those clothes and other pelf into his apartment and, as he talked with the girl, he wished for some woman his own age, or at least twenty-five, who was not either married or one of those so badly divorced that their pain was not only infectious but also produced in them anger at all men, making him feel he was a tenuous exception who, at any moment, would not be. They met with women's groups, shrank each other's heads without a professional in the room, and came away with their anger so prodded they were like warriors. He had tried two of those and, bored and weary, had fled. Once with honey-blonde Donna, the last one, he had left a bar to enter a night of freezing rain, ten minutes to chip his windshield clear while she sat in the car; then driving home so slowly and tensely he could feel his heart beating, he said: 'Probably some man froze all this fucking rain too.' Perhaps because she was as frightened as he was, she gently, teasingly, said 'MCP,' and patted his shoulder.

He only argued with Donna once. He believed in most of what women wanted, believed women and men should work together to free themselves, believed *The Wild Palms* had said it first and as well as anyone since. Some trifles about the movement had piqued him: they had appropriated a word he loved, mostly because of its comic root, and he could no longer have the Cold War fun of calling someone a chauvinist. And, on his two marches in Washington during the Vietnam War, he had been angered by the women who took their turn on the speakers' platform and tried to equate dishwashing with being napalmed. The only important feeling he had about these women was he wished they had some joy. The night he argued with Donna he was drunk and, though he kept trying not to see the *Ms.* on her coffee table, it was finally all he could see, and he said abruptly: 'Donna, just as an unknown, average, .260-hitting writer, who sometimes writes a story and tries to publish it, or a piece of a novel, I've got to say one thing: I hate totalitarian magazines whether they're called *Ms.* or *Penthouse*.'

'Totalitarian?'

'That.' He picked up *Ms.* and dropped it on its cover so all he saw was an advertisement encouraging young girls to start working on lung cancer now, older women to keep at it. 'They hate literature. They just want something that supports their position. It's like trying to publish in China, for Christ's sake.' Then, because he was angry at magazines and nothing else, and she was suddenly an angry feminist, they fought.

The fight ended when it was over, so it wasn't serious. But one of the reasons he finally left her, chose loneliness instead, was what she read. She did not read him. This hurt him a little, but not much; mostly, he was baffled. He could not understand why she would make love with him when she was not interested in his work. Because to him, his work was the best of himself. He believed most men who were fortunate enough to have work they loved saw themselves in the same way. Yet Donna's affection was only for what he was at night, when he was relaxing from that day's work, and forgetting tomorrow's, in much the same way he saw most movies that came to town, no matter what they were. And his bantering night-self was so unimportant to him that often, at his desk in the morning, he felt he had not spent last evening with Donna; someone else had talked with her, made love with her; some old, close friend of his.

Typed on a sheet of paper, thumbtacked to the wall over his desk, was this from *Heart of Darkness: No, I don't like work. I had rather laze about and think of all the fine things that can be done. I don't like work—no man does—but I like what is in the work—the chance to find yourself. Your own reality—for yourself, not others—what no other man can ever know. They can only see the mere show, and never can tell what it really means.* A woman had to know that: simply know it, that was all. He did not need praise from her, he rarely liked to talk about his work, and he had no delusions about it: he liked most novels he read better than he liked his own. But the work was his, and its final quality did not matter so much as the hours it demanded from him. It made the passage of time concrete, measurable. It gave him confidence, not in the work itself, but in Hank Allison: after a morning at the desk he had earned his day on earth. When he did not work, except by choice, he disliked himself. If these days occurred in succession because of school work, hangovers, lack of will, sickness, he lost touch with himself, felt vague and abstract, felt himself becoming whomever he was with. So he thought Donna knew little more about him than she would if, never having met him, she came across his discarded clothing and wallet on her bedroom floor. At times this made him lonely; it also made him think of Edith, all of her he had not known during their marriage, especially the final three polygamous years; and with no way now to undo, to soothe, to heal, he loved her and grieved for what she had suffered: the loneliness of not being fully known.

One night in Donna's bed, lying tensely beside her peaceful, post-orgasmic flesh, in the dark yet seeing in his mind the bedroom cluttered with antique chairs and dressing table and family pictures on the wall and, resting on the mantel of the sealed fireplace, faces of her grandparents and parents and herself with her two children, a son and daughter, he wondered why he was with her. He knew it was because of loneliness, but why her, with her colliding values, her liberated body which she had shared—offered actually—on their second date, lying here among the testaments of family, marriage, traditions? He suspected that her feminism existed solely because, as her marriage ended, her husband had become mean. He was behind on child support; often he broke dates with the children. Hank believed she was happy now, in these moments this night, because she had just made love, her children slept healthy down the hall, and she was lying amid her antiques and photographs of her life, on a four-poster bed that had been her great-aunt's. When he tired of trying to understand her, he said: 'I don't know why you like me.'

'Why *Hank*.'

Her voice was wrong: she thought he felt unloved, needed comfort. He left the bed to piss, to break the mood. When he returned and covered himself he said: 'You're not interested in my work. That's me. All you see is what's left over. I don't think that's me.'

'I've hurt you, and it was stupid and selfish. Bring them over tomorrow night. I'll read them in order.'

'Wait.' He spoke with gentle seriousness, as he did at times with Sharon, when they were discussing a problem she was having or a difference between them, and he wanted her to hear only calm father-words, and not to listen for or worry about his own emotions beneath them. 'I'm not hurt. I just don't understand how you can feel for me, and know nothing at all about that part of my life. Maybe two-thirds of it; only about an eighth of my day, in hours, but usually two-thirds of it, which is all of it except sleeping; no matter what I'm doing, it's down there inside me, I can feel it at work; whether I'm with Sharon or you or teaching; or anything.' He was about to explain that too, but veered away: some nights with Donna he had the same trouble he would have with Monica much later; but Donna either had not noticed or, more likely, because she had been with more men, she had simply understood; probably she had her own nights like that, as they moved together in that passion which, true as it was, did not totally absorb them, but existed in tandem with them.

'What about my work?' she said.

There was no edge on her voice; not yet; but he could sense the blade against whetstone in her heart. He watched her eyes, kept his voice the same, though with a twinge of impatience he felt he *was* talking to Sharon. Why was he so often comforting women? He wished he could see himself as they saw him: his face, his body, his gestures; wished he could hear the voice they heard. For now he felt like a mean lover, and he did not want to be, but maybe he was and could not do anything about it; or maybe (he hoped) he simply appeared that way. Whatever, he was sad and confused and lonely, felt lost and homeless and womanless, though he lay in bed with a good woman, a good companion; and he needed answers, or even just one, yet now he must give answers, and in a controlled and comforting voice whose demand on him clenched his fists, tightened his arms.

'It's not,' he said. 'You told me it wasn't. We were eating at Ten Center Street, and you said: "It's not work; I wouldn't grace it with the name. It's just a job till I find out what I really want to do."' He was still tense, but her face softened with his voice.

'You're right,' she said.

'I also know about your job. I've listened. I can tell you your typical day. But mostly with me you talk about your children and rearing them alone and shithead Max not coming through with the money and not seeing the children when he's supposed to, because he's become a chic-freak smoking dope all day with young ass and bragging about leaving the engineering rat-race, when the truth is he was laid off with the rest of the poor bastards during the recession, and he talks about opening a bar when he can hardly afford to drink at one because he's drawing unemployment. And you mostly talk about men and women. And how everything's changed since you and Max bought this house and it's got you muddled and sad and pissed-off and you want to do something about it, for yourself and other women too if you could think of a way, but you don't know how yet. I don't mean any of this as an insult. You talk about these things because that's who you are right now, that's your struggle, and it never bores me. Because I care about you and because I'm going through my version of the same thing. Everything's changed for me too. When we were pregnant—'

'We?'

'Of course we. Not just Edith. I didn't vomit and my pants size didn't change and my breasts didn't swell and I didn't feel any pain. But it was we. It always is, unless some prick pretends it isn't.'

'Like Max.'

'I don't know what he felt then. You said he was different then—' He waved an arm at the dark room, was about to say *He liked all this stuff*, but did not.

'What did *you* feel?' she said.

'Guilt. Fear. I'd read *A Farewell to Arms* too recently. Three or four years earlier, but for me that was too recently.' He saw in her face she did not know the book, and he was about to explain, but thought that would be a worse mistake than his mentioning it. 'I was afraid she'd die. Off and on, until it was over. While she was delivering I hated my hard-on that had been so important whatever night it seemed so important and the diaphragm wasn't enough.'

'Men shouldn't feel that way.'

'Should and shouldn't don't have much to do with feelings. Anyway, we got married. We were in graduate school and we didn't know any feminists. We were too busy, and our friends were other young couples who were busting their asses to pay bills and stay in school. It made sense then, graduate school: there were jobs waiting. And I saw Edith as a wife in I suppose the same way my father saw my mother. Which somewhat resembles a nineteenth-century aristocrat, I guess: some asshole out of Balzac or Tolstoy.' (This time, remembering his marriage, he did not even notice that literature had moved into the bed again, like a troublesome cat.) 'Well, not that bad. But bad enough. I don't think I knew it, most of the time. Or maybe I just believed I was right, *it* was right. It's the only way I had ever seen marriage. I'm not excusing myself. It gets down to this: I nearly drowned her in my shit creek till one night she found a paddle and broke it over my head. Then she shoved the handle through me. I still feel the splinters. All of which is to say I'm not just politely nodding my head when you talk about trouble between men and women. You're talking to a comrade in arms, and I lost too.'

Goddamn: he had gotten off the track again, for now she held him with both arms, pulled him against her, and he let her quietly hold him a while, then he shifted, got an arm around her, pulled her head to his shoulder so he was talking to her hair, and said: 'All of which got us away from the original question. You're a lovely woman. You could have as many kinds of men as you're lucky enough to meet—doctor lawyer Indian chief—so what I want to ask is, why me? A man you met at a party, you came up and said "You have foam on your moustache," and I licked it off and you said "I like watching men lick beer from their moustaches." Why in the world me?'

She turned and kissed him long, then raising her face above his, she said: 'Because you're so *alive*.'

As if she had suddenly pulled the blankets from him, a chill went up his back and touched his heart, which felt now dry and withered, late autumn's leaf about to fall slowly through his body. Feeling her bones against him, he thought of her as a skeleton lying amid the antiques in the dark, a skeleton with a voice struggling for life, with words that were the rote of pain and anger from the weekly meetings of women. Then he felt like crying for her. It seemed that, compared to hers, his own life was full and complex and invigorating. He wished he knew a secret, and that he could give it to her: could lay his hand on her forehead and she would sleep and wake tomorrow with the same dreary job as a bank teller, the same mother-duties, and confusion and loneliness and the need to feel her life was something solid she was sculpting, yet with an excited spirit ready to engage the day, to kick it and claw it and gouge its eyes until it gave her the joy she deserved. But he had nothing to tell her, nothing to give. He held her quietly, for a long time. Then he rose and dressed. He never spent the night with her. She did not want the children, who were three and five, to know; nor did Hank; and it was implicit between them that since their affair had begun impetuously soon, it was tenuous, was at very best—or least—a trial affair. There would probably be another man, and another, and her children should not grow up seeing that male succession at breakfast. He leaned over and kissed her, whispered sweetly, then drove home.

The point was, finally, that Donna did not read. He guessed all men did not have to love women who were interested in their work; somehow a veterinarian could leave his work with its odors in the shower before dinner, spend his evening with a beloved woman who did not want a house pet. But he could not. Literature was what he turned to for passion and excitement, where he entered a world of questions he could not answer, so he finished a novel or poem or story feeling blessed with humility, with awe of life, with the knowledge that he knew so little about how one was supposed to live. So, better to have the company of a girl who loved literature and simply had not read much because she was young, far more exciting to listen to a girl's delight at her first reading of *Play It As It Lays* or *Fat City*, than to be with a woman in her thirties who did not read because she had chosen not to, had gone to the magazines and television.

Two nights later they went to dinner and, with coffee and brandy, sipping the courage to hurt her, he spoke about their starting too fast, becoming lovers too soon, before they really knew each other; he said their histories were very different, and being sudden lovers blurred their ability to see whether they were really—he paused, waiting for a series of concrete words besides the one word *compatible*, wanting his speech to at least sound different from the ones other men and women were hearing across the land that night. During his pause she said: 'Compatible.'

Then relief filled her face as quickly as pain does, the pain he had predicted, and for an instant he was hurt. Then he smiled at his fleeting pride. He was happy: she had wanted out too. Then she told him she had been three days late last week and her waiting had made her think about the two of them, she had been frightened, and had wanted to stop the affair. But not their friendship. They ordered second brandies and talked, without shyness, about their children. They split the bill, he drove her home, and they kissed goodnight at her door.

As he leaves Lori in the car in front of Edith's house he kisses her quickly, says he loves her. Edith opens the door: small body, long black hair, her eyes and mouth smiling like an old friend. He supposes that is what she is now and, because they have Sharon, in some way they are still married. Though he cannot define each scent, the house smells feminine to him. Like Donna, Edith does not let lovers stay the night, and for the same reasons. Hank knows this because, in their second year of divorce, when he could ask the question without risking too deep a wound, he did. Now he asks: 'What kind of smell does a man bring into a house?'

'Bad ones.'

'I smell bacon and the Sunday paper. Both neuter. But there's something female. Or non-male.'

'It's your imagination. But there *has* been a drought.'

'I'm sorry. What happened to what's-his-face?'

She shrugs, and for a moment the smile leaves her eyes: not sadness but resignation or perhaps foreknowledge of it, years of it. Then she looks at him more closely.

'What happened?' she says.

'Something shitty.'

'With Lori?'

'No.'

'Good. I think she's the one.'

'Really? Why?'

'I don't know. I hope you can keep her. What is it? Work?'

'No. I'll talk to you tonight. Where's Sharon?'

'Cleaning her room. I'll get her.'

She goes to the foot of the stairs and calls: 'Sharon, Dad's here.'

'I'm sorry about the drought,' he says.

'What the hell. I should have been a teacher so I'd have more livestock to pasture with. It's all right now, did you know that? For women. A friend of mine is having an affair with one of her students. She's thirty-seven and he's nineteen.'

She is not attacking him; those days are long past. He is sorry for her, knows her problem is geographical too, that she would do better in Boston. He is grateful and deeply respects her for staying here so he and Sharon can be near each other, but he can only tell her such things on the phone when he's had some drinks.

Sharon comes down in jeans and a sweater, carrying a windbreaker. He hugs her and they kiss. Her new breasts make him uncomfortable; he rarely looks at them, and when he embraces her he doesn't know where to put them, what to do about their small insistence against him. They both kiss Edith and walk arm-in-arm to the car. Lori opens the door, and Sharon gets into the back seat.

Sharon and Lori get along well, and sometimes talk like two teen-aged girl friends, as if he's not there. That they are both teen-agers, one in her first year of it, the other in her last, gives Hank both a smile and a shiver. He wonders if someday he will have a girl who is Sharon's age. It could happen in five years. And who, he wonders as he drives on a country road winding east, ever started the myth that a young girl gave an older man his youth again? Not that he would want his confused youth again. But they were supposed to make you feel younger. All he knows is that with Lori he feels unattractive, balding, flabby. That she wakes with a hangover look-ing strong and fresh, and is; while at thirty he lost that resilience and now a bad hangover affects his day like the flu. Remembering how in his twenties he could wake six hours after closing a bar, then eat breakfast and write, he feels old. And when people glance at him and Lori while, in Boston, they walk holding hands, or enter a restaurant, he feels old. The beach is worse: he watches the lithe young men and wonders if Lori watches them too, and his knowing that most of them, probably all except the obsessively vain and those who are simply exempt by nature, will in a few years have enough flesh at their waists to fill a woman's hands, does not help. He feels old. Yet with Donna and the divorcée before her, he had felt young, too young, his spirit quickly wearied by their gravity. So, again, no answers: all he knows is that whoever spread the word about young girls had not been an older man in love with one.

Sharon and Lori are talking about school and their teachers and homework and how they discipline themselves to do it, how they choose which work to do first (Lori works in descending order, beginning with the course she likes most: Sharon does the opposite; they both end with science). Last summer Sharon started and stopped smoking; quit when Edith kissed her just after running, and smelled Sharon's breath and hair; which she might not have, she told Hank on the phone, if her sense of smell hadn't been cleansed of her own cigarettes by an hour's run. Hank liked that: he had a notion that kids got away with smoking now because their parents didn't kiss them much; when he was a boy, he and his friends had chewed gum and rubbed lemon juice on their fingers before going home, because someone always kissed them hello. Edith talked to Sharon, and that night Hank took her to dinner and talked to her, pleaded with her, and she promised him, as she had Edith, that she was not hooked, had smoked maybe two packs, and from now on, she said, she would not give in to peer pressure. That was the night Hank and Edith started worrying about dope, talked on the phone about it, and he wondered how divorced parents who were too hurt and angry to talk to each other dealt with what their children were doing. Now, at least once a month, while he and Sharon cook dinner in his small kitchen, he mentions dope. She tells him not to worry, she's seen enough of the freaks at school, starting with their joints on the bus at seven in the morning.

He is not deeply worried about dope, because he trusts Sharon, knows she is sensible; that she tried cigarettes with her girl friends because at thirteen she wouldn't think of death; but he is as certain as he can be that, seeing the stoned and fruitless days of the young people around her, she will take care of herself.

What really worries him about Sharon has to do with him and Lori, and with him and Monica, and with the two girls before Monica. It also has to do with Edith: although her lovers have not spent the night, have probably not even used the house, by now Sharon must know Edith has had them. But he doesn't worry much about Edith, because he feels so confused, guilty, embarrassed, honest and dishonest about himself and his lovers and Sharon, that he has little energy left to worry about Edith's responsibilities. Also, he understands very little about mothers and daughters, the currents that run between them. But about Sharon he knows this: with each of his young girl friends—she did not meet Donna or the divorcée before her—she has been shy, has wanted to be their friend, more to them than her father's daughter. He has also sensed jealousy, which has disturbed him, and he doesn't know whether Sharon feels the girl is taking her mother's place, or her own, in his life. Always he has talked with her about his girl friends, and pretended they were not lovers. Yet he knows that she knows. So he is hung on his own petard: he does not want her to have lovers early, before she has grown enough to protect herself from pain. He wants to warn her that, until some vague age, a young boy will stick it in anything and say anything that will let him stick it. He doesn't know when he will tell her this. He does not want her girlhood and young womanhood to become a series of lovers, he does not want her to become cynical and casual about making love. He does not, in fact, want her to be like his girl friends. Yet, by having four whom she's known in five years, and two whom she hasn't, that is exactly the way he is showing her how to live.

Lori makes things better. When he became her friend, she had had one quick and brutal affair with a co-worker in a restaurant in Maine where they both waited tables the summer before she came to college. He hurt her physically, confused her about what she was doing with him, and after two weeks she stopped. So she was more the sort of girl he wanted Sharon to be. And Lori—shy, secretive not by choice, brooding (though it didn't appear on her smooth face; he had to look at her drooping lip-corners)—was warm and talkative with Sharon, enjoyed being with her, and Hank thought they were good for each other: Sharon, with her new breasts and menses, her sophistication that came from enduring divorce and having parents who were not always honest with her yet tried to be as often as they could, for the two purposes of helping her with divorce and preparing her to face the implacable and repetitive pains in a world that, when they were much younger, neither of them had foreseen. On the other hand Lori: with her quiet, tender father, his voice seldom heard, his presence seeming to ask permission for itself, and her loud mother whose dominance was always under a banner of concern for her daughter and, beneath that (Hank guessed), Lori's belief that her father was, had been, and would be a cuckold, and not only that but one without vengeance, neither rage nor demand nor even the retaliatory relief of some side-pussy of his own. So as Hank listens he thinks Sharon needs warm recognition from Lori, and that Lori needs to be able to talk, giggle, be silly, say whatever she wants, and from Sharon (and yes: him at the wheel beside her) she draws the peace to be able to talk without feeling that someone is standing behind her, about to clamp a hand on her shoulder and tell her she's wrong.

Wondering about Sharon and Lori gives him some respite but it is not complete. For all during the drive there is the cool hollow of sadness around his heart, and something is wrong with his body. Gravity is more intense: his head and shoulders and torso are pulled downward to the car seat. He crosses the bridge to the island, turns right into the game preserve, driving past the booth which is unmanned now that summer is over. To their right is the salt marsh, to their left dunes so high they cannot see the ocean. He parks facing a dune, and walking between Lori and Sharon, holding their hands, he starts climbing the grass-tufted slope of sand; his body is still heavy.

At the dune's top the sea breeze strikes them cool but not cold, coming over water that is deep blue, for the air is dry, and they stop. They stand deeply inhaling the air from the sea. On the crest of the dune, his eyes watering from the breeze, holding Lori's and Sharon's hands, breathing the ocean-smell he loves, Hank suddenly does not know what he will do about last year's dead fetus, last night's dream of her on the summer beach with him and Sharon; he cannot imagine the rest of his life. He sees himself growing older, writing and running and teaching, but that is all, and his tears now are not from the breeze.

'Let's go,' he says, and they walk southward, releasing each other's hands so they can file between the low shrubs on the dune's top. He turns back to the girls and points at Canadian geese far out in the marsh, even their distant silhouettes looking fat, and he thinks of one roasting, the woman—who? his mother? he sees no face—bending over to open the oven door, peering in, basting. They walk quietly. He can feel them all, free of house-wood and car-metal that surround most of their time, feeling the hard sand underfoot, the crisp brown shrubs scratching their pants, their eyes looking ahead and down the slopes of the dune, out at the marsh with its grass and, in places, shimmer of standing water, and its life of tiny creatures they can feel but not see; and at the ocean, choppy and white-capped, and he imagines a giant squid and killer whale struggling in a dance miles deep among mountains and valleys. For an instant he hopes Lori is at least a bit sad, then knows that is asking too much.

They walk nearly two miles, where the dune ends, and beneath them the island ends too at the river which flows through the marsh, into the sea. The river is narrow and, where it meets the sea, the water is lake-gentle. It is shallow and, in low tide, Hank and Sharon have waded out to a long sandbar opposite the river's mouth. Hank goes down a steep, winding path, and they move slowly. At the bottom they cross the short distance of sand and watch the end of the river, and look southeast where the coast below them curves sharply out to sea. They turn and walk up the beach, the sand cool and soft. He is walking slightly ahead of them, holding back just enough to be with them and still alone; for he feels something else behind him too, so strongly that his impulse is to turn and confront it before it leaps on him. He wants to run until his body feels light again. They move closer to the beach and walk beside washed-up kelp and green seaweed. He stops and turns to Lori and Sharon. Their faces are wind-pink, their hair blows across cheeks and eyes.

'I don't know where the car is,' he says. 'But I know a restaurant it can get us to.'

Sharon points at the dune.

'On the other side,' she says.

'Oh. I thought I parked it in the surf.'

'It's *right* over there.'

'No.'

He looks at the dune.

'You want to bet?'

'Not with you. You'd bet a dinner at the Copley against a hamburger at Wendy's.'

'Okay. What's the Copley?'

'A place I'm not taking you. Lori and I go Dutch.'

'That expensive, huh?'

'We go everywhere Dutch. You can't tell me that part of the dune looks different.'

'See the lifeguard tower?'

He looks north behind him, perhaps a half-mile away. Sharon talks to his back.

'When we climbed the dune I looked that way and saw it.'

He looks at her. 'If you're right, I'll buy you a meal.'

'You already said you'd do that.'

'Right. Let's climb, ladies.'

He leads them up and, at the top, they see the car to the south.

'I was a bit off,' Sharon says.

'No more than a hundred yards.'

The restaurant is nearby, on the mainland road that curves away from the island; and it is there, seated and facing Sharon and Lori, that whatever pursued him on the beach strikes him: lands howling on his back. He can do nothing about it but look at Sharon's cheerful face while he feels, in the empty chair beside him, the daughter salined or vacuumed from Monica a year ago. The waitress is large and smiling, a New England country woman with big, strong-looking hands, and she asks if they'd like something to drink. Sharon wants a Shirley Temple, Lori wants a margarita, and Hank wants to be drunk. But he is wary. When his spirit is low, when he

can barely feel it at all, just something damp and flat lying over his
guts, when even speaking and eating demand effort, and he wants
to lie down and let the world spin while he yearns for days of un-
consciousness, he does not drink. The only cure then is a long run.
It does not destroy what is attacking him, but it restores his spirit,
and he can move into the world again, look at people, touch them,
talk. Only once in his life it has not worked: the day after Edith told
him to leave. He would like to run now. Whatever leaped on his
back has settled there, more like a deadly snake than a mad dog. He
must be still and quiet. He remembers one of his favorite scenes in
literature, in Kipling: 'Rikki-Tikki-Tavi,' when Nagaina the
mother cobra comes to the veranda where the family is eating,
coiled and raised to strike the small boy, the three of them – father,
mother, son – statues at their breakfast table.

'A mongoose,' he says.

'He'll ask me how to make that one.'

'It comes with a cobra egg in its mouth.' She is looking down at
him, her eyes amused yet holding on to caution too, perhaps anger,
waiting to see if this is harassment or friendly joking. 'It's the last
egg in the nest. He's killed the others. He comes up behind the
cobra and she turns on him just long enough for the father to reach
over the table and grab his son and pull him away.'

'Sounds like a good one,' she says. 'Must start with rum and keep
building.'

She is smiling now, and he is ashamed, for he sees in her quickly
tender eyes that she knows something is wrong.

'I'm sorry,' he says.

'For what? I like a good story. If we had cobras around here I
swear to God I'd go live up ten flights of stairs in Boston and never
see grass or stars again. You going to drink that?'

'I'll have a Coke with a wedge of lime.'

'So that's a mongoose. I think I'll call it that, see what he comes
up with. Now I like Jackson. But he's his own man behind the bar.
Any time—*every* time—somebody orders a sombrero, he says, What
do you think this is, a dairy bar? Doesn't matter who they are. He
makes them, but he always says that. Won't make a frozen daiquiri.
Nobody orders them anyway. Maybe five-six a year. He just looks
at them and says, Too much trouble; I'll quit my job first. Young
guy came in the other night and ordered a flintlock. Ever hear of
that one?'

'No.'

'Neither did Jackson. He said, Go home and watch Daniel Boone, and he went to the other end of the bar till finally the guy goes down there and asks can he have a beer. Jackson looks at him a while then opens up the bottle and says, You want a glass with that or a powder horn?'

Hank keeps smiling, thinking that on another day he would stay here for hours, drinking long after his meal, so he could banter with this woman with the crinkles at her eyes and the large hands he guesses have held many a happy man. He could get into his country-western mood and find the songs on the jukebox and ask about her children and wonder how many heartbreaks she had given and received.

'Better just tell him Coke then,' he says. 'You order a mongoose and he'll send me the snake.'

'He's a bit of one himself. Coke with a wedge,' and she is gone. He looks at Lori. She understands, and he glances away from her, down at the red paper placemat. When the waitress brings their drinks, they order food, taking a long time because Sharon cannot decide and the waitress, who is not busy this early in the afternoon, enjoys helping her, calls her Honey, tells her the veal cutlet is really pork tenderloin but it's good anyway, the fisherman's platter is too big but if she doesn't stuff on the fries she might eat most of the fish, with maybe some help from the mongoose-drinker. Sharon orders a sirloin, and Hank is glad: he wants to watch her eating meat.

When it comes he does watch, eating his haddock without pleasure or attention: Sharon is hungry and she forks and cuts fast, and he watches the brown and pink bite go into her mouth, watches her lips close on it and her jaws working and the delight on her face. He remembers the smell of the sea, the feel of her hand in his, the sound of her breath beside him. *Life*, he thinks, and imagines the taste of steak in her mouth, the meat becoming part of her, and as his heart celebrates these pleasures it grieves, for he can see only the flesh now, Sharon's, and the flesh of the world: its terrain and its seasons of golden and red, then white, then mud and rain and green, and the blue and green months with their sun burning then tanning her skin. All trials of the spirit seem nothing compared to this: his grave and shameful talk with Monica and her parents, Monica's tears and seven more months of gestation, his taking the girl home, blanket-wrapped on his lap on the plane: cries in the night and diapers, formula and his impatience and frustration and anger as he powdered the pink peach of her girlhood, staying home with her at night and finding babysitters so he could teach—all this goes through his mind like blown ashes, for he can only feel the flesh: Sharon's and his and the daughter in the chair beside him: she is a small child now, has lived long enough to love the sun on her face and the taste of steak. And for the first time in his life he understands that grief is not of the mind but the body. He can dull his mind, knock it out with booze and sleeping pills. But he can do nothing about his pierced body as he watches Sharon eat, can do nothing about its pieces sitting beside him in the body of a daughter, nor about the part of it that was torn from him last October, that seems still to live wherever they dumped it in the hospital in New York. He offers Sharon dessert. The waitress says the apple pie is hot and homemade, just out of the oven. Sharon orders it with vanilla ice cream, and Hank watches her mouth open wide for the cold-hot bites, and hears the sea waves again, and sees the long rubbery brown kelp washed up on the sand.

He does not phone Edith that night because Lori stays with him. She ought to go back to the dormitory: Friday night she walked to his house with clothes and books in a knapsack, and if she goes back now she can say she spent the weekend in Boston. If anyone asks. No one does, because her friends know where she is. Tomorrow she will have to wake at six while the students are still sleeping and no one is at work except the kitchen staff and one security guard who might see her walking from the direction of Hank's apartment, not the bus stop. The security guard and kitchen staff are not interested; even if they were, their gossip doesn't travel upward to the administration; student, secretarial, and faculty gossip does. Lori and Hank have been doing this for nearly a year, with a near-celibate respite last summer when, except for her one day off a week, they saw each other in Maine, after she had finished waitressing for the night. The drive from his apartment was only an hour, but he decided, grinning at himself, that it meant he truly loved her, that he had not just turned to her during the school year because he was lonely. He had not done anything so adolescent since he had been one: at ten he met her in the restaurant, they went to a bar for a couple of hours, then to her house for coffee in the kitchen, talking quietly while her parents slept; they kissed goodnight for a long time, then he drove home. He did not even consider making love in the car, told her if he did that, hair would grow on his bald spot, his love handles would disappear, and he'd probably get pimples. Some nights her family, or part of it, was at the restaurant, and they all went out together: father, mother, and one or both of her sisters home for a weekend. Hank liked her father, though he was hard to talk with, for he rarely spoke; Lori's mother did most of that, and the two sisters did most of the rest. Everyone pretended Hank and Lori were friends, not lovers, and although Hank wanted it that way, it made him uncomfortable, increased his guilt around Lori's father, and kept him fairly quiet. Often he wanted to take Mr. Meadows aside and tell him he and Lori were lovers and that he loved her and was not using her. He felt none of this with Mrs. Meadows, perhaps because as father of a daughter he imagined Mr. Meadows's concern. Hank danced with all the women in the family and the mother was foxier on the floor than her daughters. She told Hank how pretty she was by joking about how old she was, about her lost figure (the body he held was as firm as Lori's); she asked if he wanted to go to the parking lot for some fresh air, smiling in a way that made him believe and disbelieve the invitation; she did not ask what he was doing with Lori, but when she talked about Lori she looked at him, as they danced, with various expressions: interrogation, dislike, and, most disconcerting of all, jealousy and lasciviousness. On Lori's day off each week she drove down to Hank's, telling her mother the beach was better there, sand instead of rocks; she needed to get out of town for a day; Hank did all that driving back and forth and she owed him one day of visiting him; told her mother all sorts of surface truths her mother did not believe, and on that day they made love and after dinner she drove home again.

Hank does not call Edith Sunday night because he does not know whether or not his turning to her will hurt Lori, and he does not have the energy to ask her. When he realizes that is the only reason, he then wonders if he has the energy to love. He does not remember the woman he was with, or the specific causes, or even the season or calendar year, but he remembers feeling like this before, and he is frightened by its familiarity, its reminder that so much of his life demands energy. He imagines poverty, hunger, oppression, exile, imprisonment: all those lives out there whose suffering is so much worse than his, their endurance so superior, that his own battles could earn only their scorn. He knows all this is true, but it doesn't help, and he makes a salty dog for Lori and, after hesitating, one for himself. Halfway through his drink, as they lie propped on the bed—he has no chairs except the one at his desk—watching *All in the Family*, he decides not to have a second drink. He has become mute, as if the day-long downward-pulling heaviness of his body is trying to paralyze him. So he holds Lori's hand. At nine they undress and get under the covers and watch *The New Centurions*. When George C. Scott kills himself, they wipe their eyes; when Stacey Keach dies, they wipe them again, and Lori says: 'Shit.' Hank wishes he had armed enemies and a .38 and a riot gun. He thinks he would rather fight that way than by watching television and staying sober and trying to speak. He goes through the apartment turning out lights, then gets into bed and tightly holds Lori.

'I still can't,' he says.

'I know.'

He wants to tell her—and in fact does in his mind—how much he loves her, how grateful he is that she was with him all day, quietly knowing his pain, and that as bad as it was, the day would have been worse without her; that she might even have given him and Sharon the day, for without her he might not have been able to get out of bed this morning. But silence has him and the only way he can break it is with tears as deep and wrenching as last night's, and he will not go through that again, does not know if he can bear that emptying again and afterward have something left over for whatever it is he has to do.

Some time in the night he dreams of him and Sharon lying on the blanket at the beach, the fetus curled pink and sweetly beside him, and asleep he knows as if awake that he is dreaming, that in the morning he will wake with it.

Monday night he eats a sandwich, standing in the kitchen by the telephone, and calls Jack and asks him to go out for a drink after dinner. Then he phones Edith. When she asks what happened he starts to tell her but can only repeat *I* three times and say *Monica*; then he is crying and cursing his tears and slapping the wall with his hand. Edith tells him to take his time (they *are* forever married, he thinks) and finally with her comforting he stops crying and tells the whole story in one long sentence, and Edith says: 'That little bitch. She didn't even let you *know*? *I* could have taken it. I would have taken your baby.'

'*I* would have.'

'You would?'

'You're Goddamned right. I didn't even get a fucking shot at it. That's why she didn't let me know. She knew I'd have fought it.'

'You keep surprising me. That's what happens in marriage, right? People keep changing.'

'Who says I changed?'

'I just didn't know you felt that way.'

'I never had to before.'

'I'm sorry, baby. I never did like that girl. Too much mischief in those eyes.'

'It was worse than that.'

'Too many lies deciding which would come out first.'

'That's her.'

'I really would have taken it. If things had gotten bad for you.'

'I know.'

'Is there anything I can do?'

'Forgive me.'

'For what?'

'Everything.'

'You are. Sharon was very happy when she came home yesterday.'

Hank's drinks are bourbon, beer, gin, and tequila, and he knows where each will take him. Bourbon will keep him in the same mood he's in when he starts to drink; beer does the same. Either of them, if he drinks enough, will sharpen his focus on his mood, but will not change it, nor take it too far. So they are reliable drinks when he is feeling either good or bad. He has never had a depressed or mean tequila drunk; it always brings him up, and he likes to use it most when he is relaxed and happy after a good day's work. He can also trust it when he is sad. He likes gin rickeys, and his favorite drink is a martini, but he does not trust gin, and drinks it very carefully: it is unpredictable, can take him any place, can suddenly—when he happily began an evening—tap some anger or sorrow he did not even know he had. Since meeting Lori, who loves tequila, he has been replacing the juniper with the cactus.

Tonight, with Jack, he drank gin rickeys, and it is not until he is

lying in bed and remembering the fight he has just won that he can
actually see it. Timmy's is a neighborhood bar, long and narrow,
with only a restroom for men. Beyond its wall is the restaurant,
with booths on both sides and one line of tables in the middle; the
waitresses in there get drinks through a half door behind the bartender; when customers are in the dining room, the door is kept
closed on the noise from the bar. Students rarely drink on the bar
side; they stay in the dining room.

Tonight the bar was lined with regulars, working men whose
ages are in every decade between twenty and seventy. Two strangers, men in their mid-twenties, stood beside Hank. Their hands
were tough, dirty-fingernailed, and their faces confident. Hank
noticed this because he was trying to guess what they did for a
living. Some of the young men who drank at Timmy's were out of
work and drawing unemployment and it showed in their eyes.
After the second drink Jack said: 'It's either woman-trouble or
work-trouble. Which one?'

'Neither.'

'It's got to be. It's always one or the other, with a man. Or
money.'

'Nope.'

'Jesus. Are we here to talk about it?'

'No, just to shoot the shit.'

Johnny McCarthy brought their drinks: in his mid-twenties, he
is working his way through law school; yet always behind the bar,
even when he is taking exams, he is merry; he boxed for Notre
Dame five or six years ago and looks and moves as though he still
could. Hank paid for the round, heard 'nigger' beside him, missed
the rest of the young man's sentence, and asked Jack if he ran today.

'No, I got fucked into a meeting. Did you?'

'Just a short one by the campus. Let's run Kenoza tomorrow.'

'Good.'

'I'll pick you up.'

The talk to his right was louder, and he tried not to hear it as he
and Jack talked about teaching, punctuated once by the man bumping his right side, an accident probably but no apology for it; then
more talk until he heard 'Lee' and, still listening to Jack and talking
to him, he also listened to blond big-shouldered cocky asshole on
his right cursing Hank's favorite man on the Red Sox, that smooth
pitcher, that competitor. In his bed he cannot count the gin rickeys

or the time that passed before he heard 'Lee,' then turned and no longer saw the broad shoulders. Drunk, he felt big and strong and fast and, most of all, an anger that had to be released, an anger so intense that it felt like hatred too. As a grown man he had come close to fighting several times, in bars, but he never had because always, just short of saying the final words that would do it, he had images of the consequences: it was not fear of being hurt; he had played football in high school and was not unduly afraid of pain; it was the image of the fight's end: the bartender, usually a friend, sober and disgusted as he ejected Hank; or, worse, cops, sober and solemn and ready for a little action themselves, and he could not get past those images of dignity-loss, of shame, of being pulled up from the floor where he rolled and fought like a dog. So always he had stopped, had felt like a coward till next morning when he was glad he had stopped. But this time he turned to the man and said: 'You don't know what the fuck you're talking about.'

The man stepped back to give himself room.

'What's that?'

'Lee's the best clutch pitcher on the staff.'

'Fucking loudmouth spaceman is what he is.'

'Oh that's it. I thought I heard nigger a while back. You don't like what he *says*, is that it?' He could feel rather than hear the silence in the bar, could hear Johnny across the bar talking to him, urging, his voice soft and friendly. 'It's bussing, is that it? You don't like Lee because he's for bussing? Pissed you off when he didn't like the war?'

'Fuck *him*. I was *in* Nam, motherfucker, and I don't want to fucking hear you again: you drink with that other cunt you're with.'

'I'm glad you didn't get killed over there,' Hank said, his voice low, surprising him, and he turned away, nodded at Johnny, then he reached for his glass, confused, too many images now—and in his bed smiling he can understand it: dead children and women and scared soldiers and dead soldiers; and in Washington he and Jack quietly crying as they watched the veterans march, old eyes and mouths on their young bodies or what was left of some of them: the legless black with his right arm raised as a friend pushed his wheelchair, the empty sleeves, empty trouser-legs on that cold Inauguration Day; in his bed he can understand it: the man had given him a glimpse of what might have been his long suffering in Vietnam, for a moment he had become a man instead of an asshole with a voice.

Then Hank surprised himself again: his rage came back, and into his drink he said: 'Fuck you anyway.'

They were standing side by side, nearly touching: they turned together, Hank's left fist already swinging, and his right followed it, coming up from below and behind his waist; then he seemed to be watching himself from the noise and grasping hands around him, felt the hands slipping from him as he kept swinging, and the self he was watching was calm and existed in a circle of silence, as if he were a hurricane watching its own eye. The man was off-balance from Hank's first two punches, so he could not get his feet and body set, and all his blows on Hank's arms, ribs, side of the head, came while going backward and trying to plant his feet and get his weight forward; and Hank drove inside and with short punches went for the blood at the nose and mouth. Then the man was against the wall, and Hank felt lifted and thrown though his feet did not leave the floor; the small of his back was pressed against the bar's edge, his arms spread and held to the bar by each wrist in Johnny's tight hands. Then it was Jack holding his wrists, talking to him, and over Jack's shoulder he watched Johnny push aside the two regulars holding the man against the wall. The man's friend was there, yelling, cursing. Johnny turned to him, one hand on the blond's chest, and said: 'I'm sick of this shit. Open your mouth again and you'll look like your friend there.' Then he turned to Jack: 'Will you get Hank the fuck *out* of here.'

Then he was outside, arm-in-arm with Jack, and he was laughing.

'Are you all right?'

He could feel Jack trembling; he was trembling too.

'I feel *great*,' he said.

'You tore his ass. You crazy bastard, I didn't know you could fight.'

'I can't,' Hank said, sagging from Jack's arm as he laughed. 'I just did, that's all.'

He is awake a long time but it is excitement and when finally he sleeps he is still happy. The dream is familiar now: it comes earlier than usual, or Hank feels that it does, and next morning at ten he wakes to that and much more. He is grateful the sun is coming in; it doesn't help, but a grey sky would be worse: he lies thinking of Johnny's anger last night, and he wonders who the man is, and hopes that somewhere he is lying with a gentle woman who last night washed his cuts. Then he is sad. It has been this way all his life, as long as he can remember, even with bullies in grade school, and he has never understood it: he can hate a man, want to hurt him or see him hurt; but if he imagines the man going home to a woman (as the bullies went to their mothers) he is sad. He imagines the man last night entering his apartment, the woman hurrying to his face, the man vulnerable with her as he is with no one else, as he can be with no one else, loving her as she washes each cut—*Does that hurt? Yes*—the man becoming a boy again as she gently cleans him, knowing this is the deepest part of himself beneath all the layers of growing up and being a man among men and soldiering: this—and he can show it only to her, and she is the only one in his life who can love it.

'I hope he finds me and beats shit out of me,' Hank says aloud. Then he can smile: he does not want the shit beat out of him. He drives to Jack's house. In the car, when Hank tells him how he feels now, Jack says: 'Fuck that guy; he wanted a fight all night. And after school we'll go see Johnny. He'll start laughing as soon as he sees you.' Immediately Hank knows this is true. He wonders what men without friends do on the day after they've been drunken assholes.

At Lake Kenoza he parks at the city tennis courts and locks his wallet and their windbreakers in the car. They start slowly, running on a dirt road, in the open still, the sun warm on Hank's face: he looks at the large pond to his left. The purple loose-strife is gone now; in summer it grows bright purple among the reeds near the pond. The road curves around the pond, which is separated from the lake by a finger of tree-grown earth. As they leave the pond they enter the woods, the road sun-dappled now, deeply rutted, so he has to keep glancing down at it as he also watches the lake to his left; the road is close to it, just up the slope from its bank lapped by waves in the breeze; to his right the earth rises, thick with trees. He and Jack talk while they run.

He wishes Lori ran. He has never had a woman who did. Edith started after their marriage ended. Running is the most intimate part of his friendship with Jack. Hank does not understand precisely why this is true. Perhaps it has something to do with the rhythm of their feet and breath. But there is more: it is, Hank thinks, setting free the flesh: as they approach the bend marking the second mile, the road staying by the lake and moving deeper into the woods which rise farther and farther to their right, he is no longer distracted by anything: he sees the lake and road and woods and Jack's swinging arms and reaching legs as he could never see them if he were simply walking, or standing still. It is this: even in lovemaking the body can become a voyeur of its own pleasure. But in the willful exertion of running, nothing can distract the flesh from itself.

Which is why he waits for the long hill that comes at the middle of their nearly six-mile run. They are close to it now, and are both afraid of it, and know this about each other. The road climbs away from the lake and they go up it, then leave it, onto a dirt trail dropping to the lake again. Here the lake's bank is sheer, there are rocks at its base, pebbles on the sand; to the right is the slope of the hill, steep, covered brown with pine needles, nearly all its trees are pines, and looking up there Hank cannot see the top of the hill or even the sky; always here he thinks of *For Whom the Bell Tolls*, sees Robert Jordan and Anselmo in the opening pages, lying up there among the pines. The trail often rises and falls, and then it goes down and to the right and up and they are on it: the long curving deceptive hill. It took Hank nearly a year to stop believing the next crest was the last one: short of breath, legs hurting, he looks up the road which is so steep and long that he cannot see beyond the next crest; he has never counted them, or the curves between them; he does not want to know. He prefers to run knowing only that it will get worse; and by doing this he always has that weary beat of joy when he sees that finally, a quarter of a mile or so ahead, is the top.

'Monet again,' Jack says.

Hank looks past him, down the hill; between the pines he can see sweat-blurred flashes of the lake; but it is the sun on the trees he's looking at. Jack is right; the sun touches the trees like Monet. Now they run harder, to reach the top, end the pain, and slowly the road levels and they shorten their strides: fast dry breaths, and Jack shakes his hand; they are at the center of the top of the hill, and suddenly, shaking Jack's hand and running beside him, Hank sees the dream again; the hill has not worked, he has run out of cures, and he releases Jack's hand and shouts through his own gasping: 'I can't get cafucking*tharsis*—'

Going downhill now, watching the road so he won't turn an ankle in a rut, he tells Jack about Monica; and the dream, which is with him now as he talks past trees and lake, talks all the way out of the woods into the sunlight where finally he stops talking for their last sprint to the tennis courts, the car, the water fountain.

'Marry Lori,' Jack says, as he bends toward the fountain; he walks away gargling, then spits out the water and returns. 'The fucking country's gone crazy,' he says. 'Marry her.'

Lori worries too much. Sometimes she thinks if she could stop worrying about so many parts of her life, and focus on her few real problems, there would be an end to those times, which are coming at least weekly now so she is afraid of an ulcer, when she is eating and it seems her food drops onto tense muscles and lies there undigested and after the meal it is still there and she is nauseated; and she could stop smoking so much; and she could stop staring at her school work at night instead of doing it; and she could ask questions in class, and could say what she was thinking when the teacher tried to start a discussion, instead of sitting there with her stomach tightening and feeling sorry for him because no one else is talking either. She could talk to her friends at school, girls and boys; she talks to them now, but usually only about what they are saying; she doesn't think they even realize this, but she knows it is why they like her and think of her as sweet and kind, their faces warm when she joins them at a table in the dining room or snack bar; but they don't know any of her secrets, and they are good friends who would listen, so it is her fault. She has been able to talk to Hank, so he knows more about her than anyone, but still she has not talked to him enough. She suspects though—and this makes her feel safely loved—that he understands more about her than she has told him.

Yet on the one night, two weeks ago, when she tried to separate her smaller problems from her essential ones, made parallel lists on a legal pad, she found that they were all connected, so the vertical lists, beginning with *my stomach* in the left column and *career* in the right column, became a letter to herself.

As she wrote it she was both excited and frightened: excited because she was beginning to see herself, and lovingly, on the paper on her desk; and frightened because she did not know where the writing was taking her; and because it might take her no place at all, might end on the very next page, in mid-sentence— Her first line was: *My name is Lori Meadows.* She wrote that she was nineteen years old, would be twenty in January, was a sophomore in college

and was screwed up. But as soon as those two words appeared on
the yellow page, she did not believe them. She was a C student.
That was in her file in the registrar's office: 2.4 next to her name.
Her mother said she would never get to graduate school like that.
Lori always nodded, always said *I know I know I'll bring it up*. She
never asked her mother what she was supposed to study in graduate
school. She was all right, she wrote, except when she thought
about the future. She liked going to her classes and sometimes she
even came out excited; but then at night she could not study. Hank
told her it was easy: she only had to spend two or three hours on
school nights going over the notes from that day's classes and reading the assignments, she would be free by nine every night, and
when exams came there would be no cramming, no all-nighters, all
she would have to do was go over the notes again and the passages
she had marked in the books. She loved the books. She loved
owning them, and the way they looked on the shelves in her small
room. But at night she didn't want to open them. Hank said he
studied that way all through college and was on the dean's list
every semester. But he was smarter than she was, and she worried
about that too. But maybe that wasn't it. He was writing then;
before he got out of college he wrote a novel and burned it. She
would have to ask him if he studied like that so he'd have time to
write, or if that was just the way he did things.

She didn't have any reason to study like that except to make
grades and she didn't know what to make grades for except so she
wouldn't feel like a dumb shit, and so her mother wouldn't start in
on her. So at night she talked with people or went to Hank's. At
least she didn't smoke dope. She didn't smoke it at all, but she was
thinking of those who just went to their rooms and turned on the
stereo and smoked themselves to sleep. Often in February, or even
before Christmas, they packed their things and went home. In the
morning she woke in panic because she hadn't done her work. Last
year she got a D in biology because she couldn't memorize, but she
liked the classes. But she could memorize. She just didn't. She got
Bs last year in Hank's literature courses because she had a crush on
him and she liked the stories and novels he assigned and she could
write about them on tests. And she'd probably get a B or A in his
Chekhov course this fall. Maybe it was love last year, not a crush.
They were drinking friends then, in September, and often she went
drinking with him and Monica and sometimes just she and Hank

walked down to Timmy's and sat in a booth in the dining room. She could talk to him then too. But she fell in love with him when he started taking her out after Monica, and when he made love with her so gently the first time and she came for the first time with a man, but if she hadn't had the crush she wouldn't have fallen in love holding hands on Boylston Street and stopping in the bookstore and making love that night, so maybe it was called a crush when you were in love without touching.

She didn't understand about school. She was not lazy. She worked hard learning to ride and won three cups for jumping before she was fifteen and then she stopped riding except for fun. Some girls stayed with horses, at a certain age, and they didn't change after that; they didn't go for boys. At least the girls she had known. She worked hard at the restaurant last summer and the summer before. She knew everything about those two summers, the work and what she had read and the beach and her friends, loving her quiet father and loving her mother too, wishing she and her father could talk and touch, watching him, wondering what he thought, what pictures were in his mind when she entered a room and he looked up at her, and his face loved her; and wishing she could talk to her mother instead of just listen to the words that seemed to come as long as her mother was awake, like a radio left on; but this radio was dangerous, sometimes it was witty, sometimes cheerful, sometimes just small talk, but each day there were always other things, nearly always subtle, sometimes even with a smile: warnings, reprimands, disapprovals, threats, most of them general, having to do with things as vague as growth, the future, love, being a woman. None of these was vague but they were when her mother talked about them: cryptic, her voice implying more than the words; her mother never spoke as if, in the world, there was a plan. And when Lori listened closely enough to this she heard or felt she heard the real cause: some brittle disappointment in her mother's voice, and she wanted to say *Are you unhappy Mother? What is it you want? What is it you want for me?*

For they had never had any real trouble. Lori had avoided dope because the first time she smoked it she didn't like it, she only got very sleepy and very hungry at once and was suddenly asleep at the party; and she was afraid to swallow anything, did not want something down in her stomach where she could not throw it away. She was obedient, and had always been. She was pretty, as her sisters were. She had a notion, which she didn't want, that if she were not pretty, her mother would not forgive her for that. They had never really quarrelled. She had watched her mother flirt with boys who came for her or her sisters, and with men, in front of her father; had watched her father's face, not quite grim, mostly calm. She knew her mother needed to flirt, see her effect on the boys who blushed and the men who did not. Her mother flirted with Hank too, but when he wasn't there she frowned when Lori spoke of him. *He's too old for you*, she said. *We're just friends. What kind of friends? I get lonely at school; he's good to talk to. This is summer. He's still my friend.* Wishing she could say *I'm in love* and *What does too old mean? That he'll die first? I could drown tomorrow.* She had told Hank. He said *It's not age. It's money. If I were a doctor or a Republican senator she'd bring us coffee in bed.*

She did not know if her mother did more than flirt. But all through the years there were times when her mother would go away, tell husband and daughters she needed a vacation, and she would go to Mexico, or the Caribbean, and return a week or two later with a tan and presents for everyone; and when Lori was fifteen she realized that for at least two years she had been trying not to wonder what a flirtatious, pretty and slender woman did alone at Puerto Vallarta, Martinique . . . Now the words on the legal pad told her exactly what her mother did and she understood why her father was even gentler than usual as he cooked for the three daughters while his wife screwed men she had met hours before. Why did her mother need that? It frightened her, as though it were an illness that ran in the women in the family, and she was ashamed that there were men walking the earth who had screwed her mother, who might crazily someday even meet her, realize she was the daughter of that six-day woman winters ago, and how could her mother do that to her—to them?

She did not know why she made love to Blake summer before last; could remember, as she wrote, moments in the restaurant when they smiled at each other as they hurried with trays, and then drank at the bar when the kitchen closed and they were done for the night. It was simply, she knew now, the camaraderie of people working together, an assurance that they were not really carriers of trays, smiling servants, charming targets of well-mannered abuse. He could have been a woman. Then at the night's end, after their drinks, Lori and the woman would have separated, as they would at the summer's end; by the time the leaves fell they would fondly think of each other, in their separate schools, as summer friends, waitress friends. But because he was a man, that affinity of co-workers, especially those with menial jobs, grew to passion and all its tributaries of humor and tenderness and wanting to know and be known; and she was eighteen, the last virgin among her friends and in her home; the last virgin on the block, her sisters teased.

It was August, she had been working all summer, school was coming. Blake was going back to Illinois, it seemed time: time to complete or begin or both, and there was tequila and cheer, the very sound of her laugh seeming different to her, something of freedom in it; there was the dirt path near the cliff's edge over the sea and rocky beach, and tenderly she walked with him and tenderly she kissed him and went to the earth with him and was not afraid, was ready, here on the cliff she had walked as a child, so much better than in a dormitory, waves slapping rocks as if they knew she was up there between them and the moving clouds and moon and stars. Then she was afraid: the slow tenderness of the walk was gone with her clothes he removed too quickly; she lay waiting, her eyes shut, listening to his clothes sliding from his skin, then too soon he was in her, big and she was tight, and everything was fast and painful and she cried, not only that night but every night after work, not because it always hurt, but because she couldn't tell him how to make it better and finally after two weeks when the summer was ending and he came, then rolled away and sat naked looking at the sea while beside him she lay softly crying, he said: *You're screwed up*. She said nothing. She got up fast and dressed and was on the path before he called to her to wait. She did not. She walked faster. But she knew he would catch up with her, so she crouched behind a pine tree, heard him coming, watched him trot past. Then she left the tree and sat near the cliff's edge and watched the ocean, listening. When she was certain she heard only wind and waves, she rose and walked down the path.

She did not want to walk the four miles home. She went to a bar where she knew her girl friends would be. She found their table; they waved and beckoned as she went to them. Monica was there. They had pitchers of beer and were laughing and on the bandstand a group was singing like Crosby Stills Nash and Young: the same songs, the same style. Her friends were talking to her: she was smiling, talking, accepting a mug. But she was angry. She did not know why and it made her feel unpredictable and moody like her mother, and guilty because her friends had not hurt her, it was Blake, yet he was only a shard of pain inside her anger. Yet writing about it over a year later she understood, and was delighted at the understanding till she paused and put her pen in her mouth and sucked on it and wondered if tonight she could have understood this without Hank. Had he taught her to see? She felt diminished. Her long-time voice with its long-time epithet whispered at her spine: *You're a dumb shit*. Then she was angry. At herself. It was Chekhov, that wonderful man dead too young; his story, when the old doctor said: *Why do you hate freedom so?* Chekhov who wrote about the perils, even the evil, of mediocrity. Hank merely assigned the stories and talked about them. And wasn't that really why she was in school? She stopped writing. Made a dash, indented. Wrote about the bar again, her friends, her anger, or else she would forget and she must get that down quickly because she had started to discover something else and if she didn't get back to the bar now she might never.

It was the people singing, and her friends' clapping praise. While she sat with the pains of Blake's attacks: the one with his cock, the one with his tongue, the one with his heart. And her friends were listening to four boys in their early twenties who were content to imitate someone else. While her betrayal on the cliff called for poetry or an act of revenge. Up *there*. On *that* cliff, where in the brightest daylight of sun on ocean she had lain beside her sisters; where she and her friends had gone with sandwiches and apples in the days of dirty hands and knees, up *there* she had tried for love and felt nothing but that cruel cock— And she walked down alone, with some bravery against pain, with some pride in her bravery, and re-entered a lowland of laughter and mediocrity, where she could never explain what had happened up there above the sea. The guitars and voices taunted her: the safe musicians who practiced to albums. Her friends' laughter drained her.

But what was that before? The anger, the *You dumb shit* voice— Yes: Hank. It was Chekhov. And first of all, she had no way of knowing whether tonight's understanding of her anger in that bar over a year ago came from reading Chekhov. But it didn't matter. What if she had learned from reading, even from hearing Hank talk about Chekhov? That didn't mean she was too dumb to understand her own life without someone else's help. It meant she was getting smarter. Now she wrote with joy, with love for herself in the world. Wasn't that what she was in school for? To enter classrooms and to hear? And if that made her understand her life better, wasn't that enough and wasn't that why she could not study for the grades for the graduate school which would give her a job she could not even imagine and therefore could not imagine the graduate school either? Wasn't she in fact an intelligent young woman trying to learn how to live, and if no profession pulled at her, if she could not see herself with a desk and office and clothes and manners to match them, that only meant she was like most people. This fall Hank talking in class about 'The Kiss' and what people had to endure when they had jobs instead of vocations; Ryabovich, with his dull career, existing more in the daydreams he constructed from the accidental kiss than he did in the saddle of his horse.

She wanted to phone Hank and tell him but she did not want to stop writing, and now it was time to write about Hank anyway. Already she was with her second lover and she had tried not to think about the future but it kept talking to her anyway at times when she was alone, but she would not talk back, would not give words to her fear, but now her pen moved fast because her monologue with her future had been there for some time and she knew every word of it though she had refused, by going to sleep or going to talk to someone, ever to listen to it. Already two lovers and she wished she could cancel the first and, if she and Hank broke up, there would be a third and she would be going the way of her sisters who had recovered, she thought, too many times from too many lovers, were growing tougher through repeated pain; were growing, she thought, cynical; and when they visited home, they talked about love but never permanent love anymore, and all the time she *knew* but wouldn't say because they still talked to her like a baby sister and because she didn't want to loosen what she saw as a fragile hold on their lives, she knew what they needed was marriage. Two lovers were enough. Three seemed deadly. If she could not stay with the third, it seemed the next numbers were all the same, whether four or fifteen: some path of failure, some sequence of repetitions that would change her, take her further and further from the Lori she was beginning to love tonight.

And now here was Hank on a sunny October Saturday, having for the first time since she had known him cancelled his day with Sharon, walking beside her, on his back a nylon knapsack he said held wine and their lunch, a blanket folded over his left arm, his right arm loosely around her waist as they walked on his running road she had never seen except in her mind when he talked about it. And he was happy, his boyish happiness that she loved, for the first time since last Saturday night when she told him about Monica because she could not hide from him any longer something she knew he would want to know. Tuesday night she had gone to his apartment and he told her of his fight Monday and that he and Jack had just been to Timmy's where he had apologized to Johnny and bought the bar a round, and he said Jack had been right. Johnny had grinned and said: *The middleweight champ of Timmy's* as soon as he walked in; and he told her about running with Jack and how it hadn't worked. She slept with him that night and Wednesday and Thursday and Friday, and he held her and talked. He did not tell her he still couldn't make love. He did not even mention it. During those four nights she felt he was talking to spirits, different ones who kept appearing above them where he gazed, felt that he was struggling with some, agreeing with others, and lying beside him she was watching a strange play.

He said Jack was right. The country had gone fucking crazy. He said I'll bet ninety percent of abortions are because somebody's making love with somebody they shouldn't. So were too many people. So had he, for too long. But no more. Things were screwed up and the women had lost again. A sexual revolution and a liberation movement and look what it got them. Guys didn't carry rubbers anymore. Women were expected to be on the pill or have an IUD and expected also to have their hearts as ready as their wombs. And women were even less free than before, except for the roundheels, and there were more of them around now but he didn't know any men who took them any more seriously than the roundheels from the old days of rubbers in the wallet and slow courting. Goddamn. The others (*Like you*, he said to Lori) are trapped. Used to be a young woman when they were called girls could date different guys and nobody had a hold on her, could date three guys in one weekend; by the end of a year in college she might have dated six, ten, any number, gone places, had fun, been herself. Now girls are supposed to fuck. Most students don't even date: just go to the dormitory room and drink and smoke dope and get laid. Guy doesn't even have to work for it. But then he's got the girl. Unless she's a roundheel, and nobody gives a shit about them. But the good ones. Like you. What they do is go through some little marriages. First one breaks up, then there's another guy. Same thing. Three days or three room-visits or whatever later, and they're lovers. Sombody else meets her, wants to take her to Boston to hear some music, see a play, she can't. Boy friend says no. Can't blame him; she'd say no if he wanted to take somebody to hear some music. Girl gets out of college and what she's had is two or three monogamous affairs, even shared the same room. Call that freedom? Men win again. Girls have to make sure they don't get pregnant, they have to make love, have to stay faithful. Some revolution. Some liberation. And everybody's so fucking happy, you noticed that? Jack is right, Goddamnit; Jack is right. He's glad now they stuck it out. He and Terry. He said I've got a good friend who's also my wife and I've got two good children, and the three of them make the house a good nest, and I sit and look out the window at the parade going by: some of my students are marching and some of my buddies, men and women, and the drum majorette is Aphrodite and she's pissed off and she's leading that parade to some bad place. I don't think it's the Styx either. It's some place where their cocks will stay hard and their pussies wet, some big open field with brown grass and not one tree, and nobody's going to say anything funny there. Nobody'll laugh. All you'll hear is pants and grunts. Maybe Aphrodite will laugh, I don't know. But I don't think she's that mean. Just a trifle pissed-off at all this trifling around.

'It's beautiful,' Lori says, as they enter the woods and she can see the lake.

'This is the first time I've walked it,' Hank says.

'It is? You've never brought a woman here?'

'No. Not even Sharon.'

'Why?'

'Never thought about it. When I think of this place I think of running. I've never even been here after it snows. Too slippery.'

'Not for walking. With boots.'

'No.'

'Can we come here in winter?'

'Sure.'

He moves his arm from her waist and takes her hand. They walk slowly. An hour passes before they start up the long hill; he looks down the slope at sun on the pines, and their needles on the earth, at boulders, and the lake between branches. At the top he says: 'Blackberries grow here.'

'Do you and Jack ever pick them?'

'We say we will. But when we get to the top we just sort of look at them as we gasp on by.'

He turns left into the woods, and they climb again, a short slope above the road; then they are out of the trees, standing on a wide green hill, looking down and beyond at the Merrimack valley, the distant winding river, and farms and cleared earth; surrounding all the houses and fields, and bordering the river, are the red and yellow autumn trees. He unfolds the blanket and she helps him spread it on the grass. He takes off the pack and brings out a bottle of claret, devilled eggs wrapped in foil, a half-gallon jug of apple cider, two apples, a pound of Jarlsberg cheese, Syrian bread, and a summer sausage. She is smiling.

'Cider?'

She nods and takes the jug from him and he watches the muscle in her forearm as she holds it up and drinks, watching her throat moving, her small mouth. When she hands him the jug he drinks, then opens the wine with a corkscrew from the pack.

'I didn't bother with glasses.' They pass the bottle. She lightly kisses him and says: 'You went to a lot of trouble. I thought you'd just buy a couple of subs.'

They eat quietly, looking at the valley. Then Hank lies on his back while Lori sits smoking. When she puts out the cigarette she returns it to her pack.

'That does it,' he says.

'What?'

'Anybody who'd take a stinking butt home instead of leaving it here ought to be loved forever.'

She lies beside him, rests her head on his right shoulder, and he says: 'I think when we started making love I wasn't in love with you. I felt like you were one of my best friends, and I needed someone to keep me going. I figured you'd be like the other young ones, give me a year, maybe a little more, then move on. But I chose that over staring at my walls at night. I wasn't thinking much about you. Then after a few months I didn't have to think about you anyway, because I was in love, so I knew I wasn't going to hurt you. I figured you'd leave me, and I'd just take a day at a time till you did. Like I did with Monica. I should never have made love with Monica. I haven't had the dream since Monday after the fight—'

'—She shouldn't have made love with you.'

'Same thing. I can't do that again. Ever. With anyone. Unless both of us are ready for whatever happens. No more playing with semen and womb if getting pregnant means solitude and death instead of living. And that's all I mean: living. Nobody's got to do a merry dance, have the faulty rubber bronzed. But living. Worry; hope the rabbit doesn't die; keep the Tampax ready; get drunk when the rabbit dies; but laugh too. So I can't make love with you. I'm going to court you. And if someday you say you'll marry me, then it'll be all right, and —'

'—It's all right now.'

She kisses him, the small mouth, the slow tongue that always feels to him shy and trusting. Then she pulls him so his breast covers hers and she holds his face up and says: 'I want to finish college.' She smiles. 'For the fun of it. But we're engaged.'

'That's almost three years. What if we get pregnant?'

'Then we'll get married and I'll go to school till the baby comes and I'll finish later, when I can.'

'You've thought about it before?'

'Yes.'

'For how long?'

'I don't know. But longer than you.'

'Are you going to tell your folks?'

'Sure.'

'They won't like it.'

'She won't. My father won't mind.'

'We might as well do it in the old scared-shitless way: drive up there together and tell them.'

'I'd like that.'

'Do you want a ring?'

'No. Something else.'

'What?'

'I don't know. We'll find something.'

'I like this. So next Saturday we go to Boston and find something. And we don't know what it is. But it'll mean we're getting married.'

'Yes.'

'And that night we go to your folks' for dinner and we say we have a little announcement to make.'

'Yes.'

'And your mother will hate it but she'll try not to show it. And your father will blush and grin and shake my hand.'

'Maybe he'll even hug me.'

'And for three years your mother will hope some rich guy steals you from me, and your father will just go on about his business.'

'That's it.' Then she presses both palms against his jaw and says: 'And we're never going to get a divorce. And we're not going to have American children. We're going to bring them up the way you and Edith were.'

'Look what that got us.'

'A good daughter.'

'You really think she's all right?'

'Man, that chick's got her shit together,' she says, then she is laughing and he tries to kiss her as she turns away with her laughter and when it stops she says: 'Clean tongues and clean lungs and no Monicas and Blakes. That's how we'll bring them up. Let's make love.'

'The Trojan warriors are at home.'

'You really *did* think you'd have to court me. Then let's go home.'

He kisses her once, then kneels, uncorks the wine bottle, holds it to her lips while she raises her head to swallow; then he drinks and returns the cork and puts the bottle in the pack. As he stands and slips his arms through the straps, Lori shakes out the blanket, and they fold it.

'Can I keep this in my room at school?'

'Sure.'

She rests it over her arm and takes his hand and looks down at the valley. Then she turns to the woods, and quietly they leave the hill and go down through the trees to the road above the lake.

'It took us a long time to get here,' she says. 'Did you say this is the halfway point?'

'Right about where we're standing.'

'We didn't walk very fast. It'll be quicker, going back.'

'It always is,' he says, and starts walking.

Finding a Girl in America
was set in Janson on a VIP composing system. Janson is an old-style face, first issued by Anton Janson in Leipzig between 1660 and 1687, and is typical of the Low Country designs broadly disseminated throughout Europe and the British Isles during the seventeenth century. The VIP version of this eminently readable and widely employed typeface is based upon type cast from the original matrices, now in the possession of the Stempel Type Foundry in Frankfurt, Germany. The book has been printed and bound by Haddon Craftsmen, Scranton, Pennsylvania.